MARGARET HAFFNER

Snowblind

THE CRIME CLUB

A  *HarperCollins Publishers*

First published in Great Britain in 1993
by The Crime Club, an imprint of
HarperCollins Publishers, 77–85 Fulham Palace Road,
Hammersmith, London W6 8JB

9 8 7 6 5 4 3 2 1

Margaret Haffner asserts the moral right to be identified
as the author of this work.

This is a work of fiction. All the characters
in it are fictitious, and no resemblance is
intended to any living persons.

A catalogue record for this book is
available from the British Library

ISBN 0 00 232409 1

Photoset in Linotron Baskerville by
Rowland Phototypesetting Ltd
Bury St Edmunds, Suffolk
Printed and bound in Great Britain by
HarperCollins Book Manufacturing, Glasgow

For Ted Wood,
with thanks for his encouragement

PROLOGUE

September, 1985

Phillip Loew staggered and fell again to the frozen ground. He fumbled at his shoulder and his hand came away wet with blood. His blood. As his vision blurred with pain he clenched his teeth against rising panic. Hard-driven snow blasted his face and the icy wind tore the breath from his lungs. He gasped for air.

Struggling to his feet, Phillip strained to see through the shifting veil of snow. Whichever way he turned, spicules of ice lashed at his face, and his eyes streamed. Was his assailant still out there somewhere? It didn't matter; he had to get back to camp. He swung his head from side to side like a deer scenting the breeze. Which way? He couldn't afford to guess wrong. 'If the wind is coming from the west . . .' He turned his left cheek to the strongest of the icy blasts and stumbled forward. Hand pressed to the bullet wound, blood still oozed between his fingers. He choked back a wild, hysterical laugh.

He'd been walking for what seemed like hours when he blundered against an arch of ice across a frozen stream bed. As his knees buckled, he slid down its smooth side to lie crumpled beneath it. He reached painfully for his backpack and the food it contained but the pack was gone. 'Rest . . . just for a minute . . .'

Considering the severity of his wound and the abysmal weather conditions, Phillip Loew had done well, but then he was a strong, determined young man. In fact he had struggled far enough to get back to the camp. It was a shame he'd been going in circles.

CHAPTER 1

May, 1986

Simon Hollingford watched as the immense load of equipment disappeared into the belly of the Hercules transport plane. It was hard to believe a group of eight people could need this mountain of supplies. 'What is all this stuff?' he wondered aloud.

'Scientific equipment, food, tents, arctic gear for starters,' a voice answered from behind.

He turned to see a woman whose short-cropped hair and workmanlike attire did little to conceal a very feminine face and form. Unconsciously Simon straightened his six foot one inch body, pulled in his stomach muscles and brushed his unruly brown hair back over his small bald spot. It sprang back immediately.

'We've cut back to the bare minimum,' she was saying. 'As it is, I've had to leave three absolutely irreplaceable plankton nets behind, not to mention my second litre of Lugol's iodine. It's scandalous that they expect us to do our work under these restrictions.' Her tone was lighter than the words.

'I don't think we've been introduced,' Simon murmured.

Holding out a friendly hand, she identified herself. 'I'm Anne Colautti. Plankton.'

'Simon Hollingford. Brawn,' Simon returned, giving the warm, tanned hand a hearty shake.

'So I see.' Anne nodded appreciatively, then turned back to watch the loading proceed.

Armed forces uniforms were everywhere at this military base just outside Winnipeg. It was a giant anthill of organized chaos but in among the khaki-clad workers he saw more brightly dressed individuals. The rest of his scientific party, Simon mused?

By the time the gear stacked on the tarmac was swallowed up, one of these civilians, a distinguished man of sixty-odd years, came up on Simon's right. The young Warrant Officer, Jean Beaulieu, approached from the opposite side.

'You folks might as well sit in the canteen and have a coffee, Dr Karnot,' the officer said to the older man. 'We've got to load our own gear now.'

'How long will it take?' the scientist asked.

'Forty-five minutes. Maybe an hour.'

'How much more can you get on that plane?' Simon couldn't help asking.

The Warrant Officer pointed towards a tank and another mountain of crates being manœuvred towards the Hercules.

'All that?' Karnot sounded dismayed.

'Plus a little more which isn't up here yet,' returned Beaulieu. 'The canteen's at the far end on the basement level.' A hint of a grin crossed his youthful countenance. 'Don't forget the army motto: "Hurry up and wait!"'

Simon turned to Dr Karnot. 'I'm Simon Hollingford, your radio operator and Man Friday.' He held out his hand.

Karnot gripped it and nodded graciously. 'Sylvester's relative.'

'Brother-in-law. He's the one who talked me into coming along and now he's backed out himself!'

'Too bad, but you'll be too busy for socializing, Mr Hollingford. This isn't a holiday!' Karnot nodded dismissively and headed for the canteen at a brisk pace. Simon followed behind less enthusiastically. It was his holiday even if it wasn't Karnot's. How had he let Sylvester talk him into this?

'It'll be great, Simon,' his freckle-faced relative had assured him. 'You maintain radio contact with Resolute, lug a few boxes, and the rest of the time's your own . . . just what you need while the inquiry's completed. Even the Commissioner can't bug you way up on Bathurst Island. Essentially you're getting a free vacation in the high arctic!'

'I'll get you for this, Syl,' Simon promised under his breath as he sauntered towards the canteen.

Balancing a cup of what purported to be coffee, Simon eased his bulk into a tiny opening around the green formica table with the rest of his group. Speaking to the youngish man on his left, he held out his hand to introduce himself. The stranger limply touched his hand. 'Dr Colautti. Tony Colautti,' he amended with a slight flush as if realizing the pretention of the title among a host of fellow Ph.Ds. 'My wife, Anne,' he added, gesturing towards the woman at his other side. It was the blonde from the landing field.

'We've met.' Simon smiled a greeting but Anne only nodded.

Simon's expectations took another dive but just then a friendly voice accosted him.

'Hi.' A wiry, grey-haired woman with tanned, leathery skin, and penetrating grey eyes, grasped Simon's hand with remarkable strength and pumped vigorously. 'Viola Legget.'

'Simon Hollingford.'

'You must be our new colleague, the radio operator. Thank heavens you could make it!'

'Thank heavens?'

'Yeah. If you hadn't come we would've been stuck with a soldier. The army won't let us go off without a radio operator.'

'Soldiers are bad?'

'No, not bad,' Viola laughed, 'but all they do is make radio reports to Resolute twice a day. We'll get more work out of a civilian with no superior officer to protect him.'

'It sounds like I'm going to be slave labour,' Simon protested, only half in jest.

'Nonsense. Glad to have you along, Simon, you'll love it. Just love it!' Her words were more like a command than a statement, but her enthusiasm was encouraging.

'I'm sure I will, ma'am,' Simon replied politely.

'Don't "ma'am", me, young man. I'm not your mother.

It's Viola to my friends. The Old Bag to my enemies. You'd best choose.'

'Can I get you something to drink, Viola?' he asked, noticing that the table was empty in front of her.

Viola barked with laughter. She jiggled Anne's elbow and cackled into her ear. 'Our new friend here wants to buy me a drink.'

Anne smiled, her reserve softening a little. 'How's he to know the brutal truth about flying on a Hercules? Give the poor man a break.'

Simon's eyebrow shot up as he spread his arms wide. 'What are you two talking about?'

'Look around, young man. Use your eyes. What do you see?' Viola demanded.

Obediently, Simon studied the table and its occupants. Including himself, there were five men, and two women, all, as far as he knew, part of this expedition. A low murmur of conversation rose from the group. Simon caught a few isolated words—tents, pH meters, experimental design—but he knew this wasn't what Viola meant. Assorted doughnuts and sandwiches, in various states of demolition, sat on the table with the drinks. Five drinks. 'Ah-ha!' Simon declared with a flourish.

'Well, Holmes?' demanded Viola.

'Only the men are drinking.'

'Very good. Why?'

'Alas, my dear Watson,' said Simon, entering into the spirit, 'it's all too clear. From the few facts before me I can only deduce there are limited toilet facilities on the aircraft.' Simon produced his conclusion with more confidence than he felt.

'Well done,' Viola congratulated. '*I* deduce you are someone who can use his eyes and his brains at the same time. We'll make a scientist of you yet, young man.'

'It's Simon to my friends, Young Man only to Old Bags.'

'*Touché.*' Viola snatched up a tired-looking sandwich. After eyeing it doubtfully she shrugged and took a bite. She grimaced. 'Very dry. I've never had a sawdust sandwich before. I don't recommend it.' She tossed the rest away. 'Have you met everyone, Simon?'

'Not yet.'

'Come over by me and I'll give you a run-down.' Viola detached herself from the group clustered around the table and with a conspiratorial index finger motioned him to join her.

'You've met Anne and Tony?'

'Yes.'

Viola snorted. 'I don't know what's come over Tony lately—he used to be a great guy even if he wasn't much of a scientist. But Anne's worth ten of him, scientifically and personally. She's a darn good limnologist no matter what that dried-up Jeff Jost says. Jeff's the shadow over there in the corner. He's with the Geological Survey. His type gives civil servants a bad name.'

Simon appraised Jeff—a florid fifty-year-old with the figure of a pear and the expression of a prune. Another charming companion, he thought sourly. Damn Sylvester. Would he be any better off with this lot than he'd be at home?

Viola's fingers bit into Simon's arm as she hunched her-self even closer, grey eyes flashing. 'See that tall man beside Jeff? The one with his nose in the air?'

Simon nodded. This was the autocratic man who had questioned the Warrant Officer. In Simon's opinion, the white goatee was a trifle overdone.

'That's Eric Karnot. Birds. He's quite good, though I'd never tell him so. His opinion of himself is already over-inflated. He's followed his feathered flocks all over the globe, taking photos and writing monographs. I hear he's even done one of those glossy coffee-table books about tropi-cal birds. Very elegant, I understand. Eric's the golden boy of Bellwood College.' Viola paused to give Simon time to admire his classic profile.

'What and where is Bellwood?' Simon asked. 'I'd never heard of it until my brother-in-law mentioned this expedition.'

'Not surprised—we're a small university. We have a reasonable reputation although Eric's really the only "name" professor we've got. Bellwood owes its reputation to him. And Wally Gingras.' Here Viola indicated the slovenly figure beside Eric Karnot. The contrast between the latter's crisp, fashionable appearance and Wally Gingras's unkempt person was startling. It was hard to believe they represented the same species.

In response to Hollingford's raised eyebrow, Viola chuckled and continued in her penetrating whisper. 'He isn't your idea of a bright light? Dung's his thing.'

'You can't be serious!'

'Wally's a world authority on microbial ecology or "dung decomposition" in arctic habitats. A very erudite field, I assure you.'

'No kidding.' Rubbing his chin thoughtfully, Simon studied Wally again. He was a short man, with greasy, yellow-grey hair hanging in lifeless hanks over his thread-bare shirt collar. Thick lenses made his pale blue eyes bulge forward, and across the bridge of his bulbous nose a wad of adhesive tape held his glasses together. Simon guessed Wally to be about fifty-five and imagined he could smell him from where he was standing, fifteen or twenty feet away. Hope I don't have to share a tent with him, Simon worried.

'Isn't it strange how so many people's personalities match their field of expertise?' Viola nudged Simon to regain his attention.

'After that comment, I'm forced to ask what you do,' Simon remarked.

Giving a crack of laughter, Viola poked his chest with a bony finger. 'Mammals in general, musk oxen in particular.'

'And what should I infer from that?'

'Whatever you like, Young Man!'

Three hours later, Simon felt on the point of physical disintegration. Ever since the engines of the Hercules transport plane revved up, his body had vibrated like jelly in an earthquake. His very molecules were resonating in unison, about to finally split apart. And it wasn't just the vibration. The sound waves themselves took possession of his brain.

Simon forced himself to re-examine his surroundings. He and his fellow sufferers sat strapped in web 'seats' slung just inches off the dull green metal floor. The accommodations could have been designed by the Inquisition's Torquemada during a particularly bad attack of indigestion. The looming bulk of the tank three feet in front of him effectively eliminated any leg room. Fortunately, numbness had finally set in and his legs no longer felt cramped, but whether he would ever walk again was debatable. When Viola gave him a cheery wave from her comfortable seat in the assistant navigator's chair he forced a smile in response. So much for equality!

Only a lucky few had been issued earplugs and Simon wasn't among them. His eardrums were on the point of implosion.

To distract himself, Simon studied the young woman, Joan Winik, seated beside Viola. She hadn't been part of the group in the canteen. A pain in the ass—wasn't that how Viola had described her? She appeared anorexic and somewhat grim. Her long dark hair hung in a loose pony tail and, on her, the escaping tendrils looked messy rather than sexy. Maybe it's those straight black eyebrows which make her look so angry, Simon decided, and the rude message on her sweat shirt. She dozed in her comfortable seat.

Simon groaned and shifted position, but he didn't dare get up again, not after the last fiasco. When his leg cramps were at their worst, he had joined Private Schmidt in a stroll between the women's seats and the freight. Pacing the six steps permitted in each direction, he fiddled idly with a steel funnel hanging from a string.

The private tapped him on the shoulder and said something.

Simon shook his head. 'I couldn't hear you. Speak louder!'

'Stop playing with the urinal!' Schmidt yelled.

It took a second for the message to register. When it did, Simon hurled down the funnel. It swung back and forth on its string, mocking him. Simon glanced around. Thank God he couldn't hear the snickers! He'd slunk back to his web seat, vowing never to move again. So much for his brilliant deductive powers. Par for the course, of late.

The Hercules plane put down at Resolute, a tiny outpost on Cornwallis Island. At 75° latitude, it was the farthest north Simon had even been. Even at ten p.m., when they arrived, the sun shone with a distant, feeble light. The expedition members bedded down in the temporary army camp.

In the army mess the next morning, Simon breezed through the food line. Most of the soldiers had finished breakfast long before and the tent was almost empty.

The Colonel in charge motioned him over to where he sat alone at a long table. 'Mr Hollingford, isn't it?'

'Yes, Colonel. Thanks for the hospitality.'

Colonel Fernald grunted. 'Don't thank me. Orders.' However, after fortifying himself with another swig of the excellent coffee, Fernald relented. 'Glad to have you all here, actually. It does my men good to see that some people actually *want* to come north.'

'This isn't a popular spot?'

'No, but we're only here for three months. We're having exercises to test our men and equipment.'

'Wouldn't it be more sensible to test in the winter?' asked Simon.

'We're going to be doing that too,' Fernald replied. 'Another popular idea. But manœuvring in summer isn't all that easy either—no roads, lots of fog, hills, cliffs, sand and gravel, deep coastal indentations to cross, not to mention polar bears, wolves, and musk oxen.'

'It sounds challenging,' Simon commented, through his mouthful of bacon.

'Just getting all the stuff here was half the battle!' Fernald declared with feeling. 'Even now, weeks into the exercise, we're still bringing up odds and ends.'

Simon's thoughts went back to the tank which had added such discomfort to his flight the day before. Was it an odd or an end? 'Logistical problems, eh?' he remarked with sympathy.

Fernald snorted. 'You know what our biggest problem is? The weather at this godforsaken airport! The place is fogged in like it was Newfoundland. Every flight has to be postponed three or four times.' Colonel Fernald stared morosely at the series of wet rings his coffee mug had made on the white surface of the mess table.

'We got in OK yesterday,' Simon reminded him.

'You were damn lucky. But I'll bet we can't get you to Polar Bear Pass today. Didn't you notice the fog rolling in?'

'Can't say that I did,' Simon replied. 'The sun was shining when I came across.'

Colonel Fernald tapped the table with his coffee spoon and shifted in his chair. He cleared his throat. 'Hollingford . . . I've heard you've had a little trouble recently.'

Simon sighed. He'd been foolish to think he could escape his problems by running away. 'A drug-dealer claims I beat him up when I arrested him.'

Fernald stopped tapping the spoon and looked Simon straight in the eye. 'Did you?'

Simon shrugged. 'I hit him. He had a knife and was planning to use it.'

'The charges against the man were dropped. And no knife was found.'

'You've been well briefed.' Simon felt a nerve jumping in his cheek and clenched his teeth.

'I like to know the people I'm responsible for. And I don't want any trouble.' Colonel Fernald hadn't raised his voice but a warning had been uttered nevertheless.

'Neither do I.'

'Good. We understand each other.' Fernald pushed himself away from the table, shoved his tray of dirty dishes into the rack and headed for the door. Simon saw him nod briefly at Tony and Anne who were on their way in.

Anne got through the food line first and came to sit beside Simon. Tony frowned but followed her. His brooding presence limited the conversation to dull platitudes.

Simon wolfed down the rest of his breakfast. 'Think I'll go have a look around,' he said, pushing back his chair.

'Mind if I join you?' Anne popped up too.

'Not at all.' Simon hid his surprise as he waited for her to collect her things. Tony, barely into his heaping plateful, frowned ominously, but Anne ignored him.

Once they left the mess tent, Anne took the lead, proceeding down the slight grade to the left. The sunlight, so bright when Simon got up, was watery now and an iridescent halo circled all the lights. They walked in silence until they cleared the huddle of khaki and grey tents and approached the edge of a long, narrow bay. Across a hundred metres of water, the opposite shore wavered indistinctly in the gathering mist. Like a watercolour in muted tones of blue and grey, its outlines blurred. The water itself, an incredible grey-blue, was dotted with crazily shaped splashes of white. Ice.

'Look!' Anne pointed to an ice sculpture to their left, close to shore. 'A cowboy hat.'

'And an eagle's head.' He indicated a much larger formation, farther out in the bay. 'This is better than cloud-watching.' Along the shore to his right another ice buttress intruded on to the shore. Its silhouette reminded him of an old, bad-tempered man. The smile faded from his face. How was Duncan managing their father? Simon hadn't been away from home for more than three or four days in years. Dad had become so hard to handle . . .

The raucous cry of a gull brought Simon back to Cornwallis Island and Anne. Forget the old man, he told himself. Have fun for once. He directed his attention to the other shore. Hills, low and rolling, ranged at right-angles to the grey and barren coastline. Between the two largest peaks the valley was white with ice and unmelted snow—a mini glacier ending at the sea. With the hazy sky, the grey hills, the white ice and the grey-blue water, the effect was unreal and dreamlike.

The dream had a musical score, too, a wild, disembodied wail which gradually penetrated Simon's consciousness.

'Huskies. In the Inuit village around the headland,' Anne explained.

Simon looked around. Although the army encampment was still enshrouded in mist, the higher land beyond was momentarily visible through a break in the fog. Endless hills of stones disappeared into the mist. Even the hardy arctic plants had given up on the place, leaving the field to the never-ending gravel. And the grey fog was the same depressing colour as the landscape. 'Why would anyone live here?' he wondered aloud.

'The Inuit didn't pick this spot themselves. They were relocated from northern Quebec to make way for the James Bay hydro project.'

'It sounds like a government idea.'

Anne took his arm. 'Don't look so glum. Polar Bear Pass, where we're going, is nothing like this. It's paradise in comparison.'

'I'll believe that when I see it,' Simon replied as they started back. 'Are you looking forward to this expedition?'

'You bet! My specialty's arctic plankton. It's a little difficult to study that subject at good ol' Bellwood U.'

'Do you come north often?'

'Every year, money permitting. We were at Polar Bear Pass on Bathurst Island last year too.' Anne kicked a pile of gravel with her booted foot. 'I go where others are going —to sponge transportation, food and lodging.'

'Do you think we'll get there today?' Simon asked, remembering the Colonel's gloomy forecast.

Anne studied the sky. 'Maybe. Colonel Fernald told us to be packed and ready to go by ten-thirty this morning.' She laughed. 'I feel for the guy—he didn't really want to see us again, you know. Not after last year.'

'What happened?'

Anne looked at him, her head cocked to one side. 'Your

relative—the one who fixed you up for this gig—didn't tell you?'

Simon shook his head. Another score to settle with Sylvester?

'One of our group, Phillip Loew, got lost last time,' Anne explained. 'We never found him.'

Simon halted in his tracks. 'You mean he just vanished?'

'Not exactly.' She ran her fingers through her hair and then shook it back into place. 'It was late in the year . . . end of September . . . and we had a blizzard. Phillip never made it back to camp. The army, the RCMP, everybody looked for him but we never found him. Must've frozen to death.'

Simon gave a low whistle. 'No wonder Sylvester forgot to mention it. He knows I'm allergic to dead bodies.' He shook his head in disbelief. 'Thousands of square miles of nothing and I have to head for the place with the corpse.' A busman's holiday for sure.

They approached the camp where a bustle of activity surrounded two helicopters. Under the watchful eye of Warrant Officer Beaulieu, the other members of the expedition were cramming the mountains of gear into these machines. Tony glared at his wife, who stiffened momentarily but turned away without saying anything. She and Simon pitched in as they all scrambled to be ready for the first signs of the fog thinning.

CHAPTER 2

As Simon watched the two helicopters disappear into the cobalt blue sky, panic momentarily gripped his heart. There's nothing to worry about, he admonished himself. You've left all your troubles fifteen hundred miles to the south . . . nothing but peace and tranquillity for four weeks.

Simon was standing a little apart from the others as the choppers took off but the huddled group was visible out of

the corner of his eye. They too were watching their link
with the familiar world vanish.

Eric was first to shake himself free of the spell. 'Let's get
this camp organized!' He pointed down the gentle slope.
'Four sleeping tents in a circle with supply tents off to the
side.'

Eric took command, barking orders with more force than
Colonel Fernald had mustered. Simon joined his tent mate,
the unprepossessing Wally Gingras, to put up their shelter.

The army had supplied large, circular tents of heavy
green canvas. All the poles and pegs were neatly rolled in
the cloth but Simon couldn't find the instructions.

Wally hurled impatient directions at Simon. 'Over there
. . . no, *there* . . .'

Simon tried to steady the centre pole while Wally
pounded pegs into the frozen earth with a small wooden
mallet.

'No, not like that! It's not straight,' Wally complained.
Simon bit his tongue and swung the tip of the tent post a
millimetre to the left.

'Hold it now! There. That's got it. No . . . not quite . . .'

Standing back for a better view, Simon thought it looked
fine, but Wally still wasn't satisfied.

'It tilts to the left and we've put the doorway on the
outside of the circle. We'll have to fix it.'

'No way,' Simon protested. 'It doesn't lean and I want
the door facing the scenery, not the neighbours.'

'But it's facing into the prevailing wind.'

'Then we'll keep the flap down.' Simon stretched his
cramped arms. 'I'm going to unpack my equipment, Wally,
so if you want to change the tent around, do it yourself.'
Simon made his way back to the mound of supplies.

'Hey, you, Hollingford!' Jeff, his disapproving scowl
glued to his face, loomed up behind him. 'How about helping with the supply tent?'

'Sure thing.'

'Put it here.' Jeff let the tent bag fall at his feet and
walked away.

'You're welcome,' Simon said under his breath as he bent to unroll the kit. He struggled for some minutes to do the impossible before he heard a chuckle in his ear.

'Need some assistance?' Viola asked. 'Joan and I finally got our tent up so I'll help you while I'm still in practice. I forget from year to year how to erect these damn things . . .' In minutes the tent stood taut and tall.

'There.' Viola smiled. 'Teamwork. Now let's move the food into the second supply tent.'

By eleven that evening some semblance of order had been established and Eric called a halt for the night. Although the sun still rested along the southern horizon they were tired and anxious for sleep.

'Who's for cocoa?' Anne asked as the activity level died down.

'Me,' they chorused. Every sleeping tent had a single-burner Coleman stove and she and Jeff each brought one out into the circle and lit it with practised skill. As they waited for the water from the nearby stream to boil, every-one found something, a collecting pail or sample crate, to sit on. Simon felt the cold penetrating through his windbreaker now that he'd stopped moving about. He donned the government issue green parka and white mittens. Others did the same and they looked like a chorus of green frogs perched on their respective logs.

'Just like last year,' Viola commented with satisfaction.

'Not quite,' a nasal voice intoned. 'Dear Phillip isn't here to annoy us.'

'Wally!' Anne said, shocked.

'Don't give me any of that "don't speak ill of the dead" crap, Anne. You can't tell me you miss the bastard.'

'That comment is in very poor taste, Wally.' Eric spoke with authority. Wally spat between his boots, following the script of a 'B' movie.

'Phillip himself was in poor taste,' Joan declared with characteristic vitriol. 'Thanks to his stupidity, I lost three weeks of field time.'

'You can't accuse him of stupidity,' Viola put in quietly.

'No one knew that storm was coming up. It could just as easily have been you lost out there in the blizzard.'

Joan tossed her head. 'Not me.'

Anne shivered. 'Poor Phillip. Do you suppose we'll find his body?'

Her husband snorted. 'The RCMP spent three weeks last year looking. If they couldn't find him then, we're sure not going to find him now!' He shifted around so that his back was towards her.

'They didn't even find his pack . . .' Anne murmured, red-faced.

Joan sprang up from her crate and planted herself in front of Eric. 'I think Phillip came to a fitting end. It's appropriate a man willing to sell out this land to an oil company should end up having his body here. Maybe in a few million years *he'll* be oil!' She stirred her hot chocolate so savagely that it slopped out on to her parka. 'Shit.'

'You're exaggerating,' Eric protested. 'Besides, he was my son. Have a little consideration for my feelings.'

'Your stepson, Eric, there's a difference,' Wally said in a voice hollow with pain.

'A technicality.'

Joan put her hand on her hip and pointed her finger at Eric. 'Don't try to con us. We all know you couldn't stand each other!' Eric shifted his feet, ready to spring up but Anne leaped into the breach. 'Have some more cocoa, Eric,' she urged, waving the pot of water and a drink packet between the potential combatants. Eric hesitated momentarily, but relaxed again. Joan laughed harshly and headed for her tent. Simon felt a twinge of disappointment—the conversation was just getting interesting.

Before turning in, Simon decided to uncrate the radio—his major charge. The tent farthest from the circle contained the scientific stores and doubled as the communications centre, a grandiose name for one short-wave radio. The instrument was well wrapped in bubble pack inside a heavy crate. Colonel Fernald's radio operator had provided instructions but basically the radio was idiot proof. Twice daily Simon was to check in with the army camp, once at 0800 and once at 2000 hours, starting the next morning. He'd have to be up early to erect the aerial in time for his first report.

Carefully he set the radio on a sturdy crate which had contained the emergency medical supplies. Joan, as the senior Red Cross graduate present, had taken these to her tent. As well as the usual disinfectants, splints, antibiotics and painkillers, there were several ice-packed vials of blood for emergency use. Duplicate medical histories of everyone had been provided—one copy Joan kept next to the medical supplies and the other Simon now hung on the side of the radio. He skimmed the medical histories—nothing interesting—and they showed an average cross section of North Americans with respect to blood type—three A's, four O's and a B.

Easing herself silently into her sleeping-bag, Anne tried not to disturb her husband who lay, similarly shrouded, on the far side of their tent.

'So you finally decided to join me.'

Sighing, she answered. 'Viola and I were completing the sanitation facilities.' Why am I explaining, she asked herself? It's my right to go to the toilet! But anything for peace.

'I heard you. So did everyone in camp, I expect. Do you have to keep the rest of us up half the night with your stupid chatter?'

'Good night.' Anne wiggled farther into the down bag as if hoping it would shield her from her husband's inexplicable anger and her own silent misery. Sleep was long in coming to both sides of the battleground.

Simon finished rigging the aerial before anyone got up. The wires drooped like a clothes line between the supports. Functional, if not artistic, he decided. When Anne appeared, Simon had just completed tying a series of makeshift red bows on to the thin wire.

'What do you think?' Simon asked, indicating his contraption.

'Colonel Fernald would have you peeling potatoes for a year! Good thing you're not in his outfit!' Anne giggled.

Simon enjoyed the friendly banter they exchanged when Tony wasn't around. 'I'm anxious to see if it works. I wish Eric had let me set up last night.'

Yawning, Anne headed for the sixth tent where they'd stored the food boxes. 'I hate the way the sun shines in the middle of the night. I have trouble sleeping when it feels like high noon, don't you?' she asked, stooping to enter the tent.

'I can sleep anytime, anywhere I get the chance.'

'Let's see . . .' Anne pried the lid off one of the crates marked BREAKFAST. It contained thirty-six white cardboard boxes, each labelled in bold red letters. The first layer read 'mushroom omelette', the second, 'bacon and eggs', and the last, 'sausages'. 'What takes your fancy, Simon?'

'I'll try the bacon and eggs.'

'I'll have sausages,' Anne decided, removing two boxes. 'I'll boil some water.'

Simon bumped into Joan as he headed back to his tent.

'What's this rat's nest?' she jeered, pointing at the sagging aerial.

'My "rats' nest" is your only link with civilization,' he retorted. 'Be careful how you insult it!'

By the time the water was boiling, everyone was up. They all hovered around the two stoves set up in the middle of the circle.

'Let's see what we've got here.' Viola ripped open her meal box and tipped out the contents. 'One chocolate bar. One packet of instant coffee. One packet of orange crystals. Crackers—I'll keep those for later. Plastic cutlery, napkin, cream and sugar packets. And this.' She held up a slim foil package about eight inches by five. 'This is bacon and eggs?' She eyed it doubtfully but dropped it into the pot of water to heat.

While the eight foil pouches simmered in the water, the others sipped coffee or hot chocolate.

Jeff turned to Simon. 'What's your job in real life? Obviously you're no scientist.'

'I'm a policeman.'

Several heads jerked up.

'Sylvester didn't tell me that,' Eric accused.

'That's where I learned how to operate a radio.'

'Hell! Here I am, trying to get away from the Establishment, and who comes along but a damned cop!' Joan shook her head in disgust.

'I'm on holiday,' Simon protested.

'Once a cop, always a cop.'

'Policemen aren't needed up here,' Wally mumbled. 'Should stay where you belong.'

'Breakfast must be ready by now,' Viola interrupted, shooting Simon a pleading glance.

Simon's lips thinned but instead of retorting he gingerly gripped the corner of his package and lifted it out of the hot water. He slit the top of the envelope and squeezed up the contents. His bacon and eggs emerged as a rectangular pressed grey mass with unidentifiable bits of brown embedded in it. He sniffed cautiously and nibbled a corner. He wrinkled his nose.

'Well?' Eric demanded.

'Tastes like cardboard with a chemical aftershock.'

'It can't be that bad.'

They all reached for their pouches. Anne's sausages were a suspicious reddish grey and laden with nitrates. Viola's mushroom omelette resembled the bacon and eggs but had grey bits instead of brown.

'We can't live on this!' Eric exploded. 'No wonder the army used us as guinea pigs—there'd be a mutiny if they gave this stuff to their own men!'

'They're poisoning us with chemicals.' Joan spat her mouthful back into the pouch.

'Maybe the other meals are better . . .' Anne ventured. Tony glared at her and her voice trailed off.

In the end, they ate chocolate bars and instant beverages for breakfast and didn't linger over the meal.

They shoved all the combustible garbage, the boxes, paper packets, and napkins into one carton, and the foil and plastic into another. What they couldn't burn, they'd take with them when they left.

As the others bustled in and out of the storage tent in search of stray equipment, Simon tried to raise the Cornwallis Island army camp on the radio.

'This is Victor Echo 8735. Come in, Viking,' Simon intoned.

'Thinks he's Lorne Greene,' Jeff commented under his breath as he squeezed by the communications centre.

Loud static crackled in Simon's earphones. 'This is Victor Echo 8735,' he repeated again and again, fine-tuning the frequency knob and fiddling with the other controls.

At last he removed the earphones and turned off the set. While he re-examined his antenna, Jeff stood to one side, pointedly examining his watch.

Simon went over to him. 'Go on ahead, Jeff. I won't be long once I've got the radio tent to myself. I'll catch up.'

'I doubt it. I travel fast.'

'I won't be long behind you,' Simon said. 'Surely you can start your sampling series without me.'

'Certainly I can. You're not conducting the survey, you're carrying the specimens.'

'I promise I'll be there to lug your stuff around, Dr Jost,' Simon responded through gritted teeth.

'Do you know where the cliffs are, Hollingford?'

'I have a topographical map. If you mark the spot, I'll find it.'

'OK, but I can't say you're off to a good start,' Jeff commented, turning on his heel.

'Don't take any notice of the old fraud, Simon,' Viola advised him with a friendly slap on the shoulder. 'He talks that way to God. I'm heading north as well, though not with Mister Personality. Don't scare my musk oxen!'

'It's more likely to be the other way round,' Simon laughed.

An hour later Simon sat back on his heels, mission accomplished. He was free to haul rocks for the next twelve hours if he hurried after Jeff. But instead, he drew a small sketchbook from his pack and began a line drawing of a burst of fragile yellow flowers pushing up from a tuft of leaves in the gravelly terrain. The Almighty Jeff could wait.

A half-mile upstream, Anne Colautti marked off a tiny pond for the installation of a conductivity meter and a temperature probe. But her mind wasn't really on the job at hand and this distressed her. Until recently her work could always take her out of herself, erasing any non-scientific problems from her mind, but not any more. Instead of taking careful notes describing why she'd chosen this site as representative of an ice-wedge polygon locale, she was sitting on the cold earth, hands tucked into her parka sleeves, on the verge of tears. At least she was alone.

Pull yourself together, woman. Anne hauled her hip waders out of her bulging pack and struggled into them. As usual, she hadn't been able to find a pair small enough to fit and, even with layers of socks, her feet were lost in the boots. She hitched the straps over her shoulders, knotted them a few times to take up the slack, and then fastened them in front.

Now encased in unyielding rubber, she moved awkwardly and almost fell as she slid into the pool. 'Damn.' A gurgle and a slurp were followed by a rush of bubbles breaking the surface as her boots sank to the ankles in the ooze at the bottom. She leaned over to get her probes from the bank and then started forward. But the suction of the bottom marl held tightly and, when she lifted her foot, the boot stayed behind. Its rubber leg tripped her up and, fighting for balance all the way, she fell with a splash.

'Damn! DAMN! DAMN!' Her voice shrilled with an edge of hysteria, and as it echoed she caught the note. 'Dear

God. I'm losing control!' Anne bit her lip hard. 'Relax. Breathe. Be calm.'

She was sitting neck deep in frigid water. Her full boots weighed her down and her jacket floated up around her ears. But the shock of cold helped her focus and she soon wiggled out of the boots and stood up. She stripped off her sodden jacket, hurling it to the bank in a dripping arc. The probes followed. She felt around in the now murky water for the boots until her hand closed on the knotted straps. But the pond bottom didn't release the boots without a struggle and her feet were again ankle deep before the boots pulled free with a rude burp. She swam the three strokes to shore, hauling the offending footwear behind and clambered up exhausted and shivering on to the bank.

'Where are you, Tony?' she sniffed. Other years he'd been there laughing at her awkwardness but ready to rub her dry and kiss her warm. Now, dripping water on to everything, she rummaged in her pack looking for the skimpy towel she'd brought. Her teeth chattered like a machine-gun as she stripped off her clothes. She had to get back to camp, but the urgency of the situation didn't galvanize her as it should have.

'So I freeze to death. So what?' she muttered, pulling on the thin jumpsuit she'd packed as a precaution. Who'd care? Who? Not Tony. Not the university. Not anybody.

Hot tears coursed down Anne's cheeks. But with a determined fist, she ground the salty pools from her eyes and hauled her mind back to the present. Only her hiking boots were still dry. She managed to pull them on but her fingers were too stiff to do up the laces. She'd just emptied her pack to use as a jacket when a voice hailed her.

'Problems?' Joan jogged up. 'Fell in, did you?'

Anne nodded jerkily.

'Here. Put this on.' Joan unzipped her coat and handed it to the freezing woman.

Anne huddled into it. 'Thanks.'

'Been crying, have you?'

'No. No, it's just water.'

Joan shrugged. 'I heard you swearing. You sounded
pretty upset to me.'

'Wouldn't you be upset if your boots were too big and
they got stuck and you fell in?'

'You should be better prepared. Unless, of course, you
want to do a Phillip Loew impersonation.'

'Are you going to help me or not?' Anne sputtered
through her blue lips.

Joan shrugged again. 'OK. OK. What do you want me
to carry?'

'My clothes, my meter and those damn boots.' Anne
kicked at the offenders.

'Get going,' Joan ordered. 'I'll bring them along.'

Anne, resolutely keeping her mind on her destination,
headed for camp as fast as her frozen joints would allow.

Eric had come to Polar Bear Pass to study shore birds,
but on this first day he headed inland. His binoculars and
cameras swung from his neck in true birder fashion but
Eric didn't pay any attention to the scenery.

'Damn Wally . . .' he muttered, kicking a stone into a
shallow pond. 'Why can't he let Phillip rest in peace?' A
worry line creased his patrician brow. 'And Joan's no
better,' he announced to a nesting plover who fluttered with
agitation as he passed. 'Always stirring the pot . . .'

Eventually he worked off his spleen. He slowed to a more
leisurely pace and began scanning his surroundings, peering left and right with more intensity than the scenery
merited.

Equilibrium restored by his art, Simon set off to join Jeff.
Before leaving camp he'd studied the map. Half an hour,
he decided. Forty minutes tops. But as he walked he discovered the deceptive nature of the terrain. The tops of the
rolling hills were covered with gravel and lichen and were
easy to walk on, but as he descended each slope the ground
changed. In places it seemed to be cut into foot-wide polygons, separated from each other by grooves about two

inches wide and four to six inches deep—a pattern well
suited to twisted or broken ankles. Farther down, near the
bottom of the valleys, he encountered a spongy, sedge-
covered surface, succeeded by shallow ponds or creeks. His
hiking boots, suitable for the high ground, were useless for
forging the water barriers and within a few hundred yards
Simon's feet were drenched. For each slope he descended,
there was another to climb. After a half-hour of hard slog-
ging the six tents still looked close.

Another hour and a half of strenuous hiking brought the
unimpressive cliffs into reach. But between them and Simon
a small blue lake nestled in a fold of hills, cutting off direct
access. The shorter way around was to the west, but a herd
of musk oxen grazed there. Viola's herd? Simon halted in
indecision, watching these prehistoric-looking animals as
they browsed in the reeds.

Beside the lake Simon caught sight of a bulky pack,
Viola's by the colour, but he couldn't see her. When he
noticed a flash of light off to the left he searched for the
source and saw Viola lift her binoculars to watch the herd.
As she did, the sun glinted off the lens. For a while, he
watched the watcher as she nimbly followed the musk oxen,
making skilful use of the sparse cover and staying strategi-
cally downwind.

Viola was carrying one of the .22 calibre rifles, but a
quick look at the animals told him they wouldn't be stopped
by such a light gun. Putting his hand into the pocket of his
parka, Simon fondled his artillery simulator or 'arti-sim'.
It was a large firecracker which made the sound and light
of an artillery attack but didn't actually fire anything. The
idea was to scare off attacking animals instead of killing
them. He also carried a .303 rifle which was much more
effective on large game, but a lot heavier and more awkward
to carry than he'd anticipated. Simon sighed and headed
the long way around the lake.

It was mid-afternoon before Simon caught up with Jeff.
The scientist ignored his presence for several minutes before

acknowledging him with a rude grunt. 'Took your time, didn't you?'

'I had to detour around Viola's animals,' Simon explained. 'What do you want me to do?'

'Help me get the dimensions of this rock face.'

Jeff pulled a cloth measuring tape from his sack and passed the end to Simon. 'Hold this right here.'

It took twenty minutes to make the measurements the geologist wanted. Jeff made careful notations in his field book. 'See that outcrop over there?'

Simon nodded.

'Make the same set of measurements on it.' Jeff threw the tape and the notebook at Simon.

With no one to hold the other end of the measuring tape, Simon was forced to go to elaborate lengths to fix it in position. It took twice as long to complete the second series of data. From time to time Simon paused to admire the spectacular scenery and watch Jeff, who seemed to be drawing portions of the rock face. When Simon finished his task, he peered over Jeff's shoulder. 'Why don't you just take a photograph?'

'Differences between the layers are so slight the salient characteristics are lost in a photo.' Jeff traced his stubby finger over the rock face as he spoke. Simon made out the indicated features with difficulty. 'See the marginally larger grain in this horizon, and the softer texture indicated by the more extensive weathering?' Jeff asked.

'You could bring out the texture in your drawing better by shading,' Simon suggested.

Jeff slammed his book shut on the drawing and whirled to face him. 'When I want your advice, I'll ask for it. I'm the geologist; you're the hired help.'

'Just because I'm not a godalmighty scientist doesn't mean I'm a complete idiot!' Simon snapped.

Jeff stared at his antagonist for long seconds with icy contempt, but then, like wax softening, his expression changed. 'Can you draw?'

'Yes.'

Wordlessly Jeff handed over his book, and pointed at the rock face.

Simon outlined the features Jeff had indicated along with a couple of other subtle differences. In a matter of five minutes the job was done. Still without a word being spoken, Simon returned the sketchbook.

The geologist studied the drawing, then, looking Simon straight in the eye for the first time, he said, 'Thank you. It's perfect.'

Motioning Simon to follow, he clambered a few feet higher to a wide ledge and then turned to offer a hand to his companion. Simon didn't need the help but took it as a gesture of peace.

'Can you do the same for this section of the rock?' Jeff asked, indicating a roughly square area about a yard wide.

'No problem.'

'Would you label the sketch F-133?'

Simon nodded. He accepted the book but declined the pencil. 'I carry my own,' he said, pulling a stub from his pocket.

Gradually their tension eased, and by the time Simon had made six sketches conversation came easily. Jeff gave Simon an elementary geology lesson of the area. 'The rocks talk, Simon, if you're only able to hear them. I can look around and know how this land has changed over the millennia. I can tell this part of the world was once a tropical sea, once a beach. For a long time it lay crushed under millions of tons of ice, and when the ice melted it took tens of thousands of years for it to bounce back. In fact the land here's still rebounding.'

It was late in the day when they gathered up the equipment and split the thirty pounds of rock samples between them. By the time they reached the lake, Viola and her musk oxen were specks in the distance so they were able to take the short way around.

'You were here last year?' Simon asked as they climbed yet another hill on their route back to camp.

'We all were, except you, of course.'

'Who was radio operator?'

'Phillip Loew. We've all returned except him, though I guess he's still here somehow.' Jeff smiled a tight smile.

'What exactly happened to him?'

Jeff shrugged—no mean feat with the heavy pack. 'No one's really sure. It was last September . . . We were all going about our business as usual when an unexpected storm hit. Wally and I holed up at the IBP station—those two quonset huts on the horizon. The others were close enough to camp to get back. All except Phillip. We never saw him again.'

'I assume you searched . . .'

'Naturally. But the winter had come to stay and conditions were difficult. The RCMP searched too, and when they couldn't find him they insisted we leave immediately.'

Conversation ceased while they forded an icy stream. Jeff wore waterproof, insulated boots, ideal for the terrain. Simon looked at them enviously. The squelching sound he made as he walked attracted Jeff's attention. Clucking his tongue, he scolded, 'That's no way to operate here. You'll end up with frostbite at the very least. Tell you what: I've a spare pair of boots exactly like these. If they'll fit you can have them.'

'If necessary, I'll amputate my toes to make them fit. Thanks.'

Trying to ignore the pain of his blistered feet, Simon again turned his mind to Phillip's disappearance. 'Wally and Joan didn't like him . . . ? Phillip, I mean,' he asked.

'No one did,' Jeff replied with a short laugh. 'He was a pain in the ass. A real know-it-all.'

They laboured up the endless succession of low hills and forded the icy streams between. From one rise he spotted Anne in the distance, leaning on a pole. Her drooping posture suggested she was as tired as he was.

'I'm surprised you came back to the same spot after such a tragedy.' Simon returned yet again to the missing man.

'I didn't want to, but not because of squeamishness. I'd

rather expand my studies to another site. However, I was overruled.'

'You're a civil servant, aren't you? What are you doing in this university crowd?'

'Habit, I guess,' Jeff replied. 'I hooked up with the bunch from Bellwood College years ago when I couldn't get travel money from the Geological Survey of Canada. It's much cheaper to piggy-back on an existing expedition than to mount your own.'

Simon manœuvred his rifle from one hand to the other. He was certain it was gaining weight. 'You don't have a gun with you. Didn't Colonel Fernald say we were to carry one at all times?'

'It gets in the way. I have an arti-sim in my pocket. I'll put my faith in that.'

'Viola has hers,' Simon commented.

'Sure, but she's following those damn musk oxen all the time. I avoid anything on four legs.'

Dressed again in warm, dry clothes, Anne crouched at the side of the pond and packed up the wet things Joan hadn't been able to carry. A whole day wasted! Only two sites chosen in twelve hours and her meters weren't installed yet. In earlier years she and Tony worked eagerly together, choosing sites they used jointly. It had been one of their dreams to work together. But even last year, the collaboration was half-hearted on Tony's part. The decay in their relationship began before that. But exactly when, and why?

Sniffing dolefully, Anne began the trek back to base camp, her mind two years into the past. How happy she and Tony'd been up until then! She conducted her research in an annexe attached to Tony's lab and spilled over into his territory, but he didn't care. In fact he joked to the other faculty members that his wife was better known than he was and the wrong one was getting paid. Somewhere in that year something went wrong. Tony changed.

*

After his radio check that evening, Simon emerged from the tent to find Joan in a foul mood and cursing Wally Gingras with every breath. The man wasn't there to defend himself.

'That prick!' Joan steamed.

'What did he do?' Viola asked.

'He won't collaborate with me, that's what! Here I am, studying bacteria on this godforsaken island and he won't even let me sample one of his dung heaps!'

'There's no shortage. Use another pile,' Simon said flippantly.

'It's not the same. He's going to have all kinds of data I need . . . breakdown rates, compositional profile, and so on. But will he share his data? Oh no. I told him I'd be happy to put his name on any papers I wrote but he still said no.'

'You know he never co-authors papers,' Viola pointed out reasonably. 'He's a loner.'

'Well, it's a pretty silly attitude if you ask me.'

'I don't know. He's famous in his field so he must be doing something right,' Jeff threw in as he joined the group.

Joan grunted 'Of course you'd defend him instead of me . . .' She stomped off in a huff.

Eric and Wally didn't appear for the evening meal. Viola and Simon tried to keep a conversation going but finally subsided in defeat. Joan and Jeff spent their time glaring at each other while Anne and Tony sat apart from the rest, speaking to no one, not even each other. Compared with what was to come, it was a convivial evening.

CHAPTER 3

Polar Bear Pass was experiencing unseasonably warm weather, the temperature frequently reaching two or three degrees Celsius. It was a comfortable working temperature for most purposes and Simon was anxious to put the mild spell to good use.

'The coast is only about six miles from here, isn't it?' Simon asked one night at supper.

'About that,' Viola agreed.

'Think I'll go have a look tomorrow.'

'You only have twelve hours between radio checks and it'll take you three or four hours to get there and the same to get back,' Eric warned. 'Hardly seems worth it.'

'That still gives me a few hours to spend there. I want to see some belugas or seals or something like that.'

'You won't see much from shore except birds and you can see them here,' Tony chimed in. 'You should stay near camp in case one of us needs you.'

'But, Tony, you're always telling me how unimportant I am. Now you think I'm indispensable?'

'Hardly!'

'Then I'll go. You'll have to struggle on without me.'

'Why don't you take one of the rubber rafts?' Anne suggested. 'The blue one folds up small for carrying and then you could go for a paddle when you reach the ocean.'

'That's a great idea. I'll do that.' Simon rubbed his hands together.

'I might need it tomorrow,' Joan objected.

'Then you can use mine,' Anne replied calmly. 'I'm going to be doing microscope work.'

Joan glared at Anne and Simon in turn but said no more.

After two hours of strenuous walking, Simon could see the coastline. Three or four hours—Eric must be a slow walker! Simon smiled and picked up his pace even more but the shore didn't seem to get any closer.

'What is this? A time warp?' he grumbled as he checked his watch. Over three hours and still the ocean hovered on the horizon. Simon's buoyant mood dissipated as he slogged on, determined not to give up.

His mind turned southward. He'd made arrangements to speak to his sergeant by radio while he was on holiday and all of a sudden he wanted to hear Bill's gravelly voice. He wanted to know what was happening. Although one of the reasons for coming to Polar Bear Pass was to get away from the cloud of uncertainty hanging over him, now he felt too isolated. Had the board come to a decision? Did they believe Delio's story? Would he be suspended . . . even charged with assault? Simon felt his fists clenching. Delio's type didn't deserve to live.

And his father . . . how was he? Simon knew the old man hated unfamiliar surroundings. Duncan and Pam would take good care of him, but still . . . Simon rubbed his chin. He realized he'd soon have to put his dad in a nursing home but he wasn't looking forward to it. Even with his memory all but gone, his father instinctively fought the idea. Simon smiled ruefully. He was damned either way. Overwork or guilt would get him, but guilt was beginning to look easier to take. He couldn't cope much longer and the expense of home nursing help was prohibitive. Simon trudged along on autopilot, his mind hundreds of miles away.

He was sweating when he finally arrived at the coast, but it was well worth the effort and his spirits rose. The sky was bluer than he would ever have believed possible and the ice was either clear like crystal or blindingly white. The emerald waves, crested with froth, were transparent as well and at times he could see the sunlight through them, giving him a glimpse into an alien world.

Simon took his time inflating the rubber raft, working the foot pedal rhythmically as he absorbed his surroundings. When that small task was accomplished he perched comfortably on a sun-warmed rock and munched a granola bar. This was more like it.

He marvelled that he could smell the utter cleanliness of the air. Granted there were flowers, tiny clumps of seaweed, and salt spume, but it was none of these which he smelled, at least not individually. It was better than any of those. Simon breathed in great lungfuls, feeling the tingle right down to his toes.

His pencil flew over the pages, capturing the mystique of the landscape with a minimum of strokes as he frantically tried to gather everything into his sketchbook. Rocks and waves, lichen and gulls, ice and whales, delicate flowers and overwhelming vistas were pulled from his surroundings and restrained in two dimensions of black and white and yet they lived. To Simon these two hours were worth two years of rock-carrying, post-pounding or dung-sifting.

When he had satisfied his need to draw, Simon turned again to the raft and manhandled it over the slippery rocks to the water which seethed and raced between the black boulders. The light craft bounced on the waves and Simon almost did the splits when the raft leapt seaward while he still had one foot on shore. But at last he was safely launched and he paddled three hundred yards from shore before relaxing to survey the scene.

Almost immediately he spotted a pod of narwhal swimming towards him. Through binoculars he watched them twist and turn fluidly in their element, staying just below the surface except when they came up to blow. Simon could feel the mist of their breath on his face. Seabirds wheeled overhead, their hoarse cries carried on the wind.

Gradually Simon realized the seat of his jeans was wet. He glanced down to see his raft riding low in the water and waves washing over the side. Hell, he was sinking! Frantically he searched for the leak. Not the valve. Not under him. Not on the gunwales. His probing fingers searched over the side and down under the water line but within seconds they were numb from cold. He felt what he thought was the hole but he couldn't be sure.

He watched the dancing bubbles in horror. Were they getting more numerous? Was the hole getting bigger? He shifted, trying to see the gash but with every move the waves washed inside faster and the raft settled deeper into the water. It no longer danced on the waves but rode sluggishly, reluctantly, up and down on the swell. The shore looked a long way off.

The repair kit! With a rush of relief Simon remembered the repair kit kept in the pouch of each raft. The patches were supposed to stick even to wet rubber. Keeping his body as still as possible, he stretched to retrieve the kit from its storage place. Nothing. Simon leaned forward, recklessly causing a flood of water to wash in board. His fingers scrabbled in the corners of the pouch but it was no use. The repair kit was gone. He was in real trouble.

Tentatively he began paddling, altering his stroke in an attempt to minimize the water he was taking aboard while maximizing his speed towards shore. With narrowed eyes he tried to gauge his progress. It would be close. Should he swim for it? Simon tried to recall the statistics he'd read about survival times in arctic waters. Why hadn't he paid more attention? Was it thirty seconds or thirty minutes?

'Not thirty minutes,' he decided aloud. 'Five minutes, maybe?'

He tried to judge the distance to shore—two hundred yards at least. But he'd been terribly mistaken in his estimate while walking to the coast—maybe he was wrong again. And he wasn't a strong swimmer.

'You're a fool to be out here alone,' he cursed himself as he fought panic. 'Paddle, idiot.' He paddled desperately, awkwardly, trying to ignore the slopping of the water as it gurgled around his numb legs. The bottom edge of his jacket was submerged now and it acted like a wick, pulling the water upward, soaking his vest and shirt. Only his fear was keeping him warm.

The rubber boat was slowly folding up around him, trapping him in a rubber strait-jacket. He had to stretch to reach up and over the edge of the boat to keep the paddle in the water. The pressure of the collapsing boat was squeezing his legs painfully. When shore was still thirty yards away Simon knew he would soon be unable to kick free of the boat's ever tighter embrace. He gritted his teeth and used every ounce of his strength on the puny paddle. Simon's muscles were screaming in protest and the water was up to his chin when the bottom of the raft dragged on the stones. For a moment he was too dazed to realize he'd made it to shore but at last he staggered to his feet, fought off the raft, and struggled for the rocks. He collapsed in a wet heap, shivering with cold and exhaustion.

Ten minutes later, teeth chattering uncontrollably,

Simon knew he would have to move. If he stayed still he would die of hypothermia. With numb fingers he fumbled at his zipper, then let the jacket plop to the hard stone where it lay weeping on to the gravel. He pulled on the dry toque he'd left on shore and each hair on his head was grateful for the warmth. He jumped up and down flapping his arms like an arthritic penguin.

'I've got to get dry,' he whispered hoarsely. He looked around. There was nothing to burn and besides, his matches were useless now. Why had he spurned the waterproof kind?

He stripped off his soaking clothes and wrung them out as much as his numb fingers could manage. Then with a shudder he wriggled back into the damp garments. Not much of an improvement, but it was the best he could do.

'Camp,' he mumbled. 'Camp,' he repeated clearly, forcing himself to action.

It was a nightmare journey. Time after time he stumbled and fell because his feet were too numb to feel the uneven surface. He was getting colder, not warmer, and a rime of ice formed on the seams of his clothing. The sun had disappeared behind an ominous cloud bank. 'You don't want to join Phillip Loew as a permanent resident,' he told himself as he scrambled up yet another hill. 'One more hour. Walk just one more hour and you'll be home.' He descended the next slope and splashed through the inevitable stream at the bottom. A thin film of ice tinkled into a thousand crystals.

'Simon? Simon?'

The voice penetrated Simon's daze at last and he peered around for the source.

'Simon!' Anne hurried up to him. He faltered to a halt. 'Oh my God,' she cried. 'You're frozen!' She briskly rubbed his arms and back, stretching her slender arms around his shivering body. 'You poor thing,' she murmured.

Gradually his shivering diminished to the point where he could talk. 'Thanks.'

'Can you walk now? We must get you back to camp.'

Simon nodded wearily. 'I know. How much farther?'
'Not far. Come on.'

'Had a good close look at the water, did you?' Eric asked
when Simon appeared at supper that night.
'Too close.'
'Let that be a lesson to you.' Eric's goatee bristled righ-
teously. 'We don't need any accidents this year.'
'Serves him right,' Joan remarked. 'He's supposed to be
working.'
'You should be thanking me, not criticizing,' Simon
retorted. 'If I hadn't taken that raft you might've been the
one to sink.'
'I only go out on ponds and most of those aren't more
than waist deep. And I wouldn't have lost the raft.'
'You shouldn't have gone out alone,' Jeff chided. 'One of
us should've gone with you. We know the dangers.'
'The rest of us have work to do. I know *I* have no time
to spare for sight-seeing.' Tony sneered at Simon.
'Let's just be grateful he's still alive,' Viola exclaimed as
she executed a final flourish to the vigorous back rub she
was giving the victim. Simon drew his blankets tighter and
cradled his hot chocolate. Would he ever get warm?
'It was thoughtful of Anne to go looking for you.' Eric
directed his words at Simon but it was Tony he watched.
'Especially since Simon wasn't even missing,' Tony
hissed, glaring at his wife.
'I wasn't looking for him,' Anne retorted, 'but it was
lucky I was out that way.' She stood up, her hands on her
hips. 'What's wrong with you people anyway? You're acting
like you wanted Simon to have an accident . . .'
Tony had the grace to blush but neither Joan nor Eric
turned a hair. 'Don't be melodramatic, my dear,' Eric said
in his most irritating manner. 'Sit down and finish your
dinner like a good girl.'
Anne gritted her teeth and stomped off.
Viola clucked her tongue. 'Don't bait her, Eric.' She
turned to Simon. 'I've made you some more hot chocolate.'

Viola thrust yet another scalding mug into Simon's hands. 'We'll get you warm, don't worry.'

As Simon drank his chocolate he glanced again at Wally. Wally hadn't contributed to the conversation but his yellowed eyes darted among his companions as if seeking hidden meanings in their words.

When Simon woke the next morning, even his feet were warm. For a few minutes he lay in his bag, savouring the comfortable glow in his fingers and toes. He squinted at his watch and groaned. Seven-thirty. He heard muffled clatter. The others were already up.

After a static-filled radio check, Simon grabbed a couple of chocolate bars and headed out in the direction of the IBP station where Wally and Jeff had waited out the storm which killed Phillip. This station lay in a north-easterly direction from their base camp, and its two small quonset huts huddled in the middle distance. Like all things on Bathurst Island, however, it was farther away than it looked and it took Simon an hour and a half of brisk hiking up and down the long low hills to get there.

Until now he had avoided visiting this vestige of the International Biological Program because he instinctively resented its human blight on an otherwise barren and wild landscape. It comforted Simon to know that when his expedition departed they'd leave no sign of their intrusion; no building, no hearth, no garbage. It would be as if they'd never come, except for a few less insects, bacteria and plankton, and a few minor scars on the unyielding rocks. They were even careful not to thaw the permafrost under their tents, keeping the atmosphere indoors only marginally warmer than outside. He smiled as he remembered Viola telling him about the radio operator on a previous expedition.

'That private was so lazy,' she railed, 'he just stayed in his tent all day. Stove going full blast. Can you believe it? All the way up here at government expense and all he does is sit in his goddamn tent? Two radio contacts a day—that's

all he did. Wouldn't even help carry gear.' She brushed a
hand through her grey hair. 'Anyway, he got his come-
uppance. His stove melted the permafrost under his tent
and he woke up one morning in a swamp. I laughed so
hard . . . Problem was, the darn swamp kept spreading like
mould on bread till we all had to move our tents.'

By the time Simon jogged up to the IBP site, he'd unzipped his parka and shed his heavy mitts, retaining only
the thin gloves he usually wore inside them. His scarlet
toque was riding high over his ears like a rooster's comb,
so he swept it off and crammed it into his pocket.

According to Jeff, Polar Bear Pass had been intensively
studied during the United Nations organized year of exploration and research. Scientists posted on Bathurst Island
had semi-permanent quarters and a rough runway had
been scraped into the terrain. A squat, ladder-like aerial,
minus its windsock, was all that remained of the airstrip
and the two low grey huts were the remnants of the camp
itself.

These huts, side by side, were each about five metres
long and two high at the vault of their curved roofs. The
door on one gaped open on a lone hinge and Simon peered
into the gloomy, empty interior. There were no windows,
and the dark, cold tunnel enveloped him in its sense of
desolation. Simon slammed the door shut but as soon as he
let go it clanged open again, echoing hollowly across the
barrens. He approached the second hut almost reluctantly
and gave its door a tentative shove. Nothing. He fumbled
at the frozen latch and with difficulty swung the hasp free.
A good shove from his shoulder made the stiff hinges
screech in protest but the door opened. He stooped and
entered.

Boxes, maybe thirty or forty, were piled along the walls
and the majority were still sealed. They'd been there twelve
years, left as emergency rations for anyone marooned in this
wasteland. Staying low to avoid banging his head, Simon
hauled one crate to the shaft of light coming from the doorway. The rest of the interior remained in deep shadow

and even the air had the closed, lifeless feel common to all long-deserted buildings. Breathing it, Simon's lungs still hungered for more oxygen, as if this dead air could no longer support life.

He tried to shake off his gloom by opening the carton. Sixteen large jars of instant coffee confronted him. One was only half full. Wally and Jeff? Or the IBP scientists? He kicked the box back to its former position and, with his eyes now adjusting to the gloom, read the labels on the others. Beside the coffee was a case of instant hot chocolate and under that a box labelled potatoes. Jeff and Wally could have managed for quite a while provided they could keep themselves warm. The next rifled crate Simon examined contained fuel canisters and a tiny stove. Not the Hilton, Simon decided, but the hut would have seemed very welcoming indeed to men trapped in a blizzard.

Curious to see how twelve-year-old potatoes looked, he bent over their box and ran his finger under the flap. The top of the carton gave way easily. Glue must be rotten, Simon thought ... potatoes likely are too. But inside, instead of vegetables, he found a lump of dirty green canvas. He began to re-close the carton but curiosity stopped him. He grabbed an edge of the cloth and pulled, but it was jammed in tightly and wouldn't yield. Simon wedged the carton between his feet and yanked, almost toppling backward as the canvas came free. He turned the bundle over in his hands and saw the pockets and leather straps of a backpack—a well-used one from the look of it. It felt heavy. He untangled the straps and set the pack upright on top of the coffee carton. When he smoothed out the creases Simon noticed the initials P.L. written in faded magic marker on the flap.

'P.L.,' Simon murmured. 'Phillip Loew?' He worked open the cord knotted around the mouth of the bag and peered in. He recognized the outline of a small soil corer and a rock chisel. He lifted the tools out and dug deeper to find a field notebook, plastic sample bags, blank tags and a crushed chocolate bar. Even before he found Phillip's name scribbled on the flyleaf of the notebook he felt sure he'd found the pack of the missing man.

Simon sat back on his heels, a frown corrugating his forehead. What was Phillip's pack doing crammed inside a potato carton at the IBP station? No wonder the RCMP hadn't found it—or Phillip either for that matter. According to Jeff, they'd concentrated their search in the Pass itself.

Simon twisted around, peering deeper into the gloom. Was Phillip's body here too? He sprang up and walked towards the rear of the quonset hut, every nerve at attention. He methodically searched the few areas hidden by the boxes. Nothing. He headed for the rectangle of light framed by the doorway, then crossed the few yards of open ground to the other building and stepped inside. The hut was as empty as he'd thought.

Chewing his lip, Simon returned to where he'd left Phillip's pack. He repacked the bag, knotted it shut and slung it over his shoulder. As he surveyed the hut one last time he saw the notebook lying on the ground. He scooped it up and shoved it in his pocket. From the doorway he looked back. How much longer would the food stored here stay edible? When would the next traveller take shelter in this bleak sanctuary? How much longer would the quonset hut itself stand? Everything was completely still, totally quiet, and Simon felt as if he were the only living thing left on the earth. He stepped from the gloom back into the world of sunlight, birdsongs, and life. As he pulled the door shut the dissonant protest of the hinges signalled his return from an alien landscape.

As he crested a hill Simon spotted Eric and Viola not far away. Eric was gripping her arm and she seemed to be protesting. 'Hello! Eric!' Simon shouted.

They turned and stared at him. Viola waved weakly. By the time Simon reached them she'd pulled away from Eric.

'Something wrong, Vi?' Simon asked.

'Nothing. Nothing at all,' she replied hurriedly. 'You look excited, though. What's up?'

Simon held out the backpack he'd discovered. 'Recognize this?' He looked from one stunned expression to the other.

'It's Phillip's,' Viola whispered. 'Isn't it, Eric?'

Eric cleared his throat as Simon silently pointed out the initials. 'Yes, it's Phillip's.' He reached out to take it from Simon. 'Where'd you find it?'

'At the IBP station.'

'The IBP station?' Viola's voice rose in disbelief as she shook her head. 'Impossible.'

'That's where I found it,' Simon assured her. 'In a carton marked potatoes.'

'In a carton? What on earth would it be doing in a carton?'

'Good question, Eric. I didn't see any sign of Phillip himself.'

'Of course not,' Viola said. 'Jeff and Wally would've found him if he'd been there. They spent two days at the station during the storm, remember.'

'And they would've mentioned the pack if they'd seen it,' Simon murmured. 'I don't understand.'

'Meanwhile, Simon, I'd like to keep Phillip's pack,' Eric said. 'His mother may want to see it ... a last reminder ...'

'Sure,' Simon agreed. 'It belongs to you more than anyone else.'

As the group sat around that evening, waiting for their foil pouches to heat, Jeff groaned and stretched out his legs. 'God, I'm tired! This terrain really takes it out of you. And then lugging rocks too ... Think I'll spend tomorrow cataloguing my samples.'

Joan smirked. 'Can't stay the pace, Jeff? Getting a little soft? Too old for field work?' She rose and moved lithely around behind him. 'Shall I get you a hot-water bottle?' She bent to put her mouth close to his ear. 'Your knitting?'

'Put a sock in it, Joan. I'm in better shape than you are.' He brushed her away and turned to Simon. 'Did I hear you found Phillip's pack at the IBP station?'

'Yeah. Packed in a cardboard box.'

Joan, half way back to her seat, stopped and stared.
'How'd it get there?'

Simon scanned the circle of faces. 'You tell me. I understood he had it with him when he disappeared.'

Anne winced. 'You don't suppose Phillip himself's there
too . . .'

'I looked. No Phillip.' Simon stirred the simmering water
with a stick. The silver packages bobbed around, a skin of
bubbles clinging to their sides like tiny jewels. 'The funny
thing is,' he continued thoughtfully, 'the pack was *stuffed*
into the carton . . . squashed down so the top flaps could
be closed. And the top was re-glued.' Simon tried lifting a
packet, balanced on his makeshift spatula, out of the water
but it fell back in with a plop. 'It looked to me like it had
been hidden.'

Eric's goatee vibrated as he frowned. Simon could hear
the words before Eric spoke them. 'Nonsense. You must be
mistaken.'

'You explain it, then,' Simon invited.

'I can't form an hypothesis without all the facts. It's
unscientific.'

'I can,' Joan interrupted. 'I bet Phillip put it there
himself.'

'Why?' Jeff and Viola chorused.

'Remember Phillip complaining his tent had been
searched? And his stuff rifled?'

Viola and Jeff nodded. Tony and Anne glanced at each
other.

'Well, maybe Phillip hid it to keep it safe,' Joan proposed.

'But there wasn't anything interesting in it,' Simon
objected. 'Just field notes and tools.' He turned to Eric.
'You have the bag now. Did I miss something?'

'No. It held just ordinary field supplies. Phillip wouldn't
need to hide it.' Eric glared at Joan, who shrugged and
locked her fingers behind her head.

'Just an idea, Eric. Don't lose your cool.' She looked
around. 'Anyone got a better explanation?'

Simon's eyes widened when Wally spoke up. 'Phillip hid

it so he could accuse one of us of stealing it.' He wiped his thin mouth with the back of his hand. 'It's something he'd do . . . Phillip liked to make trouble.'

'I refuse to sit here and listen to this!' Eric stood up and stalked to the stove. 'Give me my dinner. I'll eat in my tent where the company's better.'

The members of the research team settled into a routine. They rose early and had breakfast, making no attempt to socialize. Instead, each scientist was intent on getting started as quickly as possible on the day's tasks. The crate of inedible breakfasts had remained untouched since the first morning. Now everyone ate lunches in the morning since these were more appetizing, and most of the cookies and chocolate bars were secreted in parka pockets for snacks during the long day away from camp.

On this particular morning Simon had agreed to help Anne. As he lifted the huge pack to his back he recalled the snatch of conversation he'd heard the night before.

'. . . So if you could help, Tony, just for the morning . . .'

'I'm too busy. Everyone else manages alone, Anne. Don't be a baby.'

'You know it's heavy work to put in the barriers. I'm not strong enough.'

'Get your loverboy, Simon, to help. Don't think I haven't noticed you cosying up to him. It's sickening.'

'That's not true, Tony, and you know it!' Anne had replied hotly. 'But if you won't help I bet he will!'

Yes, Simon thought decisively, count on it.

'How far away are these ponds, anyway, Anne?' Simon panted under his load.

'Not that far. They're the closest suitable ones I could find.'

'And just how picky are you?'

'All I want is small size, constant depth and symmetrical shape.'

'That's reassuring,' Simon returned sarcastically as he splashed through a pond which, although it had been rejected for the study, seemed to fit the bill as far as he could see.

'I need a rest,' he announced a little later, dropping his armload of poles to the frozen ground with a clang. A knapsack full of clamps and nets clattered after it. 'This better be worth it,' Simon gasped as he stretched out, unzipping his parka as he did so.

'It will be. I'll give you an acknowledgement in my paper.'

'That'll look good on my résumé, I'm sure . . . really help me in my career.'

Anne smiled. 'Except for the fact you're a policeman, I don't know anything about you.' She eased out of her pack and sat down crosslegged. She tilted her head to one side and stared at him. 'Tell me about yourself.'

'Not much to tell . . . I'm just a boring, middle-aged, slightly overweight male.'

'Come on—not one of those things is true.' She wiggled around, searching for a smooth spot on the rough ground. 'Are you married?'

'Nope.'

Anne noticed the slight hesitation in his voice. 'You don't sound very sure. Are you divorced?'

Simon shook his head. 'Never married. I almost was, though.' He saw the question in Anne's eyes. 'Two years ago I was engaged . . . my fiancée broke it off three weeks before the wedding.'

'Oh . . .'

Simon smiled, his eyes crinkling in amusement. 'Don't look so worried—she did the right thing. Smart girl, Annette.'

'I bet it hurt,' Anne said softly, touching his arm.

'Yeah, mostly my pride, though. I had my doubts about the whole thing but I didn't have the guts to tell her.'

Anne propped her pack up behind her, leaned back and stretched out her legs. 'Why did you get engaged?'

Simon shrugged. 'We'd been dating a long time . . . seemed like the thing to do.'

Anne reflected on her own engagement. It had been such a glorious time. She'd had no doubts and neither had Tony. Or had he?

'Why did your fiancée change her mind?'

'The old story. A cop's life is too hectic, too unpredictable. I don't know how many dates I broke with her because of my job . . . I guess she decided she wasn't cut out to be a policeman's wife.' Simon could remember Annette's exact words when she told him her decision. 'I need order, Simon, and dependability. Every time we make plans I end up having to change them. Our friends can't count on us . . . I'm running out of excuses. I'm tired of going alone to parties where everyone else is in couples.' She'd pushed her long auburn hair out of her eyes in her characteristic gesture. 'And your father—if you're serious about having him live with us . . .' She shook her head vehemently. 'No. It just won't work. I'm sorry.'

Simon returned to the present. Anne was speaking to him. 'What was that?' he asked.

'I just wondered if you have another girlfriend now.'

'No one special,' he replied. No one period, he added to himself, and unless his life made a dramatic turn for the better, there never would be. He jumped to his feet and struggled into his pack. 'I'm getting cold sitting here. Come on—let's get this over with.' He jogged off at a terrific pace and Anne had to run to keep up.

When he had finally worked off his frustration he was sweating. 'Guess I got carried away,' he apologized. Then he laughed. 'Here I am, leading the way, and I don't even know where I'm going!'

'You haven't done badly,' Anne reassured him. 'See that pond over to the right?' She pointed. 'That's it. Let's have a drink and a snack and then we'll get started.'

They sat in silence for several minutes while they recuperated. As he lay, taking in great gulps of the cleanest air he had ever enjoyed, Simon put his personal problems behind him. His thoughts turned once again to the missing man of Polar Bear Pass. He was fighting the urge to treat this tragedy like a murder investigation, but his sixth sense told him something was not quite right. And both he and his partner, Bill Harkness, had a healthy respect for his hunches. 'Out here in the wilds with all these men,' Simon stammered, 'do you have trouble fending any of them off?'

Anne chuckled and turned an amused gaze on him. 'Getting the lie of the land, Simon? I'm a married woman.' A shadow crossed her face.

He laughed. 'That's not what I meant. I was thinking about Phillip, actually. Even you don't seem to have liked him much . . . I wondered if perhaps he'd been bothering you.'

'Hardly. If he'd been "bothering" anyone, as you put it, it was likely Jeff or Tony.'

'Oh.' Simon rubbed his chin. 'Then what did you have against him?'

Anne shifted around trying to get comfortable on the unyielding earth, a frown creasing her brow. 'That's hard to say. I can't think of one particular reason.' She took off her toque and ran her fingers through her short curls as she tried to crystallize the reasons for her dislike. 'He had many of Eric's characteristics but few of his redeeming features. Phillip was—how can I put it?—autocratic, opinionated. But most scientists can forgive those failings. Those adjectives describe us all to some extent!' She laughed self-consciously.

'Not all of you,' Simon protested gallantly. Anne blushed.

'Probably what bugged us the most was his pursuit of money above science. Even if some of the rest of us are after the almighty dollar instead of "knowledge", the illusive Holy Grail of science, we keep it to ourselves. Phillip was always after money from contracts, industry, foundations, the government . . .'

'I thought all scientists were looking for research money.'

'That's true, but Phillip wanted money for himself as well. Oh, he collected it under the guise of research, usually from oil and other resource-based companies, but he always factored in a hefty salary for himself. That is *not* common.'

'And everyone knew this?'

'Of course. He boasted about how he inflated his costs to cover it. Besides, if he was willing to give the answers the companies wanted, particularly about things like environmental impact, they were happy to pay him.'

'That would make him really popular with Joan,' Simon commented.

'You're not kidding. Joan is a rabid environmentalist, very unrealistic at times, and a pain in the neck, but I prefer her extreme stand to Phillip's mercenary soul.' She gasped guiltily. 'Why am I saying these things? The man is dead.'

'Probably,' Simon agreed calmly, 'but that doesn't change what he was in life.'

But Anne, upset with herself, scrambled to her feet. 'Let's get to work.'

Joan was not easily defeated, but she had met her match in Wally Gingras. No amount of coaxing, reasoning or threatening would get him to help her. 'Wally, why? I won't hurt anything. I could get my samples after all your measurements have been taken. All you'd need to do is give me a photocopy of your rough notes for that particular patch of shit.'

'I work alone. I do not collaborate, I already told you that yesterday.'

'Wally . . .'

'No! That's final. Go away.' Wally turned on his heel and stalked off, leaving Joan to fume helplessly.

She kicked at a clump of reindeer moss. Bastard. How the hell was she to get her research finished this year if Wally wouldn't cooperate? If she'd just stuck to the narrow academic road she would've been finished long ago. But with most of her time spent working for Greenpeace and Environment Now her doctorate was taking longer than the usual four or five years. And all she got for thanks was a police record for a failed attempt to set fire to a fur warehouse.

Joan held a pointed finger in the air towards Wally's

disappearing back. 'You won't stop me, you old fart,' she muttered under her breath.

'That's not very nice.'

Joan started in surprise and then twisted to face Viola. 'So? Neither is he,' Joan sneered.

'He has his reasons,' Viola replied.

'He's not the only one who's had a bad break in life . . . The rest of us manage to remain civilized.' Joan stalked away.

'Not so as you'd notice,' Viola murmured as she headed out of camp.

Using a heavy mallet, Simon attempted to drive a metal pole into the ground at the edge of a small pond. Sweat flowed freely even in the chill air and progress was slow as he fought his way inch by inch through the permafrost. Gingerly he tested the pole. A gentle shove failed to dislodge it but Simon had no doubt an energetic lemming could tip the post with moderate effort. Wiping the perspiration from his forehead, he cast around for some rocks to anchor the pole. This was only their second pond and already it was four in the afternoon.

Anne was busy stringing a fine mesh between the other pair of poles but, judging by the exclamations erupting from her vicinity, her task wasn't much easier.

'Are you sure all this is required?' Simon asked with a grunt as he heaved a large rock out of the water.

Anne rushed over to peer into the water with a worried frown. 'Don't do that. You mustn't disturb the pond any more than is absolutely necessary.'

'All I did was remove a rock! You've been walking through it!' Simon protested indignantly.

'Yes, you're right, but I had to. Aren't there any rocks on shore?'

'They're not very handy,' Simon replied shortly.

'I'm sorry,' Anne cried, immediately contrite. 'I don't mean to criticize, I really appreciate your help. Let me find you some rocks.'

'It's OK, I'll do this. You just finish with that net so we can get out of here.'

'Thanks.' Anne smiled her breathtaking smile. It almost made the labour worth while, Simon decided.

They finished their tasks and then stood back to admire their handiwork.

'Now what happens?' Simon asked.

'Well, for this particular pond I'm going to remove all the zooplankton from one side and see if the population of phytoplankton increases when the grazing pressure is diminished.'

'In English?'

Anne laughed. 'Too technical? OK. Let's see . . . With a sampling net I'm going to remove as many of the microscopic animals as possible from one side of the pond. The mesh we've just installed will keep the animals from the other side from moving in. Then in six weeks I'll sample both sides of the pond to see how many microscopic plants are present. The theory is that the side with no plant-eaters will have a higher population of plants. Clear?'

'Yes, except we've sectioned this pond into three areas, not two.'

'Good point. Into the third area I'm going to add the animals I've removed from the first section. This should lower the plant population below that in the control area.'

'Let me know how it turns out,' Simon commented.

'You won't be here then, will you?'

'No. I'm leaving after just four weeks in this vacationer's paradise. Some other poor sucker is taking my place.'

Anne came over to stand by Simon and they both stared at the scene in front of them: the grey-purple tundra, the endless blue of the sky and the utter transparency of the pond in which the entire world was repeated, upside down, in perfect detail.

'You don't like it here?' Anne laid a small hand tentatively on his forearm. Simon imagined he could feel the tingle of each fingertip even through his down jacket.

'Of course I like it. I love it, if you must know,' Simon

said. 'In just a few days Polar Bear Pass has got into my blood. It's beautiful . . . awesome . . . quiet, pure.' The last words hung in the crystal air. Again Simon's thoughts were pulled inexorably towards the missing man. If you had to die, it was a wonderful place to spend eternity.

'Yes, it's all of that,' Anne breathed, sharing his emotion. 'I've come to the arctic every year since I started my master's degree and I'm still awestruck each time. My only regret is that I have to travel with such a motley assortment of people—they intrude on this perfection.'

'Well, excuse me!' Simon exclaimed in mock indignation.

'You know I don't mean you. I'm talking about Joan, or Wally, or even Eric.'

'I can understand your objections to the first two, but Eric Karnot? I thought he was the quintessential scientist and nature-lover.'

'In more ways than you might expect,' Anne retorted with feeling. 'Remember the behaviour you were suspecting Phillip of? His stepfather was the problem, still is the problem, as far as I'm concerned. Around the university he has a reputation as a real lecher. He can't keep his hands off women.' She sighed. 'Poor Lynda—the wife is always the last to know.'

Simon gave a low whistle. 'Well, well. So the noble-looking Eric isn't quite so noble as he appears.'

'No way, and he's very persistent—almost a pain.'

'And a married man, if I'm not mistaken.'

'You're not mistaken. Three years ago when I first came up north with Eric and the crew from Bellwood College, he was recently divorced, without a good word to say for his ex-wife, and hot on my trail. The next summer he came, a newly-wed, but still on my case. Guess who he'd just married?'

'Phillip Loew's mother, I gather.'

'Yes, but whom do you suppose he had divorced just the year before?'

Simon shook his head.

'Phillip's mother.'

'Are you saying he remarried the same woman?'

'Precisely. And Phillip was furious, especially when he caught Eric prowling around me.'

'I'm not surprised. You'd think with the son right at his elbow, Eric could've controlled himself.'

'Well, he didn't, and his wife never heard anything about it since Phillip didn't live to tell the tale.'

'It's sad the baggage of civilization has to come up here with us,' Simon mused.

As she picked up the gear to move on to the next pond, Anne agreed wholeheartedly.

Wearily Tony plunked his corer down on the frozen terrain. These northern trips used to be the highlight of his year but this time it was torture. But then life itself was torture of late. He groaned aloud, longing for what he considered the innocence of his post-doctoral days.

His mind's eye saw Anne as he had first seen her, one brilliant autumn day at Hemlow College. A colleague had pointed her out where she sat, eating her lunch under a golden beech in the arboretum. Her simple white dress had been spread out around her, making a base for her graceful upper body and accentuating her pale skin and gleaming blonde hair. It had taken him a year's allotment of nerve to go up and introduce himself, but he needn't have worried; she was the friendliest, least critical person he'd ever met. He thought she was beautiful.

Very easily they had become a 'couple', informally at first, just frequenting the same functions and monopolizing each other's time. But Tony remembered the first event they'd attended as a unit—a summer tea hosted by the women's alumni, and presented in Edwardian splendour on the shady lawn of the college. Anne was seductive in a simple cotton dress and he felt awkward and inelegant, like a lump of earth on a china plate. With wonder, he realized she actually meant it when she told him she was enjoying herself and his company.

From there, it seemed a natural progression to marriage,

and he had assumed, in the patriarchal manner of his family, that Anne would sublimate her career to his own. She had, and without protest. But time and experience educated Tony in ways formal schooling could not, and now he couldn't contemplate Anne's salary-less, adjunct status without guilt overcoming him. As if he didn't have enough of that to carry already.

Removing a fur-lined glove, Tony rubbed his eyes with a heavy hand. Where the hell was he? Why? The corer, as familiar as an old friend, felt strange in his hand when he bent to retrieve it. No site in the majestic terrain seemed worth sampling and no knowledge was worth wringing from the harsh landscape. He wasn't the first to decide solitude was not good medicine for someone at war with himself.

With a supreme mental effort Tony hauled his thoughts from the abyss of despair and surveyed the vista before him. He needed a location with deep soil so he could obtain pollen buried in the peat as long as possible. Then he could accurately re-create the changes in the vegetation of the island over time. Last year's data indicated that about seven thousand years into the past was as far as the pollen record went. It hinted that for the last one thousand years the climate had been colder and drier than it had been for the two thousand years previous to that. Tony realized his findings agreed with studies done on Axel Heiberg Island and Devon Island, but that didn't really raise his self-esteem. Validating someone else's data wasn't the activity of an innovative scientist.

Carefully Tony centred the corer in an ice polygon. Grunting, he drilled deeper and deeper until he hit the basal rock, just over a metre below the surface. With impressive dexterity he pulled the sample core from the drill and encased it in plastic. A mother laying her infant in the crib couldn't have been more solicitous. The plug of earth was smooth and cold to the touch—like Phillip's soul, Tony reflected bitterly.

After his exertions, Tony paused to look around. Far in the distance he could make out tiny brown specks—musk oxen. Viola was probably skulking along behind them taking her endless notes. As his eye travelled the horizon, however, he stiffened suddenly. He would've recognized in total darkness the figure cresting the beach ridge three hundred yards to his right. Anne was heading his way.

Viola was in hot pursuit of the herd of musk oxen. Her grey hair sprang out from under her shocking pink toque at impossible angles. Her hip waders, miles too big and held over her thin shoulders with grubby string, was covered in muck—dung primarily. Wally would not have approved of her waltzing through his potential specimens.

Viola was one of the lucky few who truly enjoyed her work. Here, in this isolated grandeur, she felt totally at home and even considered herself one of the herd. Even more than when she had first begun her studies ten years before, Viola marvelled at how completely at home musk oxen were in this most inhospitable of environments. Every detail of their anatomy, physiology and behaviour had been sculpted over tens of thousands of years to adapt them to the extreme cold and sparse food resources of their range. Now, in the comparative warmth of late May, the animals had shed their dense, fine inner hair leaving only the sweeping lengths of the outer guard hairs swirling around their short legs like over-long coats. As she followed the herd, Viola gathered what discarded tufts of wool she came across, stuffing them into her knapsack to be carded, spun and woven during her exile in Ottawa. On the three winter expeditions she's managed to arrange, she wore as a talisman a soft sweater fashioned from this hair. Wearing this, she felt invincible, as if the cold could never harm her. It never had.

On her all too short field trips, Viola mostly observed. Today she watched the musk oxen browsing on the choice willows and grasses, nibbling the occasional arctic poppy as they luxuriated in the abundance of the few weeks of summer. All too soon they would be using their hoofs to scrape the thin snow from the lichen and moss which formed a staple part of their winter diet. They would eat almost anything which grew on the tundra. Musk oxen weren't choosy. But during these weeks of plenty, they could spend energy on something other than the endless search for food. The mating season would soon begin, the most exciting time for the observer, and, Viola supposed, for the musk oxen as well.

Her first encounter with these animals had given Viola a particular thrill. She had been observing a large herd from a discreet distance, unobserved by the animals—she thought. Suddenly, one of the adult bulls left the group and galloped directly towards her. He stopped, snorting, a few metres away from her cowering form. He lowered his massive forehead to his forefeet—the signal for a charge!

Viola froze, her heart pounding in her throat, unable to run or cry out. When the bull lifted his head again she saw death in his black eyes. He began the attack, moss and dirt spitting up from his thundering hooves, but at the last he altered course, wheeled to the side and charged towards another male. The titanic clash of the two seven-hundred-pound bodies rocked the tundra itself.

Viola went limp with relief when she realized what had happened—the bull had delivered a warning. She vowed never to go near musk oxen again. She hadn't kept her promise, but the warning had been effective and she treated these wild animals with great respect.

Today the warning had been given again and she sat down on a rock outcrop to catch her breath. Viola listened to the beat of her heart as it slowly settled to normal. Someday the charge might be for real.

She swept the wide expanses with her binoculars. She too recognized Anne as she made her way slowly along the top of a ridge, staying downwind and well away from the musk oxen herd. Viola gave a grunt of satisfaction—Anne was always so careful not to disturb anyone's studies. As Viola continued her visual sweep, Tony entered her field of vision. She noted his hasty departure as he spotted his wife.

A tiny sigh escaped Viola. Poor Anne. Both she and Tony

had so many sensitive spots it was difficult even to make small talk. Viola thought she knew the root of the problem between the Colauttis even though it was obvious Anne didn't. Maybe I should talk to Tony, Viola mused. He really should tell his wife what's wrong. Anne could handle it.

Banishing the Colauttis from her mind, Viola turned back to her herd. Even though they were grazing as they moved, they were deceptively fast and Viola, shouldering her rifle and her pack, had to hustle to close the gap.

When Joan returned to camp for dinner, she stuck her head into Simon's tent and found him stretched out on his cot, groaning in exhaustion. 'Can't keep up, eh, Simon? Too much soft living in your cushy job? Maybe you should join the real world.'

Simon snorted. 'You're a fine one to talk. The most I've seen you do is stoop over and collect the odd bacterial sample.' He winced as he sat up. 'I've been impersonating a pack animal and a chain-gang worker and my weary bones need rest. Thank God I've a legitimate reason for having to be back here by eight o'clock or that slave-driver Anne would have me working yet.'

'Who are you calling a slave-driver?' Anne was standing in the doorway, mock indignation on her face.

Simon threw his hand to his forehead and fell back on his bed. 'Save me! I can't take any more.'

A rare smile crossed Joan's severe countenance.

'Then I guess I'll have to take my restorative somewhere else.' Anne waved a mickey of rye in front of her.

The bottle must have had truly magical powers since the very sight of it enabled Simon to regain a sitting position. Three relatively clean cups appeared in Joan's hands.

Anne poured generous portions. They sipped in silence, appreciating the warmth as it trickled through their bodies.

Finally Simon broke the peace. 'Ah . . . human again. I may live to fight another day—and not for you, I might add, Anne.'

'But I've six more ponds to do.'

'A great scientist could arrive at the truth with four ponds. Only a plodder would need ten replicates,' Simon declared.

'And since when are you an expert?' Anne demanded.

'Since I strained my back and crippled myself for life preparing the first four ponds. Why don't you work like Joan here does, performing the occasional deep knee-bend to obtain a sample and then retreating for a well-deserved rest?'

'Unfair, Simon,' Joan protested, earnest again. 'I've been working hard. It's not my fault Wally won't collaborate with me and make my data really complete.'

'Did you ask him nicely?' Anne asked, sympathetic to Joan's complaint.

'Of course I did. I positively dripped goodwill and generosity. He simply won't consider it.'

'Poor Joan . . . and poor Wally, too. I remember when he was a great guy—quiet, but helpful and enthusiastic. He's changed so much . . .' Anne's voice died away as she remembered the Wally of five years ago.

'What happened?' Simon couldn't suppress his curiosity.

'I don't know much detail,' Anne explained. 'However, Wally's wife died four years ago and he hasn't been the same since.'

'Yeah, that's what I heard too,' Joan nodded. 'And then eighteen months ago his only son committed suicide. That's when he really went weird.'

'Was the son upset because of his mother's death?' Simon asked.

'Rumour has it there was more to it than that,' Joan offered, 'but Eric could tell you more. Or Jeff—they were great buddies till Wally changed.'

'Well, tell me what you can,' Simon urged. 'Wally makes me nervous and if I understood why he acts like he does, maybe I could deal with him better.'

'Fat chance! Think you're a psychologist as well as a cop?' Joan asked derisively.

'I heard that Scott Gingras—he was only twenty when he died—was a homosexual and a drug addict,' Anne stated baldly. 'Depending on whom you listen to, either his pusher or his lover dropped him and he couldn't cope. I understand he jumped off a tenth-floor balcony.'

'I heard he had a fight with his lover—some rich guy with lots of friends in high places, and simply went to pieces. He was high on something when he jumped—a farewell gift from the boyfriend, maybe.' Joan shrugged. 'Guess the one-two punch was more than Wally could handle.'

'That explains his hostility, at any rate,' Simon commented. 'In my job I've seen enough parents destroyed by any one of those factors. All three, gay, drugs and suicide —not many could deal with that and remain unchanged.'

Silence descended on the little group, the festive mood destroyed. Anne rose uncertainly. 'Dinner-time, I guess,' she murmured as she scuttled out of the tent, swinging the flap shut as she went.

After dinner, Simon was in a mellow mood as he headed away from the tents to make a final check along his antenna. As he tightened a guy wire, more for something to do than out of necessity, Joan appeared behind him, her black brows drawn to a straight line over her blue eyes.

'I need help tomorrow.' She jammed her fists into her pockets, pulling the jacket down taut. 'You're supposed to help any of us who need it.'

'I'd be happy to help.'

'You don't have to lie about it. I need help but I don't care if you enjoy it or not. And you won't!' Joan's large white teeth flashed briefly in satisfaction.

'What do you want me to do?' Simon asked neutrally.

'Collect dung. Lots of nice fresh shit. Weigh it. Bag it. Label it.'

'Sounds delightful.' Simon grimaced.

Joan laughed. 'I thought you'd be pleased. Kind of ironic, isn't it—a cop scooping shit for an ex-con.'

'A nice change of pace,' Simon agreed without reaction. 'See you tomorrow.'

He started to move away but Joan shifted to block his path.

'Aren't you going to ask what I was in for?'

Simon tilted his head and studied her. Her eyes flashed in defiance. 'What were you in for?' he asked.

'Arson and resisting arrest, for starters.' She kicked the ground and looked at Simon sideways. 'Still going to work for me?'

'You're an *ex*-con, I believe you said.'

'Aren't we just the model citizen!' Joan set her hands on her hips and raked him with her eyes. 'I suppose you're going to tell me I've paid my debt to society and now I'm just like you or anyone else.'

'That's the theory.'

'Well, let me tell you, mister, I don't want to be like you!' Joan shook a finger inches from Simon's face. 'Arresting people for fighting for what's right . . . supporting those who are destroying our planet . . .'

'That's not what I do. I'm with the Criminal Investigation Branch and I arrest people for murder, or kidnapping. You want them to go free?'

'I'd rather let a murderer go free than let a big conglomerate destroy our forests, pollute our air, poison our water . . . Who's doing more damage?'

'A murderer has killed a human being.' Simon fought to keep his temper. Even up here he got nothing but crap.

'So? The victim probably deserved it. A polluter kills too, you know, and not just people. Everything. And no one cares.'

'Some people do,' Simon protested. 'I'd say the people who come here care.'

'Ha! That's what you think. Take the late, great Phillip Loew. An exploiter of monumental proportions—and all the worse because he called himself an environmentalist.'

'How do you know he didn't care about such things?' Simon was ever alert to *his* favourite topic.

Joan could hardly speak coherently. She paced with short, jerky strides. 'He—he hired himself out to do en-

environmental impact studies for industrial giants.' She
brushed back her hair with a savage gesture. 'Then he told
them ex-exactly what they wanted to hear. And he made
damn sure he got his thirty pieces of silver.'

'Maybe he told the truth. You view any industry as bad.'

'For good reason!' Joan retorted. 'But as for Phillip, he
—he didn't even do any research. He just wandered around
the location for a few weeks and then wrote up his report.'
Bitterness swelled with the anger in Joan's voice. 'Take it
from me, I've had first-hand experience with Phillip's dirty
tricks.'

'What did he do?' Simon asked quickly.

'Oh, what's the point?' Joan fumed, kicking aimlessly at
the frozen ground. 'You don't care. No one cares. We'll
have destroyed the whole planet before any one even
notices. Humanity will be extinct and we'll deserve it.' The
last outburst hung in the air as Joan stalked off, back in the
direction of the camp.

CHAPTER 4

Simon made a wide sweep to locate bear dung for Joan.
He'd used only three of the dozen sample bags so far and
these, with their unsavoury contents, he carried in a small
backpack. He hadn't seen the animals which supplied the
samples: arctic foxes, rabbits and musk oxen.

As Simon reached the halfway mark in his trek he felt a
change in the weather. The sky, uniformly blue for the
morning, had turned grey in the east as a bank of cloud
reared its bulk over the horizon. The wind, noticeably
colder, picked up and slowed his pace. Now he didn't care
about seeing any animals—he just wanted to finish his job
and get to shelter.

When he spotted a musk oxen herd directly in his path
he groaned aloud. 'Damn! Do I have to go all the way
round?' He raised his binoculars to search for Viola. Per-

haps it wasn't 'her' herd. No such luck. He recognized her unmistakable pink hat between him and the animals. He examined the situation. The musk oxen were grazing in a valley while Viola crouched on the slope nearest him. If he crossed the steep-sided valley he'd be in full view of the herd. Viola had suggested half a mile as the minimum distance to avoid disturbing the animals.

Simon sighed. It wasn't his day. Shifting his pack, he turned and headed along the ridge, just far enough below the crest that the animals couldn't see him. He had covered two hundred yards when the sharp loud cracks of gunfire shattered the immense quiet. He stopped dead, instinctively crouching and turning to face the threat as another volley of sound split the air. Orange flashes and smoke rose from the far side of the valley, directly across from Viola. Memory of the army-issued artillery simulators replaced his momentary incomprehension. Who was in danger?

Simon scanned the scene. The herd of forty musk oxen milled in disarray. Then one of the large bulls seemed to take command of the group, which formed itself into a ragged phalanx. Cows and calves led the flight as the bulls kept to the rear protecting the threatened flank. The herd thundered across the narrow valley, frightened bellows mingling with the pounding of their hoofs. Viola stood frozen, directly in the line of flight, staring through her binoculars at the spectacle. 'Run, Viola!' Simon shouted. 'Run!'

She jumped, at last realizing her danger. She peered frantically in all directions, searching for shelter. She ran. Simon sprinted towards Viola, shouting and waving madly, but neither the herd nor Viola paid any attention. The thudding of hoofs, frantic animal cries, Simon's shouts and the pounding of two human hearts blotted out the peace which had filled the open spaces moments before.

Simon had three artillery simulators with him. But good as his pitching arm was, he couldn't hurl them two hundred yards. He raced to get within throwing distance, clutching the first arti-sim in his fist. Narrowing his eyes, he mentally

judged the respective distances between himself and Viola
and the musk oxen. A dead heat.

Simon halved the distance between himself and the animals and prepared to throw the first of his diversions. From
the crest of the ridge he could see Viola diving for shelter
in the lee of a large rock. Momentarily slowing his wild
pace, he twisted off the cap and scratched the head of the
arti-sim against its striking surface like a giant match. He
threw with all his strength. The arti-sim spiralled high into
the air, to hang like a prayer at the top of its arc. Then it
came plummeting down fifty yards short of the herd, on the
crest of the ridge. Its display seemed less spectacular than
the ones which had started the animals' headlong flight.
The lead cows shied slightly, but seemed unable to break
the momentum of the herd. Simon imagined he could feel
the earth trembling under their weight. He sped up again,
pulling the next arti-sim from his pocket as he ran.

His second attempt landed short as well, but again the
leaders wavered, and this time they angled slightly away
from their previous line of flight. Before Simon had time to
throw his last arti-sim, the musk oxen thundered past the
rock where Viola crouched and charged on over the ridge.

By the time Simon reached the rock, his breath was
coming in ragged gasps. He rounded the rock to see Viola
sagging forward, her head on her knees. 'Are you all right?'
he demanded urgently.

Slowly she raised her head. Blood pulsed from a deep
gash on her forehead, blinding her left eye as it dripped.
Although dazed, she quavered a reply, 'I think so . . . a
stone . . .'

Pulling off his toque, Simon used it to stanch the crimson
stream. He bunched the cloth against the wound, pressing
hard. 'Hold this,' he ordered.

Obediently she raised her hand to the crude bandage as
Simon searched for something to hold it in place.

'I have a scarf inside my coat,' Viola volunteered, her
voice steady this time.

Simon's fingers scrabbled at Viola's zipper, then yanked

free the length of pink wool. He wound it around her head, supporting the wadded toque.

'Thanks,' Viola said simply.

'I'm not much of a nurse, I'm afraid.'

Viola smiled wanly. 'I wasn't talking about your Florence Nightingale act. I meant for saving my life.'

'To be quite honest, I think you saved it yourself, but I tried.' Simon looked around. 'Where's your rifle? You always carry a .22.'

Viola hung her head and pointed vaguely behind her. 'Over there . . . near my pack. I just put it down for a minute . . .'

Simon snorted. 'Great. And I suppose you don't have any arti-sims either.'

Viola's guilty expression was answer enough. She probed her forehead with her fingertips, wincing when she touched a red swelling. 'What happened?'

'I was about to ask you the same thing.'

'I was watching two of the animals through my binoculars when I heard the blasts . . . I didn't really register what it was until the herd started acting panicky and you yelled at me.' She paused and then added softly, 'If you hadn't yelled I don't know how long I would've stood there mesmerized, watching the herd come right for me.'

Simon sat down beside her, leaning back against the stone. 'Then you didn't see who threw the firecrackers?'

'No. You didn't either?'

In his turn, Simon shook his head. 'When I heard the noise and turned around, all I saw was the smoke, the flashes, the herd, and your pink hat right in the path of the stampede. Maybe if I'd thought to look at the far ridge . . .'

They sat on the tundra in silence, each lost in thought, until finally Viola voiced the question uppermost in both their minds. 'Why?'

'I don't know. I can't think of any good reason, can you?'

'No. The herd was peaceful . . . no threat to anyone.' Again she gingerly fingered her scalp. 'Who knows how long it'll take the animals to trust me again . . .'

Another voice shattered the silence. 'Vi! Where are you? Are you OK? Viola?'

Simon slowly got to his feet and waved wearily. 'Over here!'

Eric was running down the slope where the artillery barrage had exploded. Another hurrying figure was visible over to the left. Anne. Simon frowned.

Viola got unsteadily to her feet, holding a hand to her head. With Simon's hand under her elbow, they both waited while Eric rushed up to them.

'Vi, what on earth happened?'

'I got stampeded by a herd of musk oxen,' she laughed shakily.

'I warned you something like this would happen some day. Those animals are totally unpredictable.'

'It wasn't my animals which were unpredictable,' she retorted indignantly.

'And just what is that supposed to mean?'

'Somebody started the stampede by exploding arti-sims right under their noses,' Simon explained as Viola bit her lip in pain. 'You must've heard the commotion. You didn't happen to see anyone else around here, did you?'

'Do you mean the arti-sims *caused* the stampede?'

'Yeah,' Simon asserted. 'I threw a couple more to try to turn them away from Viola but I wasn't close enough. Everything was fine till the first explosion.'

At this moment Anne arrived panting on the scene. Joan wasn't far behind, coming in from the right. Hell, thought Simon, was everyone in the area?

'Oh Viola,' Anne wailed. 'What happened? Are you all right?'

'She'd be better off if we got her back to camp and put a proper dressing on her head,' Simon said, noticing how pale Viola was looking.

'Of course. Immediately,' Eric concurred. 'Simon, you and I could make a chair of our hands and carry her back that way.' Turning to Viola, he asked solicitously, 'You could put your arms around our necks, couldn't you? We'll be very careful not to jar you more than we can possibly help . . .'

'And Joan and I can spell you,' Anne added.

'OK,' Viola whispered, adding a green tinge to her already sickly hue. 'Anne, would you get my pack, please?'

Viola gritted her teeth against nausea and faintness as she swayed over the tundra in her human sedan chair, but she was a tough lady and made no complaint. The others speculated about the cause of the incident until the steady deterioration in the weather forced them to concentrate solely on getting safely back to camp.

The headwind was viciously strong and cold, biting through their clothing and catching in their lungs, making progress difficult and conversation impossible. Viola was feeling the cold most keenly, as she sat grimly on the clenched fists of her bearers. They all thought about their warm parkas stashed snugly back at camp. No one had come prepared for such a change in the weather. Forecasts for Bathurst Island weren't very specific.

'Put me down.' Viola struggled to stand.

'What?' Eric and Simon jerked to a halt.

'Put me down. If I don't move I'll freeze,' she chattered.

'Sure?' Eric asked as they eased her down.

'Just let me lean on you.' With support on both sides, she plodded grimly through the darkening landscape. Flakes of icy snow, driven hard on the wind, attacked their naked skin like tiny needles. Never had such a short distance seemed so far. After an endless hour, they spotted the lights of the camp glowing hazily through the snow. They stumbled into the friendly circle of tents and the welcoming arms of the three waiting scientists. Amid a barrage of questions, Viola was put to bed in her tent and Joan exchanged Simon's makeshift dressing for a clean white bandage.

Eric recounted the facts, but Simon, the only eye-witness, was in demand for details. Jeff and Tony peppered him with questions.

'Coffee, hot,' was all Simon would say until he'd wrapped

himself in several more sweaters and a dry pair of socks. He sat hunched up on his cot. Jeff thrust a steaming mug into his outstretched hands.

'Is everyone here?' Simon asked after taking a scalding mouthful of the brew.

'All present and accounted for,' Jeff's calm voice answered. 'No lost sheep tonight.'

Even Wally was attracted by the drama of the situation and joined the group huddled in Simon's tent. Only Joan and Viola were absent. In a by-play as they'd arrived, Simon noticed Anne's attempt to follow the other women into their tent, but her husband had prevented her. Simon didn't know what Tony had said but she had flushed and turned aside into their own quarters. Now she was back, bundled to the point where she seemed almost spherical.

'Did anyone make the radio check?' Simon inquired.

'No,' Jeff replied with a guilty start. 'I guess we didn't think of it . . . We were worried about the rest of you. We heard the arti-sim, you know, faintly, but we decided the best course of action was to wait here.'

'Who is "we"?' Simon asked.

'Wally and I.'

'When did Tony get here?'

'And just what are you insinuating?' Tony blustered.

'Well, unless you believe a stranger is stalking Polar Bear Pass, one of us set off the arti-sims,' Simon explained calmly. 'Would anyone like to claim responsibility?'

The silence was absolute, except for the howl of the wind and the snapping of the canvas door flaps.

'It wasn't me,' Tony protested. 'Just because I got here a little later than the others doesn't mean I stampeded that herd.'

'No,' Simon agreed, 'it could've been Eric or Anne, or Joan, if they weren't together when the fireworks started.' He turned to look at Anne. 'Were you?'

Anne shifted uncomfortably. 'No, but when I saw Eric and Joan they were both running in the same direction, *towards* the trouble. Just like me.'

'That'd be easy to arrange. All you'd have to do is run like hell along the blind side of the ridge, then turn around and start hurrying back on the side where we could see you.'

'I resent your implication, Mr Hollingford.' Eric's rich, measured tones broke into the ensuing silence. 'I, for one, would never perpetrate such a foolish prank. It could be very dangerous.'

'It was very dangerous. Viola is lucky she escaped so lightly.' Simon stared at them, one after the other.

At this uncomfortable moment Joan appeared. A whirl of snowflakes entered the tent with her. 'Viola will be fine . . . it's just a bad gash on her forehead. Once I cleaned away all the blood it didn't look nearly so serious. A couple of aspirin and a good night's sleep should take care of the headache.'

'Well, that's a relief, at any rate,' Anne commented, and a murmur of agreement followed.

'I'd better report in.' Simon rose from his bunk and edged his way to the door.

'That reminds me, Viola would like to talk to you before you call Resolute.' Joan ran her fingers through her damp hair. She'd crossed the compound bareheaded and the snow had melted now, warmed by the heat of many bodies.

'Right,' Simon called over his shoulder as he went out into the night. The wind was even stronger now, and the camp seemed very frail against its power. Simon huddled into his coat and crossed to Viola's tent as quickly as possible. Joan had set up one of the tiny heaters with which they were equipped, but this tent, with its sole occupant, was much colder than the one he'd just left. 'Boy, it's got chilly,' Simon commented as he looked around for something to sit on.

'It's fine once you're in your sleeping-bag,' Viola replied, much of the old twinkle back in her voice as she propped herself up on her elbow.

'So how are you doing?' Simon inquired.

'I'll be as right as rain in the morning,' Viola replied, 'so don't go saying anything about the accident in your report to Colonel Fernald. If I know you, you were going to give a full account of the day's events.'

'The salient points,' Simon admitted. 'That's what I'm supposed to do, if you recall.'

'We can't take a chance on him over-reacting, Simon. He might just put a stop to the whole project.'

Simon sat quietly for a moment, his knees up around his ears as he squatted on Joan's cot. With a mittened hand he rubbed his cleft chin as his mind worried at the dilemma. 'It wasn't an accident, Viola,' he finally said softly.

'I know.'

'And I don't think we can pin it on a wandering psycho-path who just happened into the vicinity.'

'It does seem unlikely.'

'I don't like the alternatives we're left with,' Simon confessed. 'Whether it was a stupid prank or a malicious act, it worries me.'

'And how do you expect I feel?' Viola asked tartly.

'So why do you want me to keep it quiet?' Simon studied Viola's drawn face. She looked her age now, except for her eyes which flashed with energy.

'I already told you,' Viola replied with exasperation, pressing her fingers to her temples. Her head ached abominably, and talking made it worse. 'The good Colonel might just tell us to pack up and leave. After all, we're technically under his command . . . The death of one of the expedition members would not go down well with his superiors. Last year, when Phillip disappeared, they pulled the rest of us out as soon as possible. If disaster strikes again this year, the army will likely wash its hands of us in the future.' Viola paused. 'They'll likely wash their hands of all science expeditions and that would be a severe blow to arctic research.'

'Maybe, but it's not worth losing your life over,' Simon pointed out.

'But I haven't lost my life, and I dare say I won't.' Viola's veined hands moved expressively. 'Whoever threw those firecrackers will have learned their lesson and won't try such a dangerous stunt again.'

'But what if it wasn't a prank, but a calculated effort to hurt you . . . kill you, even?'

'I really can't think it was, Simon,' Viola pleaded. 'No one here hates me that much. No one here hates me at all, as far as I know. I'm a harmless old lady,' Viola added with unaccustomed wistfulness.

At that Simon had to laugh. 'What a whopper! You're neither old nor harmless, nor a lady for that matter, but I agree you're an unlikely target for murder.' He held his hands towards the small heater and looked sideways at her. 'I don't suppose your will leaves a fortune to anyone here?'

Viola snorted. 'What fortune? I haven't bothered with a will, but my beneficiaries will be my sisters, I suppose, as nearest living relatives. Neither of them is closer than three thousand miles and they're both better off than I am—they were "sensible" girls and married money.'

Simon grunted, scratching his head. 'You don't happen to be indulging in a spot of blackmail?'

'Would I tell you if I were?'

'Probably not.' Simon sighed. 'There goes another promising idea.' He paused. 'I know! Have you observed someone committing dastardly deeds?'

'Other than eating lunches for breakfast, you mean?'

'Something more dastardly than that,' Simon replied. Even he was guilty of this misdemeanour, but there were extenuating circumstances. Breakfasts were inedible.

Viola struggled to a sitting position so that she could look him in the eye. 'Really, Simon, there's no earthly reason why anyone here or elsewhere would try to kill me. It must've been a practical joke which got out of hand. You can't wreck everything by reporting the accident to Colonel Fernald.' A network of worry lines creased Viola's forehead as she pleaded her case. Her age had definitely caught up with her.

'All right,' Simon agreed reluctantly, 'but I'm not sure

it's a good idea. You'll have to promise me you'll be careful
. . . try to stay in sight of others while you work. And carry
some arti-sims, for heaven's sake. Your rifle didn't do you
much good lying on the ground a hundred yards away.'

'Yes, yes, I promise,' Viola declared hastily.

Simon hoisted himself to his feet with difficulty, his legs
stiff from the cramped position. 'Is there anything I can get
you before I go?'

'No, thanks. Sleep is what I need now, so go make your
innocuous report to Resolute. If they crave some excitement
tell them about our weather.'

The weather did make an acceptable excuse for the late
hour of his radio check, so Simon got off with sympathy
instead of censure when he finally placed his call.

As Viola lay in her sleeping-bag, bits and pieces of her
history rose to her mind in a jumble of unconnected vig-
nettes. Both conscious thought and fitful dreams were
mixed up in them.

Eric drifted by, not as he was now, but as he'd appeared
when Viola first met him at a wildlife symposium many
years before. They'd been attracted to each other then, as
they were in her dream, but Eric had wanted a stay-at-
home wife and Viola was too ambitious to put her career
aspirations aside to play the helpmeet, even to Eric. In
Viola's dream Eric was chasing her, yelling at her, but he
sounded like a musk ox, and gradually acquired shaggy
hair and four feet.

Suddenly, as is the way with dreams, an entire herd, with
many familiar faces included, was chasing her. Tony and
Anne were represented by a mother and child pair, but the
mother was rejecting the calf because it was albino. Joan
Winik thundered along, getting ever closer to the fleeing
Viola who could run only in slow motion. Two aged bulls
were fighting it out while they floated along, inexplicably
keeping up with the herd despite the mortal combat. Their
eyes reminded Viola of Jeff and Wally. A third bull with
green eyes and an oddly cleft chin loped along behind. This
male, seeing that the herd was about to trample Viola, tried

to turn the living steamroller aside with firecrackers blazing from his horns. Just as the lead animals bore down on her —she could see their human eyes and smell their feral breath—Viola woke with a start, heart pounding wildly and her skin sheened with sweat inside her sleeping-bag.

She must have cried out because Joan was beside her, stroking her forehead below the bandage, a worried frown creasing her face. Viola was touched by her obvious concern. 'Just a nightmare.' Her throat was parched. A hoarse frog would have sounded healthier.

'I'll get you a drink,' Joan whispered.

No more was said until Viola had sipped some iced tea. It had started as hot tea, but the weather had metamorphosed it. Joan broke the thick crust of ice on its surface, liberating the chunks to drift as ice cubes.

'Thanks,' the patient croaked before drinking thirstily. 'I'm sorry I woke you,' she apologized, sounding much more like herself.

'It must have been quite a dream.'

Viola nodded. 'Another stampede, and this time there was no last-minute refuge. I was a goner.'

'Poor dear. Try to forget it and get back to sleep. Would you like another painkiller?'

'No, thanks—it must've been them that gave me the nightmare. I rarely dream.' Viola settled herself back in her bag, the frigid air having cooled her off. Joan's teeth were chattering. 'You get back to bed before you catch your death!' the older woman admonished. 'I'll be just fine.'

Joan squeezed her hand before doing as she was bid, huddling deep into the soft down of her Wood's four-star bag and drifting quickly back to sleep.

Viola, on the other hand, had no desire to endure a re-run of her recent dream and fought her drowsiness. Her head clear now, she mulled over the list of suspects. At least three of them could be eliminated immediately, leaving only Anne and her husband, Joan and Eric . . . good old Eric. How long had she known him? Close on thirty years it was now. Even back then, as a young man, he'd had a patrician air about him. Their romance had been passionate and stormy, since Eric was determined to dominate and Viola equally determined not to submit. It was odd, in a way, because she was sure it was her very spirit and independence which he'd found so attractive. Several years after the final blow-up, they'd met again. He'd introduced a timid redhead as his wife and the small boy as her son.

'Isn't he wonderful?' Lynda Karnot had whispered when Eric had turned aside to speak to someone else. Her adoring eyes followed her husband as he worked the room. 'I'm so lucky! He's so good to us . . .'

Lynda's soft eyes hovered before Viola's when Eric had suggested a late-night rendezvous for old times' sake.

Lynda Karnot reminded Viola of Anne—another vulnerable wife. Poor girl. And Joan wasn't quite as tough as she looked either. They wouldn't have hurt me . . .

It had to have been an accident, Viola told herself sleepily. Her head was aching again but gradually frustrating conundrums gave way to fitful sleep and uneasy dreams. These too passed and Viola, at last, slept deeply. It was to be her last good sleep at Polar Bear Pass.

Simon was up early, well refreshed. It was before six o'clock in the morning and no one else was stirring. The storm had died down leaving the air crisp, cold and still, and despite the near-blizzard conditions of the night, not much snow had actually fallen. Blowing snow, not falling snow, had caused the difficult conditions.

Pulling on his heavy gloves as he walked, Simon turned his steps towards the scene of the stampede. While part of his mind was still occupied with the unfortunate event, he couldn't stop himself from gazing with wonder at the scene before him. Most of the ground was still quite bare, the greens and greys of the lichens and dwarf willows exactly as they had been the day before. But here and there drifts of snow had built up—patches of white against the dark background. The flowers still bloomed as if unaware of the freezing temperatures, each blossom framed delicately in snow crystals. The sun, well above the southern horizon, hung hugely in the startling blue of the sky, as a talisman of infinity. The brilliant light glinted on the pockets of snow and refracted into rainbows of colour. Somehow the air seemed even purer than it had before the storm.

Simon kept up a good pace, anxious to be back in time for his morning radio check. He removed his gloves and toque as both the sun and the exercise warmed him. On the leeward sides of the valleys there were large drifts, as if all the snow which fell had been gathered together in a few discreet piles. He skirted an old ice bridge, newly frosted in gleaming white, and forded the narrow stream in three long steps. As he neared his goal, the site of the arti-sim explosions, he slowed and examined the terrain in all directions. The landscape here was rougher than it was for the most part, with the beach ridge undulations closer together than they were near the camp. The ridges themselves were slashed frequently by narrow, but deeply eroded stream beds. It would be possible, Simon concluded, for someone to get a fair distance away without being seen unless someone else were traversing the same depression. He jogged on to the precise site of the explosions, pinpointed by scorch marks on the frozen ground.

Simon squatted over the burns, pushing gently at the dirt with a bare finger. The wind had blown away most of the debris but a few small bits of the casing were lodged between the polygons. He gently extracted these and examined them carefully, turning them this way and that for a thorough inspection. He took an unused arti-sim from his pocket. The casing material was identical and the transient stranger hypothesis appeared even less likely now than it had at the time of the incident. Slowly Simon straightened, letting the fragments fall between his fingers.

By the time he arrived back at the camp, everyone but Viola was up and about. Viola had reluctantly agreed to stay in bed for the day, but had warned Joan, her nurse, that one day was all she was willing to sacrifice. Evading

Tony, Anne managed to make a brief visit to Viola's bed-
side where she stood, awkwardly shy.

'I'm really sorry, Viola . . .' she began, but trailed off in
embarrassment.

'You've nothing to be sorry for, my dear, unless it was
you who spooked my animals,' Viola replied. Privately,
Viola thought she probably looked better than Anne did,
with the latter's wan expression and colourless cheeks.

'No, no . . . of course I didn't . . . that's not what I
meant. I meant I'm sorry you're hurt.'

'Not to worry. No permanent harm done.' Viola leaned
forward conspiratorially. 'I'm already perfectly recovered,
but Joan's been bullying me. I agreed to stay put for the
day just to get her off my back.'

A smile flickered over Anne's pallid face and was gone
before it had time to reach her eyes. 'No one bullies you,
Viola,' she responded with forced lightness.

'That's what you think. Joan can be a real tyrant when
you try to cross her. I don't recommend it.'

'I heard that.' Another voice chimed in and the two
looked up to see the maligned Joan enter the tent. 'One
more such remark and I'll prescribe an enema!'

Viola gave her trademark crack of laughter and even
Anne smiled as she slipped out the door.

'I'll collect more samples for you today, Joan,' Simon volunteered over his breakfast of veal cutlets.

'Oh?' Joan peered suspiciously at him from under her
black brows.

'I didn't get much yesterday, what with the weather and
the excitement. I wouldn't want you to feel you weren't
getting full benefit of my services.'

'All right.'

Simon stared steadily at her.

'Thank you,' Joan finally mumbled, reddening slightly.

'You're welcome.'

With a little planning Simon was able to meet Anne in

the supply tent. 'Want to come for a walk with me?' he asked.

Anne was flustered. 'I don't know . . . I have work to do . . . and Tony . . .'

Just at that moment Tony's nasal voice came floating over the still air. 'Anne? Where the hell are you? Where's my micrometer?'

With a nervous smile, Anne slipped away.

Sample bags in pocket, Simon set out eastward at a brisk pace. His gaze roamed around, searching for bear dung, but his stride was long and purposeful. He was again headed for the coast.

It was noon when he reached the water's edge, only a hundred feet from where he'd stumbled ashore a couple of days before. He made his way carefully over the slippery rocks, pausing frequently to study the shoreline and the shallows. The water was abnormally calm and chunks of ice sat motionless on its face. Even the clouds seemed to have paused in their flight across the sky.

'Ah-ha.' Simon spotted the blue raft resting on the bottom in three feet of water. One small pocket, still air-filled, swayed like a Portuguese man-of-war just below the surface. Simon pulled hip waders from his pack and struggled into them before cautiously entering the water, feeling for a safe footing. This time he was determined to stay dry.

The raft was awkward and bulky to pull ashore but after a good deal of swearing and sweating, Simon had it stretched out wetly on the beach. He tried to ignore the knot of tension in his stomach as he examined it.

He searched for the hole which had almost cost him his life. There it was—a straight, clean cut about an inch long. For most of its length the cut had severed only the outer skin but in the centre the second layer had also parted. His weight must have caused the final rip.

Simon refolded the raft as it had always been packed. The cut, and it was the only one, was on the inside of the packet, well away from the danger of accidental puncture.

He re-examined the damage. The cut was close to, but not on, the line of stitching around the label. It was well hidden.

A defect in manufacture, Simon wondered? The inside of the gash was bright blue, not soiled like the rest of the material. It looked fresh; cut cleanly as if by a knife. Anne had used the raft several times with no difficulty. She was much lighter, but how long could such a weak spot have held?

Simon rubbed his chin, his green eyes dark with worry. An accident? Maybe. Two accidents? He saw again the musk oxen thundering towards a terrified Viola. What the hell was going on?

CHAPTER 5

When they'd first arrived at Polar Bear Pass, everyone except Simon pitched in to do Eric's initial bird census. Simon had been excluded simply because he couldn't tell a snow goose from a long-tailed jaeger. Even Wally and Joan helped without fuss.

Using a book he borrowed from Eric, Simon worked hard on his bird identification before accompanying the great man himself. They settled down behind a blind overlooking one of the largest ponds. Eric mounted twin sets of binoculars and an expensive camera on high tech tripods. Simon eyed the equipment enviously. If only the police department were so well equipped . . . He frowned. What did he care? They were likely going to dismiss him anyway.

Eric kept up a whispered running commentary about birds in general and arctic birds in particular, but he paused now and again to direct Simon's attention to some interesting avian behaviour. He observed, talked, and made notes simultaneously. He wrote his notes in exquisite long-hand, without even looking at the page.

'How do you do that?' Simon asked, fascinated. 'I can barely think and write at the same time.'

Eric laughed good-humouredly, losing some of his
reserve and his boyish enthusiasm took over. 'I learned
that trick long ago. When I first started birding, all the
interesting things seemed to take place while I was bent
over my field book. I don't know how many rare and exciting incidents I only heard about from others when I'd been
right there on the scene. So this is how I reconciled my
mania for note-taking with my desire to see for myself. I've
perfected it over the years.'

'It would be a useful skill in my job,' Simon commented.

'I suppose it would.' Eric frowned as he recollected
Simon's profession.

The flock they were watching was composed mostly of
snow geese, their gleaming white feathers iridescent in the
sun. Sitting on the sandy gravel at the water's edge soiled
their breast plumage, but a short swim in the crystal waters
of the pond easily remedied that. They emerged from their
watery dining perfectly white except for their night-black
wing tips. The quick, muffled notes of their call punctuated
the silence, otherwise broken only by the short, descending
whistle of a snow bunting in flight.

A soaring form, high in the azure sky above them captured
Eric's attention. 'Look! Look! Do you see it?' He sprang to
his feet, scaring the nesting birds near the blind. He pointed
an urgent finger at the graceful, gliding bird.

Simon stood and stared heavenward. 'What is it?'

'It's a gyrfalcon, white phase. What the hell is it doing
way over here?'

'It's magnificent,' Simon whispered in awe.

'Isn't it!'

As the bird rode the winds above them, it barely moved
a feather, soaring effortlessly in its element, at home high
above the concerns of those doomed to crawl on the harsh
surface. Still without visible effort, using its characteristic
slow wing beat, it climbed higher, until it was only a dark
speck fading into the southern sky.

'If there is reincarnation, let me come back as one of

those,' Eric breathed almost as a prayer—to whom, Simon didn't know. Eric claimed to an atheist.

Reluctantly the two settled themselves once more behind the blind. Simon turned to his companion. 'Didn't I hear you had a pet gyrfalcon last year?'

Eric nodded. 'I found an injured juvenile gyrfalcon down near the coast. I captured it and put a splint on its wing. It got quite tame, for a falcon, anyway, and seemed reluctant to leave our camp even after its wing had healed. I put a miniature transmitter around its neck to track it, but it never went far from the camp. More faithful than a dog,' he said, laughing.

'What became of it?' Simon asked.

Eric shrugged. 'I don't really know. We were evacuated rather hurriedly last summer . . .'

'And this year? Any transmitters?'

'I've put one on a male snow bunting to see how far it wanders from the nest, but it seems to be a real homebody.'

'I'd like to see the transmitter sometime,' Simon commented. 'I'm interested in that sort of thing.'

Eric directed a sharp look at Simon but then reached into his pocket. 'I can't show you the transmitter right now, but this is the receiver.' He pressed a button. The receiver immediately emitted shrill beeping noises which rose and faded as Eric slowly swept the horizon. 'The bunting's over in that direction,' he announced, 'not more than a mile away. It's no gyrfalcon, I'm afraid.' He handed the small gadget to Simon, who turned it over in his palm. He flicked a tiny switch and the beeping noise was replaced by a flashing light. He handed it back. 'Neat.'

They glued themselves to their binoculars again but the snow geese had lost some of their charm.

'It's kind of like dining at McDonald's when you've just smelled Chateaubriand, isn't it?' Eric asked, sitting back on his heels.

'A little,' Simon admitted. 'Is the gyrfalcon rare?'

'Quite rare. The white phase is almost never seen outside Greenland and is virtually unheard of at Bathurst Island.

You normally find the grey ones around here. This one is way out of its usual range.'

'I suppose you've seen them there, in Greenland, I mean,' Simon asked wistfully.

'Of course.' A touch of Eric's usual astringent tone crept back into his voice but it vanished as quickly as it came. He was talking about his favourite topic. 'I've studied birds all over the world. Two years ago I was up the Amazon, and man, the birds there . . . Thousands of species, each more beautiful and exotic than the last. Up here you get maybe fifteen or twenty species nesting, and maybe another ten transient types. But I'll take birds anywhere I can get them, and I have to admit they're much easier to observe here, on the tundra, than deep in a rainforest.'

They watched in silence, the whisper of Eric's pencil and the occasional call of a feathered companion the only sounds. Silence in the arctic is truly silence, Simon thought.

'OK, Simon, let's see if you're a good student. Name that bird over there, the whitish one pecking at his wing feathers.'

'Easy. A male snow goose.'

'Easy now, but when you came?'

'Well, I might've got the goose part right,' Simon hedged.

'Ha! What about the smaller white one with the feathers on its feet, over there by the patch of poppies?'

'A rock ptarmigan, *Lagopus mutus*,' Simon responded promptly.

'It's not necessary to get fancy, just correct,' Eric said with some amusement.

They went over the identification of all the birds visible from that spot and Simon hesitated only once, over a purple sandpiper, which was a rarity at these latitudes. As they strolled back to camp, Simon named all the birds they saw without making an error.

'You're a careful observer,' Eric complimented him, 'though I suppose that's only to be expected with you being a policeman. I think you'll make an excellent census taker,' he decided and appointed Simon to the ranks of gatherers of avian data.

Now it was Simon's turn to do the weekly census. He positioned himself at the beginning of the transect which would lead him from the hill where the tents were perched southward across the Pass to the low cliffs beyond. Simon hadn't been there yet. In fact, no one seemed to cross this southern boundary on a regular basis.

Taking out the official census notebook, Simon licked his pencil and held it at the ready. On the left page were listed, alphabetically according to common name, all the species he was likely to encounter. All he had to do was make a check in the proper row for each bird he counted. Simon walked in a deliberate fashion, scanning both the ground and the air, and meticulously recorded the required information. Every few hundred yards he took a breather, to relax his eyes from the strain and to enjoy, rather than just inventory, his surroundings. It had turned into a beautiful day, with the snow melting into tiny rivulets making their circuitous way down the slopes to the stream beds. The two near-tragedies were temporarily forgotten.

When he finally reached the end of the transect, Simon grinned with satisfaction and stretched luxuriously. He'd been tense as he performed his first 'solo' scientific procedure, but he was proud of the job he'd done. Only one bird had given him any trouble but he had tentatively identified it as a red phalarope. 'Not bad for a rank amateur, if I do say so myself,' he declared to a nearby king eider and pocketed the field book.

It was still early in the day, so Simon decided to climb the low cliffs and explore what lay beyond to the south. It was an easy climb—the face rising in fractured dignity only twenty feet or so above the level of the Pass. From the top he had a view of a fairly level, stony plain, reminiscent of Cornwallis Island and Resolute. Plant life was so sparse that the lowlands he'd just come from looked lush in comparison. The few scrub willows were even more warped and shrivelled than those in the Pass. There seemed little to explore.

None the less, he went forward at a brisk pace determined to make the most of his vacation. He'd not likely get another chance to visit Bathurst Island. The rocky desert was criss-crossed by stream beds cut deeply into the hard tundra. The sides of these gullies were steep and the snow had not started to melt on their shadowed north slopes. Snow bridges, mounds of snow and ice across the creek beds, were more numerous here, and up to four feet high. They sparkled surrealistically in their new white frosting. An exceptionally large one, fantastically sculpted by wind and weather, attracted Simon and he slipped and slid down the slope for a closer examination. Its stark beauty was enhanced by its texture of worn marble and Simon caressed it with his bare hand, feeling for its heart and soul as he moved around it, probing its depths. Only near its base, where the new snow had piled up, was the texture yielding and he thrust his hand into its cold embrace. A chunk of ice broke off at waist height. 'Damn,' he swore, staring at the jagged break. He sought to regain the flowing line by kicking at the protruding cornice. More snow fell away. Simon's heart skipped a beat. A human hand extended stiffly from the sculpture. Beckoning death.

He leapt backward, almost tripping in his haste. Cold sweat beaded on his forehead and his blood rushed and pounded in his ears. He wanted to squeeze his eyes shut to block out the horrifying sight but despite his dread the hand held his gaze, refusing to even let him blink.

Simon stood there, staring, stunned. Then, ever so slowly, his consciousness tiptoed around the edge of his mind, testing, probing for a way to accept this new reality. 'Phillip,' he croaked. 'Holy shit! I found the goddamn body.' Simon sobbed with relief. He could deal with the corpse now. He knew where it fitted into his reality.

As his head cleared his professional self took over and he began painstakingly to chip away at the icy tomb. He used his hands, his feet and a pocket knife to dislodge the mixture of snow and ice which encased the body. After half an hour of scrabbling at the unyielding material, he had uncovered the arm, head and upper torso. Phillip was lying on his left side, with one hand extended above his head. The other was clutched close to his chest.

Simon paused, breathing hard from his exertions. He sucked at a fresh scratch on his thumb and leaned on the ice bridge, staring down at the corpse.

As he toiled, Simon's mind had been churning. He'd regained his equilibrium after the initial shock, but finding a corpse right on the heels of two suspicious accidents looked like the final straw. What would become of the expedition now? Would Eric call a halt to it? Would Colonel Fernald order them to leave? Would Eric accompany the body of his stepson back south and leave the rest of them to carry on? 'Or will he ignore the whole thing?' Simon mused aloud. 'It's hard to tell with Eric.'

He looked again at the partly exposed body, this time paying more attention to the extended hand which he'd been consciously avoiding. Hands were so . . . intimate . . . so much a part of a living personality. Simon forced himself to confront his dread. He bent down and took the outstretched hand in his own equally cold one. It was well shaped and the nails, though bluish now, were neatly manicured. No callouses. But embedded in the whorls and lines of the palm were dark stains which to Simon's well-trained eye looked like old, dried blood. Odd, in someone who had presumably frozen to death. Hesitation forgotten, Simon continued his scrutiny of the dead man.

The arm held close to the chest was frozen into that position and no amount of effort could budge it. Nor could he turn the corpse to get a better look. Even with these restrictions, however, he now noticed the brown stain on the upper chest. He knelt in the snow, face close to the body, running his numb fingers over the jacket of the dead man. He brushed away the last traces of frost. Two small, circular holes, about four inches apart, decorated the expensive parka. One was high in the shoulder and the other lower down. 'Lung,' mumbled Simon. 'Or spleen, maybe . . .' The interesting red-brown stains were centred around the punctures. Simon knew a bullet hole when he saw one.

He sat back on his heels. The sun still blazed in the afternoon sky, making rivulets of water run from the pile of snow his digging had produced. A melodious birdsong echoed on the breeze, but Simon was only dimly aware of all this. He began fingering the cleft in his chin as his brain re-engaged, examining the discovery as a cat might worry a dead bird.

Phillip had been murdered; that was true beyond a shadow of a doubt. Simon's mind flickered only for a milli-second over the comfortable explanation that an unknown stranger had done the deed. The inescapable truth was that one of last year's expedition members was responsible for the grisly sight now confronting him. And, except for the addition of himself, and the absence (until now) of Phillip, the make-up of the group was identical this year. Simon's eyes narrowed and he felt the cords in the back of his neck pull even tighter.

When in a quandary, he liked to pace. There was plenty of room, but his steps didn't take him far from the ice bridge. Phillip drew him back like a magnet before he'd wandered far, and each time he returned to this focal point Simon stooped again to re-examine the body and search for other, more palatable explanations.

In normal circumstances, when confronted with an obvi-ous crime, he knew exactly what to do and how to go about it. While he'd never actually discovered a body himself, he'd seen plenty of them during police investigations. Bodies did turn up in the oddest places, from freezers to bear traps, from cars to hotels, from ditches to penthouses, but always, in Simon's previous experience, he'd had all the facilities of a modern police force to call upon. Local constables would corral anyone in the vicinity. The identi-fication unit would examine and record the murder scene in meticulous detail. And there was always his right-hand

man, Bill Harkness, to assist him all through the ensuing
investigation. But here, he realized with dismay, he was on
his own. The echo of his morning's conversation with Private Ernie Mallow, his radio contact, reverberated.

'Yes, everything's fine, here, Ernie, except the food. How
about way down south in Resolute, over?'

'Everything's lousy including the food AND the weather,'
the private reported gloomily. 'Colonel Fernald is getting
pissed off about this fog. We're socked in again today. Nothing can get in or out. Over.'

'You guys should be happy with nothing to do. Over,'
Simon chuckled.

'Are you kidding? The Great Man is a week behind on
his schedule because of this weather, and he's taking it out
on us. Two ten-mile runs today, tent inspections, cleaning
machinery . . . all the worst jobs. Over.'

'Cheer up, Ernie, the fog can't last much longer. Over.'

Private Mallow groaned into the mike. 'That's what you
think! Our meteorological service sees no change for the
next few days. By the time it lifts we'll be frothing at the
mouth and tearing each other apart! Cabin fever—and
we've all got it, from the Colonel down to yours truly. Over.'

Simon's face creased in indecision, and his green eyes
clouded with worry as he weighed his options. On top of
everything else, the weather on Bathurst Island was also
deteriorating and he'd have to move quickly to get back to
the relative safety of the camp. He piled snow over the
exposed corpse. 'Just to preserve it,' he muttered, but he
knew he had another motive. He didn't want anyone else
stumbling on the body until he was ready.

With one long, final look at Phillip's tomb, Simon started
back, moving with surprising speed considering his mind
was not accompanying him. It stood watch over the corpse.

While the wind rose and dense, heavy grey snow clouds
piled up on the western horizon, he made his way home-
ward with a hundred questions swirling in his mind. At
present, it was impossible for Resolute to send a helicopter
for them, and along with it someone to take charge of the

situation. In the meantime, would he be farther ahead to announce his discovery as soon as he returned to camp, or hold off until something could be done about it? Should he talk to the Colonel? Should he speak to the expedition members? At least one of them wouldn't be surprised at the news.

Even as he neared camp amid the first flurry of snow-flakes, he still hadn't decided. 'Better play it by ear,' he mumbled to himself. Usually he was very decisive, but then, there wasn't much that could be classified as 'usual' about the present situation.

'Surely it didn't take you this long to do the bird count?'

Startled, Simon jerked his head up to peer at the speaker. 'What . . . ?'

Eric motioned him into his tent. Most of the others were gathered inside. 'The bird count. You did do it, didn't you?' Eric asked with a touch of exasperation.

To Simon, that slow pacing of the valley identifying and enumerating seemed days in the past, but now he remembered it had been only a few hours ago.

'Yes,' he cleared his throat as his voice came out as a hoarse croak, 'yes, I did.'

'No problems?'

Simon snapped his head around to examine Eric's face, wondering how he'd found out about Phillip. Then he felt foolish as he realized the question was about bird identification. 'Just one,' Simon replied after an awkward pause while he adopted the proper mind-set to deal with the scientific questions. He then described the one unusual specimen he'd seen on his transect. 'I tentatively put it down as a red phalarope,' Simon concluded.

'I think you're right, my boy,' Eric replied, taking an avuncular tone with his promising student. 'We'll make a scientist of you yet.'

'Where've you been all this time, Simon?' Anne asked.

'I decided to see what was beyond the south cliffs, since I was at that side of the Pass anyway,' Simon answered, surreptitiously examining the circle of faces for some sign of consternation.

'Not much over there,' Jeff commented. 'Those cliffs are even lower than the north ones. Very boring.'

'So I saw,' Simon replied. He decided to say nothing to his companions. Not yet.

'I did a few permafrost measurements over there last year,' Jeff continued, 'but it really isn't very interesting. The musk oxen don't browse on that stony soil, so there isn't even any good dung for Wally.'

'No one was over there on a regular basis last year?' Simon inquired casually.

'No. We mostly stick to the Pass. It's much richer biologically,' Eric explained.

'But what about Phillip? He was interested in rocks, not flora and fauna. Did he do any studies to the south?'

'He took a few measurements . . . did a little topography, but he was mainly interested in the coastal area,' Jeff replied. 'We all felt he was prospecting for oil deposits, even though he wouldn't admit it. He was more interested in the shale and such.'

'He was a traitor,' Joan mumbled under her breath.

'Who did he betray?' Simon turned on her.

'All of us!' Joan hissed. 'This is a biological expedition. We're supposed to cherish the natural world, not destroy it.'

'Not too long ago you told me no one here was truly devoted to the environment except you,' Simon remarked mildly. 'Was Phillip worse than the rest of us?'

'Huh! He made Allied Chemical and Amoco look like bleeding Greenpeacers!' she replied viciously.

'Come on, he wasn't all that bad,' Eric objected, quite mildly Simon thought, considering his close relationship to the deceased.

'Shit! I can't stand it in here, with all you rapists.' Joan turned on her heel and strode out into the incipient storm.

'Rapists?' Simon asked of the room at large.

'Of the environment,' Anne explained drily. 'Joan would

be happy only if we all became hunter-gatherers . . . no, strike that. Gatherers. Maybe. She hasn't been able to explain yet how five billion people are going to survive on a diet of weeds and carrion.' Anne smiled. 'Perhaps she'd prefer it if most of us didn't.'

'She's the type who gives conservationists a bad name,' Eric fumed. 'Hell, we all know we've got to take better care of our planet, but Joan turns people off instead of bringing them over to our side.' Eric echoed Simon's thoughts on the subject of Joan Winik.

'But she has a real bee in her bonnet where Phillip's concerned,' Simon commented. In a normal investigation he could have just come out and asked exactly what was on his mind.

'Probably because Phillip was on retainer from one of the big oil companies,' Viola piped up. 'Phillip really was a prick. Sorry, Eric,' she added, nodding in the stepfather's direction before continuing. 'Ol' Phil came across as a real charmer until you got to know him—then it was obvious he cared only about numero uno.'

'And handsome young men . . .' Jeff added, letting the innuendo hang like an icicle in the cold air.

Simon cleared his throat. 'Joan certainly feels very deeply for the environment.'

'Yeah, but she thinks she's the only one who does,' Jeff replied. 'The rest of us care, but we're more realistic. You can't turn the clock back fifty years, much less a thousand.'

'Joan didn't have a personal axe to grind with Phillip?'

'Not that I know of,' Eric replied, 'but anything's possible. Neither Joan nor poor Phillip are the type to confide their personal tribulations.'

The others were nodding their heads in agreement, but Simon felt dissatisfied. Joan had hinted of a personal conflict with Phillip, and so, for that matter, had Wally. Hatred gleamed dully in Wally's eyes whenever Phillip's name was mentioned. And Eric? How did he and his stepson really get along? And then there was Tony who became totally silent whenever Phillip's name was mentioned. So many mysteries . . .

'You seem awfully interested in Phillip, Simon, considering you never met him,' Jeff remarked, mildly curious.

So much for subtlety, Simon thought as he flushed faintly and fought the urge to squirm. 'Once a policeman, always a policeman, I suppose,' he responded, suppressing a nervous laugh with difficulty. 'I just can't let a mystery go unquestioned.'

'And what mystery is that?' Eric asked.

Simon gave him a close look before answering with a shrug, 'The man left camp one morning and hasn't been seen since. Ergo, a mystery.'

'But not a difficult one,' Anne replied. 'There was a severe storm . . . thank God only one of us got lost! If Phillip was far from camp when the storm hit it would've been impossible for him to get back.'

'That's for sure,' Jeff concurred. 'I was too far away to get back here, but luckily I was near the old IBP station. I holed up there for almost two days until the storm blew itself out. Believe me, even with shelter it was no picnic.'

'And you were alone . . .'

'Not alone. Wally crawled in, literally, an hour or so after I did. I don't know how he made it, visibility was minus ten feet by then.'

'And the rest of you, except Phillip, of course, were safely back at camp when the storm hit?'

'Pretty much,' Anne said with a nod. 'Oh, except for you, eh, Eric?'

Eric nodded. 'I got caught even though I was just down by the big pond. You know, Simon, the one where we were watching the snow geese.' He turned to face Simon, almost tipping the cot he was sitting on. 'It was my own damn fault, actually. I *had* noticed the gathering storm but I decided I could afford to complete my usual observation period. Crazy!' Eric shook his head in disbelief at his own stupidity. 'By the time I came to my senses, the blizzard was almost upon me—in fact I could see a wall of white closing in. Up to the edge of it, everything was perfectly clear, but beyond it I couldn't see a damn thing.' Eric fell silent for a moment, letting the others feel his fear and awe at the terrifying sight. 'My first thought was to stay in the blind and make the best of it, so, in the few minutes before the snow came, I added a few more stones to anchor the poles and lowered the canvas down over the open sides. Ha!' Eric laughed without humour. 'That was a waste of effort. It couldn't have been more than fifteen minutes before the first pole collapsed . . . in an hour my shelter was merely a heap of metal and canvas piled on top of me.' Eric's elegant hands smoothed his still perfect coiffure and he stood and attempted to pace in the cramped tent as he continued his narrative. 'Perhaps I should've stayed in the blind even at that point, but you can imagine what meagre shelter it afforded by then.'

Simon nodded in agreement. 'No kidding.'

'Anyway,' Eric continued, 'I didn't stay; I decided to head for the camp. I'm telling you, I barely made it. It took me close to two hours to go half a mile in that blizzard, and if I hadn't run into the radio antenna I would've missed the camp entirely.' Eric finished his story and looked again at Simon. 'So you see,' he added in his most professional tone, 'there is no mystery in Phillip's disappearance. Rather, if there is a puzzle, it's in the happy fact that there was only one death that day.'

'So it would seem,' Simon agreed, successfully keeping the irony out of his voice. 'But the rest of you weren't in danger?' he asked, glancing at Anne and Tony as he spoke.

'Not really,' Tony answered reluctantly. 'I suppose we might've been if the storm had lasted much longer. But as it was, we were merely cold, bored and worried about the others.' He pulled off his grey toque and ran his hand through his thinning hair. 'In other words, we were miserable but not panicked.'

Simon heaved himself off the crowded cot. 'I'll keep a wary eye on the weather from now on,' he said, starting for the door. 'Time for my radio check . . .' Outside, he studied the sky. The snowflakes now were few and small, and he could see the blue-grey dome above him. The weather hadn't deteriorated in the last couple of hours and he felt hopeful the expected storm wouldn't materialize.

He sat down at the radio as he blew on his cold fingers and considered what he should say. How much should he tell Resolute? How much *could* he tell them without alerting his companions? At last he briskly rubbed his hands together and switched on the transmitter-receiver. 'This is Victor Echo 8735 calling Viking. Come in, Viking. Victor Echo 8735 calling Viking. Come in, Viking,' he repeated.

'This is Viking. Over,' came the response, just audible through the static which crackled through the earphones like a bonfire on a hot summer night.

'Hello, Ernie,' Simon greeted his contact before asking the question foremost in his mind. 'How is the weather at the base? Over.'

'Still socked in, so no matter how bored you are, you're stuck out there. How's life at the Pass? Over.'

'Snow flurries,' Simon replied but omitted the 'over'. With painful slowness he pecked at the anachronistic morse code key attached to the side of the modern radio. He blessed Fernald's ·thoroughness.

'Get Fernald. Urgent,' he tapped out amateurishly.

'What's the problem, Hollingford? Over.' The question crackled in his headphones. Simon clamped them even tighter to his ears even though he knew no one but he could hear the private.

Simon repeated his morse code message. 'Get Fernald. Urgent.'

'I'm getting him. Wait. Over.' The friendly banter which had become the norm for these evening calls disappeared as those at both ends waited in suspense. Private Mallow was completely mystified by the unexpected change in routine and Simon himself was worried about just what he would say and how he would say it. He'd changed to morse

code to avoid being overheard but his lack of practice made
this kind of communication difficult for him.

'Colonel Fernald here. What's the problem? Over.' The
Colonel's voice boomed over the air waves, drowning out
the static.

Simon rubbed his sweaty palms together and then wiped
them on his jeans. He poised his right index finger over the
morse key and started tapping.

There was a pregnant pause before the Resolute end
snapped and sputtered into life. 'I read you as "Have found
body of Phillip Loew, lost last year. Died of two bullet
wounds. Murdered." Is that correct? Over.'

'Yes. Over,' Simon said.

'How many people know of your discovery? Over.'

Simon sighed with relief. Thank God the Colonel was on
the ball. He'd already grasped the reason for the coding of
the original message.

'Just me. Over,' Simon signalled carefully. Since it had
been Colonel Fernald who'd assisted with the expedition
the preceding year, Simon knew he was aware of the identical make-up of this year's team.

'We can't get you out now, Hollingford, there's too much
fog. What do you want to do? Over.'

'Can start quiet investigation. Over.' Simon's tensed
right hand ached from the strain and sweat beaded pro-
fusely on his brow. He knew he'd made mistakes and could
only hope he'd communicated the gist of his message.

'I'm not certain whose jurisdiction it would be, Hollingford. This may fall into the RCMP's bailiwick. I don't think
it's the army's since there are no armed forces personnel
with you. Over.'

Red tape, Simon groaned. Who the hell cared about
jurisdiction? He had a human icicle on his hands, and a
trail getting colder every minute. He flexed his fingers in
preparation for his next foray into morse code. 'The body
is exposed now and may be found by others. Over.'

There was another long pause from the Colonel before he

replied. 'Acknowledged. Call back at twenty-three hundred hours. Over.'

'Ten four, over and out,' Simon answered briskly into his microphone just as Wally ducked into the tent.

Simon watched him rummaging among the instruments in one of the large boxes. Wally was ignoring him but Simon was determined to make him talk. 'Resolute's fogged in again, Wally.'

The pause stretched uncomfortably. 'It's always fogged in, or iced in. Damn stupid place to put an airstrip,' Wally eventually mumbled, his head buried in the carton.

'What's your weather prediction?' Simon persisted.

Wally emerged from the box and directed his unfocused gaze at Simon. He licked his lips and ran a soiled hand through his greasy yellow hair. 'Clear,' he finally croaked as he returned to his task. It was the longest conversation Simon had ever had with the man.

Simon closed down the radio and considered what he should do with the three hours until Colonel Fernald's next call. When he poked his head out of the tent, he found the wind had dwindled to a light breeze and the snow had stopped. By the light from the hazy sun, hanging huge and low in the south-western sky, he could see the doorway of Viola's tent and decided to pay her an overdue visit.

Viola was no longer wrapped in her sleeping-bag recuperating on her cot. Instead, she was kneeling in the green gloom, studying her slides by the light of a lantern. Glancing up, she continued on her original train of thought, but aloud. 'You know, of all the pictures I took last year, I don't have a really good one of a clash between a pair of males.' She held out a slide. 'What do you think of this one, Simon? Doesn't quite catch the power of the event, does it?'

He examined the slide. She'd caught the challenge at a point just before the two massive bodies collided. The picture gave an impression of the speed the musk oxen reached before the clash, but the artist in him had to agree with Viola; it did lack something. 'It has the feel of a full dress rehearsal, not opening night,' he said thoughtfully.

Viola jumped up. 'Well put, Simon, that's exactly it. But I happen to know this particular collision was quite spectacular. I can't understand why it would appear half-hearted.'

He studied the picture again. 'It's the animal on the left, I think—his head's turned slightly towards the camera. Perhaps he noticed you and got distracted for an instant?'

'Maybe,' Viola allowed, as she put her head close to his and re-examined her photo. 'Whatever the reason, you're right about his attention being distracted . . . and I had great hopes for this slide . . .'

'If you'd only had your camera with you during the stampede you could've got some excellent shots.'

Viola gave a bark of laughter. 'You're right! Not many people get photos of musk ox tonsils, do they?'

Simon smiled. 'I'd say you're feeling better.'

'I'm fine. Tomorrow it's back to my usual routine, thank God. I make a dreadful patient.'

'You will be careful . . . ?'

Viola studied his face. 'You're really worried about me, aren't you?'

'Of course,' he responded lightly. 'I'd be devastated if anything happened to my favourite critic.' The offhand tone belied a deep concern. After seeing what had happened to Phillip, Simon was less inclined than ever to treat the stampede incident as a practical joke.

'Well, don't be concerned. I can take care of myself, especially now that I've been forewarned. I'll even carry one of the .303s, beastly nuisance that they are, despite the fact I couldn't hit a horse from the saddle.' Viola stood up and patted him absently on the sleeve. 'You're not my mother, you know.'

'Fortunately!' Simon ducked out of the tent.

To kill time, he strolled the length of his radio antenna, checking that all was in order. The fine strands of wire looped from post to post about twenty feet from the ground and he'd decorated each guy wire with a knotted rag to increase its visibility. The posts were anchored with gravel and stones to keep them upright in the wind and weather, but even so, he found two of them canted at a crazy angle and stopped to straighten them. Standing at the trailing end of the antenna wire, where it was coiled loosely around the last stake, Simon remembered Eric's tale and how the presence of this long landmark had guided him home. 'Maybe I should extend it another twenty-five or fifty yards,' he mused aloud, 'just to be on the safe side.'

Coming back to camp, he ran into Joan who was stretched out on the ground staring at the heavens. Despite himself, his gaze followed hers.

Without glancing at him, Joan asked conversationally, 'Have you noticed that even though it's never quite dark you can see the stars up here?'

'Yes, it's marvellous. They seem very intense in this clear air; less twinkle, I think.'

'The north star is right overhead, see?' Joan indicated with her index finger.

'Yes,' Simon answered, 'and there are Draco and Cepheus nearby.'

Joan sat up slowly and gave him a measured look.

'I'm not totally gone over to the Dark Side, you know,' he remarked.

'Maybe not,' Joan replied grudgingly. 'Just how much astronomy do you know?'

'Not much. When I first joined the police force I spent a lot of time on rural night beat. Frequently the only ones up besides myself were the stars, so I got to know them . . . it's only polite to call friends by name.'

Joan lay down again and resumed her study of the darkening vault while Simon sat down at a companionable distance.

'It helps to put things in perspective, don't you think?' Joan asked.

'Star-gazing is definitely a good cure for an over-developed ego.'

'Maybe we should invite Eric to join us.' If Simon wasn't mistaken there was a grin on Joan's face when she said this.

He smiled too. 'I don't think even the heavens in all their glory can puncture Eric's self-esteem. I'm sure he believes the stars are paying their respects to his evident superiority.'

'Him and Phillip . . . so much the same. It's hard to believe they weren't really related.' Joan paused and Simon was afraid she wasn't going to proceed, but after a moment she continued. 'That's why they didn't get along, you know. Two monumental egos each vying for position as top dog. Poor Lynda! How did she manage to live with the pair of them for so long?'

'Did Phillip live with his mother?' Simon asked. 'From what I've heard he hardly seems the type to stay tied to the apron strings.'

Joan laughed. 'No, he had a house near the university and a place in Toronto as well, I think.'

The two stared at the arched glow of the milky way. The stillness was absolute—not even a whisper of wind or a calling animal cut the night.

'Where did you first meet Phillip?' Simon asked, breaking the silence at last.

'Here. Last summer.'

'Oh . . .' He cleared his throat. 'Something you said earlier gave me the impression you knew each other from somewhere else.'

Joan gave a laugh filled with bitterness and sorrow. 'He wrecked my parents' lives, that's all . . . ruined their live-lihood.'

'How?'

But Simon had hit a nerve. She got abruptly to her feet and told him, very clearly and fluently, that she didn't want to talk about it, especially with him, a lackey of the law.

Sighing, Simon stretched out again, arranging the hood of his jacket like a pillow beneath his head as he filed away one more small kernel of information for future reference. He gazed at the breathtaking panorama spread out above him and wondered if Phillip could still appreciate it.

*

At last it was time for the call. The others had already turned in and Simon had stayed away from camp to avoid questions about his atypical behaviour. He was usually one of the first to retire, luxuriating in the unaccustomed opportunity to get a full, undisturbed eight hours of sleep.

The silence was so complete that he worried the faint tapping of the morse key would sound like pistol shots to the people bundled in their sleeping-bags, but there was nothing he could do about it. Hopefully none of them could read morse code. He was glad the radio came equipped with earphones instead of a speaker—this way Resolute could talk and he wouldn't have to interpret a morse signal from them. He flexed his fingers in preparation. As the second hand of his Timex watch reached the twelve, exactly eleven p.m., he began signalling. He'd barely started when Colonel Fernald's voice boomed through the earphones, sounding even louder in contrast to the quiet Simon had been experiencing. The static had disappeared and Simon's hopes immediately rose. Perhaps the weather had cleared at Resolute as well as in Polar Bear Pass.

'Fernald here. Over.'

'Has the fog cleared?' Simon signalled hopefully.

'Negative. It's thicker, if anything, so we still can't get you out. I've talked to National Defense, the RCMP, and your people, the Ontario Provincial Police. They're not happy, but since you're there you might as well find out what you can. Over.'

'I'll need some help from my headquarters in Toronto. Talk to Sergeant Bill Harkness. I need backgrounds on everyone here. Tell him to look for connections to Loew.'

'Affirmative. I'll arrange a radio hook-up with this Harkness fellow for tomorrow evening. Over.'

'Negative. Arrange for the morning after, at eleven.'

'When no one will be around? Over.' Fernald asked.

'Correct.'

'Anything else? Over.'

'That's it for now.'

'Ten four. Over and out.'

Simon sat back on his packing crate, leaned up against the tent post and massaged his right hand with his left. At least he was getting finger exercise from the tragedy—it might help his piano playing.

Reaching to turn off the receiver-transmitter, he turned towards the door of the tent just in time to see the canvas flap swing down into place. For a second Simon froze. Then he leapt silently to his feet and was at the door and out in two bounds. He peered about in the gloom. No one was in sight; nothing disturbed the chill silence. With furrowed brow Simon returned to the radio and shut it down for the night. For the first time he wished the radio had a case—and a lock.

CHAPTER 6

Despite Simon's claim of being able to sleep anytime, any-where, he tossed and turned, his mind a kaleidoscope of conjecture. Time passed incredibly slowly as he listened with growing annoyance to Wally's stentorian breathing. He gurgled and snorted like an angry pig. At four a.m., unrested, Simon gave up in disgust and arose to brilliant sunlight and a sky of perfect clarity. He considered re-turning to Phillip's icy tomb with equipment to disinter the body but decided against it. Phillip wasn't going anywhere, and the corpse would be better preserved in its frozen casing.

Simon quietly lit the small stove and made himself a cup of hot chocolate. As he perched on a crate sipping his drink, the image of Phillip's body hung before his eyes. He focused on the bloodstains. Now that he thought about it, their shape indicated Phillip had been standing for a least a little while after he'd been hit—the blood had run *down* his jacket. The position of the body interested him too. It suggested Phillip had died sheltering under the meagre protection of the ice bridge. That meant he'd still been mobile after he'd been shot. A shadow crossed Simon's face. How terrified Phillip must've been . . . bleeding . . . freezing . . . finally crawling under the ice bridge knowing he'd never make it back to camp. Simon shook his head. No matter what kind of man Phillip had been, no one deserved such a fate.

He needed to know just when the trigger had been pulled. He had to get information about everyone's movements but it was almost a year ago now. Would they remember what they'd done . . . what they'd seen? And at least one of them would lie. Simon sighed. The trail was cold in more ways than one. The sooner he started the investigation the better.

Time to make some notes, he thought. He rummaged around in his right parka pocket for his small sketchpad. He tried the left, also without success and then stood up to check again. In the side of his right pocket he found a slit, big enough for a pad of paper to slip through. He reached in, bending over as his arm disappeared into the lining of his coat. 'Ah-ha.' He felt the outline of a book. 'So that's what's been banging my knee,' he murmured. But when he pulled it out, it wasn't his sketchpad—it was Phillip's notebook, the one from the hidden backpack. He had forgotten to repack it.

As he flipped through, looking for a blank page, a slip of paper fell out. Simon unfolded it and spread it on his knee. 'I'll be damned,' he gasped, skimming the contents. '*Loew*,' the note read, '*sweating yet? Next time your mailbox may contain something more unpleasant than a dead rat! You'll pay in full for S.'s death. So far you've just made the down payment.*'

Questions surged in Simon's mind. Who wrote the note? Who was S.? What had Phillip done? Was the note the reason the backpack was hidden? Was it hidden by Phillip or the author of the note? Or maybe even someone else with their own reasons to muddy the water? Hold on, Simon, he told himself, go about this in an orderly manner.

He sprang up and began to pace out along the antenna wire. The key questions was S. Who'd died? He frowned as he strode along rubbing the cleft in his chin. 'S . . .' The only person even remotely connected with the expedition who'd died recently was Wally's son, but was there a connection? What had Anne said the boy's name was? He stopped dead in his tracks. 'Scott.' Simon slammed his fist into his other palm. It just might fit. That would mean Wally wrote the note. Simon pulled the letter from his pocket and stared at the unfamiliar handwriting. He'd have to get a sample of Wally's.

Simon resumed his pacing as he strained to remember what Anne and Joan had told him about Scott's death. A fall from an apartment balcony in Toronto . . . A drug pusher or a male lover . . . 'Anne said Phillip was gay,' Simon murmured, 'and Joan told me Phillip had a place in Toronto.' He was practically running now, he was so excited. Means . . . Wally, as well as everyone else, had access to the rifles. Motive . . . Wally was devastated by Scott's death and wanted revenge. Opportunity. Simon slowed. How the hell had Wally got to the IBP station a good three hours' walk from Phillip's body? Simon knew the shots had to have been fired after the storm started or they would've been heard by the others. 'But maybe they were,' Simon muttered. 'If they didn't know Phillip had been shot, no one would have had reason to mention hearing anything.' He checked his watch. Six o'clock. Still too early for anyone else to be up.

Now he was dying to talk to his sergeant, Bill Harkness. How he missed his down to earth advice. Bill, however, would never have come on an expedition like this. Food, of both high quality and copious quantity, were essential to his mental and emotional well-being. Simon chuckled as he imagined Bill's reaction to their food packets. While sufficient to sustain life, the grub on Bathurst Island would never make the Michelin guide to good eating.

Simon waited impatiently for his tent mate, Wally, to set out on his sampling route. He didn't think the scientist would take kindly to being asked for a specimen of his handwriting, so he planned to search Wally's pack while he was out. But the man wasn't cooperating. Instead of being the first out of camp as he usually was, Wally was grumbling over his collection of sample jars.

'What's wrong?' Simon finally demanded, not really expecting an answer.

But Wally surprised him again by turning around. 'The marking pen I've been using. It's rubbing off.' He gestured towards his rows of bottles. 'I have to relabel them.' He looked at his battered watch and frowned. 'It'll take me all morning to get this mess straightened out . . . if I can.'

Simon stifled a groan as he left the tent. He'd have to wait to confirm his suspicions about who wrote the threatening letter.

He'd agreed to help Anne with some measurements, so after breakfast the two of them set off, walking briskly in a westerly direction up the Pass.

'If you'd asked me I would have helped,' Tony called after his wife. 'You didn't need to get that man involved.'

Anne didn't look back, but sank her head deeper into her parka, and walked faster.

They scrambled down the gentle, scree-covered slope to the floor of the Pass without speaking. Finally Simon couldn't resist his curiosity any longer. 'What's Tony's problem?' he asked, careful to keep his tone mild and conversational.

'I don't know,' she replied curtly, angrily dashing a tear from her eye. 'I don't know!' she repeated on a wail and started to sob openly as she slowed to a halt.

Simon stared at her, embarrassed at the raw grief in her face and devoutly wishing he'd kept his mouth shut. As a homicide investigator he was familiar with grief in its myriad manifestations, but he still felt uncomfortably like a voyeur in the face of undisguised, uncontrollable sorrow.

Every person he'd ever confronted with news of death or loss had reacted differently. In a murder investigation he tended to break the news baldly, unexpectedly, to analyse the first, instantaneous reaction. Few people, however self-controlled, could turn on their defences instantly and for a brief moment he felt he could see into their souls. Often he saw a reflection of the ambiguity most people feel on the death of a friend or relative. Unalloyed regret was distressingly rare in his opinion. And even when confronted with a seemingly complete breakdown he still could sense some hint of calculation on the part of the bereaved. How upset should they be? Should they cry? Where they reacting in an appropriate manner? What was that policeman thinking?

But what Simon saw in Anne's face was different. She wasn't reacting to a sudden, shocking discovery. Her iron control, exercised rigidly for many months, was cracking just a bit, releasing just enough tension to keep the internal strain at a containable level—like a minor volcanic eruption portending a major blow-up. New emotions replaced Simon's embarrassment and he instinctively gathered her into his arms and gently stroked her hair. 'I'm sorry. I'm sorry, Anne,' he repeated as she buried her face in his chest. Gradually the sobs subsided and they stood quietly, Simon's arms still around her. He breathed the perfume of her hair.

At last Anne raised her tear-reddened face to his and stepped back reluctantly from the haven he represented. 'Thanks,' she said trying to smile through her tears. 'I needed that.'

'Any time.' A smile flickered on Simon's lips.

Anne started walking, but at a more leisurely pace this time. 'Life's funny, isn't it? You never know what's in store from one day to the next. And just when you think your future's all laid out ahead of you, the road takes an unexpected turn. Or ends completely!' She laughed, bordering still on hysteria. 'And you can't go ahead, and you can't turn back because life's a one way street. What do you do?'

Simon fought the urge to take her back into his arms. 'Maybe you should decide where it is you want to be, Anne, and then plot the course to get there . . .' He continued the road analogy for lack of a better.

His companion laughed bitterly. 'I don't know what I want any more. Not long ago I thought it was to be Tony's wife. We'd do our research side by side and make our life together. But now . . . now I don't have Tony and I don't have a job and my dreams are all dead. I don't know what to do.'

Simon stretched out his hand to Anne's wet cheek and gently wiped her tears. 'You'll be OK.'

Anne raised her moist eyes to his and then lightly touched her fingers to his hand. She looked down at her boots.

'You have a position at Bellwood, don't you?' Simon asked.

'Oh yes! Adjunct professor. No money and just a bench in Tony's lab. That will certainly solve all my problems.'

'You could move out of Tony's lab for now, I suppose, and look for another job, if that's what you really want. Now that Phillip's gone maybe Bellwood will offer you his position.'

'Phillip isn't dead, at least not officially, and he was a palæobotanist, not an ecologist.' Anne looked at Simon and shook her head, a shadow of a smile on her lips. 'You really don't know how universities work, do you? Tony Colautti's discard will not be the replacement.' She spoke with finality.

'You haven't lost Tony yet.' Simon was dismayed at how much the thought of her husband bothered him.

'Oh no?' Anne shot back. 'In case you haven't noticed, we're not exactly the picture of connubial bliss.'

'Has he asked for a divorce?'

'Not yet, but it's coming.'

'Do you want one?'

'No. Yes . . . oh, I don't know!' Anne flung her arms out. 'I'm all mixed up.' She began walking again, trying to outrace her confusion and Simon followed a stride behind.

Despite the cutting edge to the wind, it was a beautiful day and the wide expanse of wild land and endless sky freely offered up its beauty. Birds shrieked and gargled and cooed as they rode the wind or settled on the patchwork of open water. Small rustling noises of hares and lemmings in the burgeoning vegetation erupted from time to time almost beneath their feet. Although barren on first glance, this northern land was far from lifeless. The beauty was merely background to Simon and Anne.

'This situation, I mean with Tony, didn't develop overnight. It's been building for a long time.' Anne was staring at the horizon as she spoke.

'When did it start?' Simon reluctantly asked. He really didn't want to waste his precious moments with Anne talking about Tony. Besides, he had more than enough on his plate already.

'I've been puzzling over that myself.' She smiled wanly. 'Maybe a year and a half ago. Maybe a bit less. I can't pin it down any closer. But I do know when it really escalated ... when Tony really changed. It was last summer. Up here. When Phillip disappeared.'

A current charged through Simon's body and suddenly Tony's behaviour became a pressing concern. Anne felt the change in him but misread it.

'No, really, Simon. I'm sure I'm right,' she insisted, turning her wide eyes upon him. 'Even before we left Bellwood Tony'd started acting strangely whenever Phillip was near. I could tell he didn't want me around when he was talking to him. And Tony voted in favour of Phillip's tenure, something he'd always been against. He wouldn't tell me why he'd changed his mind.' Her eyes clouded and dropped to study her boots. 'Plus I think Tony saw Phillip a couple to times in Toronto—though he never said so and I didn't want to ask. Phillip was a taboo topic even before he disappeared last year. And then after that . . .' Her voice trailed off.

Simon stared politely into the middle distance for a few moments before prompting her. 'Yes?'

She shrugged. 'Then he started to give me the kind of treatment you've been privileged to witness.' She pushed her shining hair out of her eyes and scuffed the toe of her boot in the frozen ground, dislodging clumps of reindeer moss. 'When Phillip disappeared Tony insisted on searching for him long before conditions were safe. And he didn't want to leave even when the RCMP ordered us home,' she continued in a voice still husky from tears. 'They practically had to throw him on to the plane. Then he wouldn't talk to me for days . . . literally. When he did it was only to criticize me, my work, my habits, what I said, did, didn't do. Once in a while, at first, he seemed to shake it off for a few days and acted loving and considerate—smothering almost. But it never lasted. For months now he's been morose and occasionally vicious—but never physically so,' she hastened to add.

'He'd better not be,' Simon muttered under his breath.

Hearing his comment, Anne turned to face him, her eyes pleading. 'If only you'd known him before. He used to be so sunny and optimistic . . . full of plans, full of *joie de vivre*. He's not the same man now.' She led the way to the edge of a shallow pond and settled down on a smooth rock, warm from the sun.

Simon squatted beside her. He skipped a flat pebble across the blue mirror and concentric waves rippled through the reflected clouds. 'So Phillip was the cause of the change in Tony?'

'That's not what I'm saying. I was just using the Phillip incident as an example of the change in him. What could he possibly have to do with Tony's altered personality?' She shook her head. 'No. I can't see how there could be any connection.'

As the young woman sat, silent and pensive, Simon's eyes caressed her delicate face. Damn Tony Colautti. Damn Phillip Loew.

As if she felt the intensity of his regard, Anne shook herself from her reverie and smiled up at him. 'I won't embarrass you any more with my problems. Shall we get to work?'

As they measured and recorded the mass of data which Anne's sophisticated instruments had collected, Simon pondered the enigma of Tony Colautti. The Wally solution to Phillip's death really appealed to him, but evidently there were more strings to unravel in Phillip's life.

'What did you mean when you said Tony voted for Phillip's tenure?' he asked as he sloshed about in a pond.

Anne paused and squinted at him where he stood silhouetted against the sun. She put her hand to her forehead to shade her eyes. 'Well, tenure is sort of like a lifetime contract. After someone's been on staff a couple of years, all the full-time members of the department vote on whether they think a new faculty member is worthy.'

'And Tony voted in favour?'

'Yeah,' Anne answered slowly, 'and he'd always said he wouldn't. He used to say Phillip didn't care about science, only about money.'

'What about the others? Wally, for example. Did he vote in favour?'

'You've got to be kidding! He hated Phillip. He led the faction in opposition.' She bit her lip. 'Poor man . . . he's so unhappy . . .' She moved around so she didn't have to look into the sun. 'But Wally did have logical reasons for his opinion. He said since Phillip was on retainer from two large oil and mining companies, he didn't have enough time to do a proper job of teaching.'

Simon digested this bit of information. Joan must've been telling the truth about Phillip's extra-curricular activities. He hoisted an oxygen metre from the pond on to the bank and disconnected its leads. Water dribbled over the top of his hip waders and down his leg where he felt the icy dampness penetrate his jeans. 'And Eric?' he asked.

'What?' Anne looked up from her graphs. 'What about Eric?'

'Did he vote in favour of Phillip's tenure?'

Anne sat down on the bank to pull off her waders. 'He abstained . . . said he had conflict of interest.' She laughed. 'That hadn't stopped him from pulling strings to get Phillip the position at Bellwood in the first place. Guess he didn't want to vote in favour 'cause he and Phillip were mad at each other since Eric and Lynda's divorce, and he didn't want to vote against or Lynda would've been mad.' Anne pulled on her hiking boots and started collecting her gear.

'Since their remarriage Eric and Lynda have acted really lovey-dovey—around Bellwood, at least.' She pointed to the oxygen metre which still dripped on the bank. 'If you'll bring that with you, I'll install it at my next site. Let's go.'

They walked in silence, Simon carrying the apparatus and its bulky battery, Anne struggling with notes, poles and nets. It wasn't far to the next site as the crow flies, but having to avoid numerous ponds extended it into an hour's walk. Anne seemed pensive and Simon had lots to think about so they trudged along in silence.

When Simon's mind turned to the timing of Phillip's death, he cleared his throat. 'Anne . . . ?'

She slowed and twisted to look at him. 'Yes?'

'How often did you people have to use your rifles last year?'

She shifted her gear as she thought about it. 'Well, I never used mine, and I know Viola didn't either. Jeff fired his twice to scare a bear away from our camp, but I think that was all.' She laughed. 'There's really not much danger up here, Simon. It's a lot riskier crossing a street in downtown Bellwood.'

'Didn't Eric say something about firing a few rounds to help Phillip find his way back?'

The smile faded from Anne's face. 'You're right. How could I have forgotten?'

'But you didn't hear any shots earlier that day?' he asked.

She shook her head. 'Uh-huh. Why would we?'

'I was just wondering if Phillip tried to signal . . . maybe he hurt himself or something . . .' Simon prevaricated.

Her blue eyes widened. 'I never thought of that. Oh, I hope that's not true—that he was injured and we didn't hear his signal.'

'But I suppose sound carries up here,' he murmured. 'I'm sure you would've heard.'

Anne nodded. We couldn't miss any gunshots before the storm—a sound like that carries for miles and miles up here, but after the blizzard started . . . we wouldn't hear anything.'

'That's what I thought,' Simon nodded in satisfaction. 'No point in worrying about it now.' He smiled at her. 'Shall we go, slave-driver?'

Tony Colautti was also the topic of discussion elsewhere that beautiful morning. In a rare moment of camaraderie Jeff and Joan had elected to head out together. They'd witnessed Tony's treatment of his wife and felt the accusation in his voice as he had called after her and Simon.

'He has no right to treat Anne like that—the days of women's slavery are over.' Joan was vehement. She glanced belligerently over her shoulder at the object of her ire who stood immobile, watching his wife recede into the distance with Simon.

'What a bastard.' Jeff was equally disgusted. 'She should walk out on him right this minute—that would teach him. Frankly, she should've done it long ago.'

'Yeah,' Joan grunted.

Secure in the naïvety of their unmarried status, they agreed it would be a simple thing for Anne to do.

'What do you suppose is eating Tony?' Joan asked after a few minutes of rough going.

Jeff shrugged, shifting his pack to stop it digging into his spine. 'I don't know. He's even touchier than he was last summer.' So far it wasn't difficult for Jeff to keep his voice even and he congratulated himself on his physical condition. His middle-age paunch wasn't slowing him down.

'And even last summer Tony was weird—especially after the ever delightful Phillip disappeared,' Joan continued.

Jeff nodded. 'He really went off the deep end then. Even Eric didn't carry on like Tony. In fact Eric was damned cool about it if you ask me.'

Joan tossed her head. 'I'll bet he was glad. He and Phillip couldn't stand each other. That "concerned expedition leader" routine was probably all he could manage.'

'Oh, come on, they'd been part of the same family for thirty years even if they weren't blood relations. Eric must've been genuinely worried.'

'Yeah, likely,' Joan agreed. 'But Eric was worried Phillip *would* turn up again. I tell you they hated each other. Not two days before Phillip disappeared I heard him threatening Eric. Then Eric shook his fist in Phillip's face and said he could do some squealing of his own. Not precisely a loving relationship, I'd say.' She glanced over at Jeff and picked up the pace.

'Just a family squabble,' Jeff declared, matching his stride to hers. 'Anyway, regardless of how he actually felt, Eric would do the "great man" routine for the audience. It's no wonder he didn't show much emotion when Phillip vanished—hysteria wouldn't fit with his image.'

'Unlike friend Tony,' Joan put in. 'You'd think Tony had lost his one true love.'

'Maybe he did,' Jeff shot back. 'Phillip was a fag, you know.'

'But Tony isn't,' Joan pointed out, 'or he never would've landed a wife like Anne.'

'You can never be sure on that basis. People change. Or sometimes they try to change and then find they can't. Still, I suppose it's unlikely.' Jeff pictured Tony in his mind's eye. That stocky, shaggy figure, formerly given to hearty laughter and course humour didn't conform to his stereotyped picture of a homosexual.

Conversation flagged as they pushed themselves to increase the pace until they were all but running. For the moment Joan's generalized animosity waned as she drank in the pristine beauty of her surroundings. This was how the world should be; clean, alive, demanding, and empty of humans. She wasn't a fan of *Homo sapiens* and the demise of ninety per cent of its numbers wouldn't have bothered her. But her jaundiced view was temporarily suspended as she charged across the open land revelling in its beauty and the rushing of her blood.

Tony stared after his wife as long as he could bear the sight of her with Simon, then squatted in front of his knapsack. The blue nylon fabric was encrusted with mud from his core samples. Bits of tundra vegetation had embedded themselves in the dried muck giving it a shaggy, unkempt appearance. Like an automaton, Tony loaded the bag—field book, core borer, T-handle, measuring tape, chisel; all the accoutrements of the trade which used to give him so much pleasure and pride. Now . . . He sighed as he hefted the box containing the small microscope—a wedding present from Anne. The fine leather case had an engraved brass plate. '*To Tony, love forever, Anne,*' it proclaimed in ornate italic. The box was worn now, but good leather aged well and it had acquired a mellow richness. Tony held the leather case to his cheek absorbing its warmth into his despairing soul and searching for something of Anne in it. Sighing, he fell back on his heels and carefully stowed the microscope in the backpack. '*Love forever*' echoed in his mind. Forever was shorter than he could ever have anticipated. Without enthusiasm he shrugged himself into his pack, ready to start the activities expected of him. He glanced one more time after Anne and another knife drove itself into his gut. She was wrapped in Simon's arms. She'd finally done what he'd been forcing her to do. She'd found someone else.

Tony collapsed on to the hard ground and crouched, staring at the frozen earth, seeing nothing. He could feel it coming on again as he left reality behind and let the madness overtake him. He looked frozen, catatonic. No one could have borne his thoughts for long as they were buffeted about in his tortured mind.

When he regained a foothold in reality his muscles were cramped and his body ached from cold and inactivity. In slow motion he staggered to his feet and flexed his numb limbs. He looked around, at first not recognizing his surroundings. Gradually, recognition flooded through him and, with it, stomach-churning fear. Three times he'd experienced this detachment from reality and each time it was harder to come back. If it happened again would he be lost forever? Bleak as his life appeared, it was infinitely preferable to the hell of his mind's creation. Tony knew he

needed help, but the practice he'd had at hiding the real
Tony during the previous two years stood him in good stead
now. He could still function within the norm. Slowly he
picked up his familiar sack and started off. An hour was
missing from his life.

After finishing his rounds with Anne, Simon dragged himself away from her and headed off in the direction of Phillip's temporary resting place. He tried to seem casual,
strolling along looking from side to side, but he had a
purpose.

The base camp was located where it had been the previous year, on the north slope of a long low hill—on the
edge of the Pass opposite the corpse. Walking south from
the cluster of green tents, one had to climb to the crest of
the hill before descending to the Pass where the ground
was lower, softer, more lush, and broken by a generous
sprinkling of small shallow ponds. In some places in the
Pass the sedges, grasses and willows reached a towering
six inches in height—monsters compared to the usual two
inches. The largest of the ponds lay to the west. Measuring
about two hundred yards in diameter, it was almost a lake,
although even at its deepest point a man of Simon's height
could touch bottom. Eric's favourite blind—the one where
he claimed to have tried to weather the storm—was on the
far side of this. As Simon threaded his way around the
network of pools, he realized how difficult it would be to
get back to camp during a blizzard. It said a lot for Eric's
navigational skills that he'd made it at all. It also explained
why no one doubted Phillip had got lost, and presumably
died. It would be impossible to hold a straight line here on
the floor of the Pass. Even on higher ground the succession
of hills and streams forced course alterations.

Simon paused for a breather at Eric's blind. From there
he had a clear view of the entire width of the Pass and the
gentler slopes to the north and south. He was trying to
determine how easy it would have been for the killer to get
to Phillip's location unseen. Down here in the Pass there

seemed little opportunity for concealment. Presumably
Phillip had crossed this low area without attempting to
hide. Had the meeting with his killer been a planned one?
he wondered. Had they travelled together? Simon rubbed
his chin. No, someone would've mentioned it by now. Had
Phillip been followed, then? Possibly, Simon decided, but
not without the victim's knowledge.

Simon started walking again, still heading towards Phillip's icy tomb. He was again oblivious of the beauty around
him as he mulled over the problem. Eric and Viola spent
a lot of time on the valley floor and would be the most likely
to notice who was crossing to the south side. How much
Anne would notice as she mucked about in the ponds
remained to be seen. And if it were common knowledge
Phillip planned to go south that day, he would have been
easy to find.

Simon munched a chocolate bar as he headed towards
the southern barrier of hills. He skirted pond after pond,
stepping carefully to avoid bird nests and new laid eggs.
Angry parents chased him, squawking and flapping their
wings threateningly. No one would be able to slip by quietly
in nesting season.

The ground beneath his feet became drier and firmer as
he reached the first hill. He swung fifty yards west and
entered a shallow valley running back into the higher
ground. Moments later, the lowland and the far hill where
the camp was situated disappeared from view. The gully
ran quite straight and he could keep his head below the
level of the hill and his feet out of the gurgling, icy water
of the stream. He trudged on for another half-hour, then
abruptly slowed his pace. The ice bridge was in view. He
licked his dry lips as he circled closer, feeling both excited
and repelled as he anticipated sighting the dead man. Again
it was the grotesquely beckoning hand which saluted him
from the melting ice. He stopped. Only when he finally let
out a heavy sigh did he realize he'd been holding his breath.

'It's just a frozen body, that's all,' he whispered to himself
as he cautiously approached. 'What's wrong with you?' He

rubbed his chin with a gloved index finger. 'Bill . . . where are you when I need you?' He took several deep breaths, squared his shoulders and marched up to the ice bridge.

The chunks of ice he'd packed around the body had dwindled but still more or less covered the corpse. Simon rubbed his palms together and tensed. Abruptly he swept the remaining film of ice from the face of Phillip Loew. The marbled flesh felt as cold and unyielding as granite. Cocking his head to one side to get the proper perspective, Simon studied the frozen expression.

Only the whites of his eyes showed under Phillip's heavy lids and he tried not to be influenced by the sinister effect. Dark curly hair escaped from under the blue toque which capped it and one lock still curled over the wide forehead. The nose jutted straight and fine above the full-lipped mouth. The square chin resembled Simon's. Even in its bloodless state Simon knew this face had once been bronzed and glowing with health. Phillip had been a handsome man —the type with appeal for both men and women. Whether or not Phillip had been gay, he wouldn't have had difficulty finding willing partners. Simon shook his head, regretting this waste of a human life.

He chipped away the remaining ice from Phillip's torso and again studied the two neat holes. He tried to pry away the arm clutched to the chest but without breaking bone and muscle it was impossible. Lower down, Phillip's pocket gaped open and Simon automatically slid in his hand. The abrasive edge of the frozen cloth scratched his skin but he ignored the twinge of pain as his fingers closed on a scrap of paper. He eased the pocket apart and pulled the sheet free. It crackled with stiffness but quickly softened as Simon held it in his hands. 'Probably a grocery list,' he mumbled as he carefully unfolded it. The letterhead told him it was from a Saskatchewan-based mining company and his brow corrugated as he scanned the letter. '. . . *regret that you were shot at, but we have had trouble from the Winik Wilderness Camp before. We will send a support group with you if another visit to the area is necessary. . . . happy to see your assessment that an extension*

of our mining operations will have minimal environmental impact.'
Simon sat back on his heels and pursed his lips in a soundless whistle. How many Winiks were there in the country?
'I knew there was a connection. And she said she didn't
know Phillip . . .' Simon smiled in grim satisfaction before
the triumph faded from his face. First Wally, now Joan.
How many others had reason to hate the dearly departed?

Using unnecessary gentleness, he covered the corpse
again with chunks of ice. Whatever Phillip had been in life,
he deserved some respect in death.

While returning to camp Simon kept to the hill tops.
Without binoculars he could see only one person, and, from
the distinctive pink toque he guessed it was Viola. When
he spotted the herd of musk oxen nearby he was sure. Before
descending to the Pass, he swept the horizon with his binoculars. As Tony swam into focus far to his right, Simon's
mouth curled in distaste. He watched the man wrestle half-
heartedly with his corer and then mouthed an insult before
turning away.

In the direction of the IBP station Simon caught a
glimpse of Anne before she descended into a creek bed and
disappeared. In less than a minute she was back in view
and again it struck him how exposed they all were on this
treeless tundra. But by judicious planning and a little luck
it might've been possible for someone to get to Phillip's
location unobserved. After all, except for Viola and Eric
they all kept their noses to the ground. He grinned. So much
for observant scientists! If it wasn't what they studied, they
didn't see it. But then, the field season for arctic research
was a scant ten weeks and time was too precious to waste.
Simon couldn't help but be impressed by their stamina.
Work continued fourteen to sixteen hours a day, seven days
a week, except when weather intervened. Then, even if
stuck in their tents, the scientists spent the enforced break
sorting, cataloguing and preserving samples, running
chemical tests, updating field notes and studying biological
specimens with the two field microscopes.

Lost in thought, Simon blundered into one of the ponds

and teetered unsteadily in the muck. 'What the . . . ?' He came back to the present with a sharp oath. Freezing water lapped over the top of his boots and oozed down his socks to his toes. 'Stupid idiot,' he cursed. 'These boots'll take days to dry.' He sloshed out of the pond, plunked down on the bank and yanked off his footwear. A trickle of water dribbled out. He squeezed his socked feet and more water ran down his arm. 'Just great. Three miles from home and two soakers.' He yanked the sodden boots back on and stood up. As he squelched along he tried to ignore the chill which settled into his feet.

While keeping half his mind on where he was walking, Simon again considered his companions. Which one committed murder? Phillip obviously had the knack of making enemies. How many more were here in Polar Bear Pass? He had little to go on other than their personalities and their conversation.

When the discussion stayed strictly on scientific matters everyone, including Wally Gingras (and excluding Simon), took part. But weren't they unnaturally reticent about their personal affairs? Simon needed to know the root cause of Tony's weird behaviour. Was he correct about Joan's connection to Phillip? And Wally? Was it only the deaths of his family which soured him? Jeff droned on incessantly to Simon but only on non-personal topics—he divulged almost nothing about his private life. And Anne? Was she exactly what she appeared to be? Simon sighed. It would be so much easier to get basic information with the full authority and resources of the law behind him . . .

His route took him past one of the ponds he'd helped Anne partition into three sections. It was three weeks now since they'd netted the zooplankton from one end and turned them loose in the central portion. At the time Simon had been amazed by the thousands of minute creatures living in the pond. The largest of these, up to half an inch long, reminded him of ancient Phoenician galleys painted pink and cream. They swam upside down and their many waving legs looked remarkably like banks of oars pulling them through the water. The next largest, after these fairy shrimp, were brilliant red scorpion-like creatures. Anne called them copepods. Up to a quarter of an inch long, they were the *Tyrannosaurus rex* of the plankton world and stalked the smaller animals with cunning. Treachery and death existed on every scale of life, Simon mused.

Now as he examined the divided pond the differences between the sections were obvious. The side cleared of zooplankton was green with algæ. Without animals grazing on them, the tiny one-celled plants had experienced a population explosion. Everything was going according to plan but unless he made progress on his murder investigation, neither Simon nor anyone else would be around for the conclusion of the experiment. If he didn't have a solution by the time the weather cleared, everyone would be yanked out of Polar Bear Pass.

After a few proprietary adjustments to the pond barriers, he headed off. When he arrived at the blind a few minutes later he settled himself on the packing crate which served both as equipment store and stool. He began sketching the nesting snow buntings and rock ptarmigan while he mulled over the mystery in his mind.

Squatting by the side of another pond, Anne picked plankton from her net and dropped them into a small plastic jar of club soda. Here they expired, turning a uniform light beige in colour. The club soda relaxed their musculature before the tiny animals were preserved in ethanol. She wished she had a little brandy to add to the soda—she felt she could use a little relaxing herself. Groaning, she got to her feet and arched her back to ease her cramped muscles. As she looked up she saw Eric bearing down on her and returned his cheery wave with a half-hearted flick of her hand, then busied herself packing up her gear. Couldn't the man take a hint?

'So, Anne, working hard, I see.'

'As always, Eric—that's what we're here for,' she replied.

'Let me help you with that.' Eric moved forward to lift her pack.

'No, thanks. I can do it by myself.' She flushed, thinking how much like a petulant child she sounded.

'I'm sure you can,' Eric continued smoothly as he hoisted the backpack and held it out for her.

She slid into it with ill grace. 'Thanks,' she acknowledged gruffly as she slipped out from the caress of Eric's hands on her shoulders.

'Which way you heading?'

Anne hesitated. She'd planned to return to camp with her samples but it was almost supper-time and Eric was likely going that way. If, however, she said she was going to do more sampling she would actually have to do it, especially if Eric tagged along as she half-suspected he might. She opted for camp. 'I'm heading back now. I think I've done enough for one trip.'

'So have I,' Eric said. 'I'll walk with you. Shall I carry your net, and maybe your rifle?'

'Thanks.' If she was going to be stuck with his company he might as well be of some use, but the price was having her hand squeezed briefly as he took her net.

'Now that's more like it, Anne, my dear. I had this crazy notion you were trying to avoid me!'

'Why would I do that?'

'I can't imagine, so I must have been mistaken,' came the self-assured reply. Anne bit her tongue and said nothing.

'Our resident policeman is a strange one, wouldn't you say?' Eric glanced at Anne out of the corner of his eye, trying to gauge her reaction.

'I quite like him. He makes a nice change from all the science freaks. Besides, he's been very helpful.'

'But don't you think Bathurst Island is an odd choice for his vacation?'

Anne tossed her head. 'Not really. Lots of people want to come north but it's very expensive on your own. Simon had a golden opportunity for a travel bargain to a remote locale and he grabbed it.'

Eric tried a new tack. 'I notice he has given you more than one-seventh of his time, my dear. Not very egalitarian of him.'

'Maybe I asked for help more often. I've never heard him say no to anyone, even you.' Anne speeded up, anxious to shed Eric's unwanted company.

'And I suppose you didn't mind asking. After all, he's not unappealing if you go for the beefy, uneducated type.'

Stopping dead, Anne practically shouted, 'This is a ridiculous conversation, Eric. First, I asked for help when I needed help and Simon gave it to me. Secondly, Simon Hollingford is not beefy—he's just not emaciated like you are. Thirdly, he's a very intelligent man who had the sense not to waste his time getting over-educated and doing some airy-fairy job. And fourthly,' she added for good measure, 'he's pleasant company, unlike that which I'm enduring at present!' She marched ahead at a furious pace.

Eric stayed in step. Most men would have backed off after this assault but Eric Karnot was not most men. He was used to getting what he wanted and he wanted Anne. Not for one moment did be believe she wasn't flattered by his attentions, but Eric was beginning to wonder if he had a rival in the policeman. The possibility annoyed him slightly, although he couldn't consider Simon a serious obstacle. Tony he dismissed without a thought.

'Methinks I've encountered a rival for the Fair Lady's affections,' Eric declared playfully, feigning mock dismay.

'No, you haven't. My affections are not for sale. I'm married, you might recall, and to one of your own colleagues.'

'Perhaps it's Tony you should be reminding,' Eric retorted, goaded at last.

'Give me that!' Anne snapped, grabbing her net from Eric and tramping off in a fury. Eric was too experienced to pursue her. He'd no doubt she'd come around.

Anne's anger propelled her forward faster than a strong tail wind would have done. The Nerve of That Man! Her fury was all the greater because the previous year she'd been so forlorn she'd actually considered an affair with him. Now, as both Tony's and Simon's faces formed before her eyes, she'd changed her mind.

CHAPTER 7

The next morning Simon announced he'd be staying in camp to correct a problem with the radio. Anne generously volunteered to remain and help but eventually he convinced her it was a one man task. Then, to his annoyance, both Tony and Jeff hung around doing odd jobs. But by ten-thirty Tony had sharpened his corer, Jeff had tagged his last sample and they had departed in opposite directions. Simon dived back into his tent, prepared to search Wally's belongings for a sample of his handwriting. It won't be difficult, he thought, Wally has several notebooks of data. Carefully he drew the boxes out from under his tent mate's cot. Rows and rows of sample bottles confronted him, but no notebooks were visible. He lifted a few of the bottles but there was no room for anything beneath them—the boxes were made for the sample bottles. 'That's funny,' Simon muttered. 'I could've sworn he kept them under here.' He shoved the samples back under the bed and reached for Wally's duffel-bag. Instinctively he wrinkled his nose as he pawed through Wally's dirty clothes, but he found nothing resembling notes. Why would he carry all his papers with him, Simon wondered? They'd be unnecessary weight . . . He sat back on his haunches, remembering how much Joan wanted Wally's data. She wouldn't steal it . . . would she? But Wally didn't trust her, that was certain . . . Simon got up in disgust and brushed off his jeans. So much for that.

He made another cup of ersatz coffee while he waited impatiently for his eleven a.m. radio link with Sergeant Bill Harkness.

Bill usually sat in when Simon interviewed witnesses and his character assessments were uncannily accurate. For a man who appeared serene and phlegmatic (except where food was concerned), he sometimes expressed very cynical views about his fellow men. In his fifties now, and out of uniform into civilian clothes, Bill bore an amazing resemblance to Alfred Hitchcock. His only vice, as far as his friends knew, was gluttony, and he fought a losing battle against perfecting Hitchcock's pear-shaped figure.

Simon whistled tunelessly through his teeth. He doubted the motive for Phillip's murder was centred in Polar Bear Pass. The threads leading to his death had to be rooted in the past and Bill would have to help trace them backwards in time and distance. Up here, he needed to verify means and opportunity. Simon shook his head in disgust. Great work! As far as he could tell, everyone had the means and no one had the opportunity.

He checked his watch yet again. Eleven o'clock. He clamped the earphones on to his head as he took one last look out the open tent flap. No stray scientists had appeared but Simon hoped the connection to Bill would be clear so he could talk quietly.

A voice crackled in his ears. 'Victor Echo 8735, this is Viking, come in, please. Over.'

Simon recognized the voice of Colonel Fernald as he responded.

'I have your connection, Hollingford, please hold. Over.'

Simon faintly heard him say, 'Go ahead,' and then the familiar southern Ontario twang of his sergeant boomed in his ears.

'So you take your work with you even to the top of the world.'

'Not willingly, Bill, not willingly,' Simon laughed.

The reception was adequate, but static bursts crackled at irregular intervals across the miles. Simon hoped he'd get his business completed before he lost the connection. They dispensed with radio protocol.

'Your bombshell caused quite a flap higher up, Simon— a little problem of jurisdiction. The only reason we've won the first skirmish is that you're Johnny on the spot. The boss wasn't too pleased about that . . .'

'Let's hope we won't regret it, Bill. Progress is slow at this end. What have you got for me?'

'Where do you want to start?'

'Give me the victim first, I think.'

'Right.'

There was a pause and Simon could hear papers rattling.

Bill cleared his throat. 'Phillip Cameron Loew. Age thirty-three. Born Belleville, Ontario. Parents Edgar and Lynda Loew. Father died in a car accident when the son was two years old. Mother married scientist Eric Karnot three years later and the family moved to Bellwood where they've been ever since.' Bill cleared his throat. 'After graduating he did private consulting. That continued even after he took the job at . . .' Static drowned out the rest of Bill's sentence.

Simon adjusted the headset and fine-tuned the gain. 'Bill? Are you still there?

'. . . ill here, but you're faint.'

'Then let's get to Scott Gingras,' Simon said urgently. 'Did you get anything on Wally's son? Was his death definitely an accident?'

Bill laughed harshly, setting off a coughing fit. When he finally regained control his voice came in short gasps. 'Sorry. Got another damn cold.' He cleared his throat with rich gurgles which came clearly through a pause in the static. 'About Gingras. It was likely suicide, but . . . a verdict of accidental death.'

Bill was fading in and out. It was the poor weather at Resolute which was causing the trouble. Simon grimaced in disgust. The technology was available to give a clear signal over the two thousand miles to Bill, but he didn't have it with him. The radio he had was barely strong enough to pick up Resolute, a couple of hundred miles away.

'. . . the autopsy report on the kid,' Bill was saying. '. . . multiple internal injuries; ruptured spleen, ruptured liver, . . . pelvis, fractured skull . . . death from a fall . . .

prior to impact . . . cocaine in blood and brain tissue . . .
ains AB . . . victim's blood type . . . note.'

'A suicide note?' Simon shouted into his mouthpiece.

'"*It's better this way. Always, Scott,*"' Bill concluded, obviously not hearing his superior's question.

'His handwriting?' Simon asked.

'What?'

'Scott's writing?' Simon screamed, with an apprehensive glance out the tent door.

'Yeah. And his prints.'

'Whose apartment?'

'. . . an't hear you, Si . . .'

Simon repeated the question.

'. . . oew's.'

'Did he deal cocaine?' If Phillip had supplied Scott with cocaine he could understand Wally blaming him for his son's death.

'. . . but no proof.'

The conversation stalled for a minute while Simon digested this information. In the interest of speed he wasn't taking notes so he hoped his memory would hang on to the essentials. 'Did Gingras know all this?'

Bill's answer faded completely into the background of static which ebbed and flowed in the ether. 'Damn,' Simon muttered, frantically turning knobs. Bill's voice tantalized him again.

'. . . effery Jost . . . emanding details of the investigation.'

'About Scott Gingras's death?' Simon asked.

'Yes. He . . .'

Static crackled and spat in Simon's ears. No amount of knob twirling helped. 'What did you find out about Tony Colautti?' he yelled into the headset, hoping a few more phrases would penetrate the angry buzzing.

'. . . squeaky clean . . . parking ticket . . . Toronto . . .'

Above the snapping in the headset Simon thought he heard another noise. 'Just a sec, Bill . . .' Slipping off the earphones, he hurried to the doorway and looked out. Nothing. He hesitated. Should he check the tents? He hovered indecisively and looked back at the radio. If the reception kept getting worse he'd soon be able to hear nothing . . . Simon went back into the tent and resumed the conversation. 'Joan Winik?' he asked. 'Anything on her?'

For a change, Bill's reply was clear. 'The computer's developed a glitch about names starting with "W". I'll dig it out the old-fashioned way. I don't know why we had to go computerized . . . Winik grew up somewhere in northern Saskatchewan and she's an environmental activist . . . some say an extremist. That's all I've got so far.'

'Ah,' Simon breathed in satisfaction. Winik Wilderness Camp was bound to be the connection. It was in Saskatchewan. He put his hand down hard on the edge of a rough crate. 'Damn!' he exclaimed, rubbing his scratched palm on his jeans.

'What did you say?' Bill asked. 'I didn't catch it.'

Simon sighed. 'There's one other thing, Bill. Someone stampeded the musk oxen and almost killed Viola.'

'Say again?' Bill too was yelling over the noise.

Simon repeated what he'd said. 'But if it was a murder attempt it was pretty sloppy,' he concluded.

'. . . someone wants . . . pedition terminated,' Bill suggested. '. . . doesn't want . . . ody found.'

Simon gave a low whistle. Bill just might be right. Maybe no one had it in for Viola after all and the stampede was just a means to an end. In which case not telling Colonel Fernald had scuppered the plan.

'That may also explain the sabotage to my raft,' Simon said.

'What sabotage?' Even over the radio Simon could hear the sharp edge of worry in his friend's voice.

'No damage done,' Simon reassured him.

'. . . like the sound of it, Simon. Be care . . .'

Unexpectedly, Colonel Fernald spoke up. Simon had forgotten he was listening. 'Any other incidents you failed to mention? Over,' the Colonel demanded.

'No, sir, none, and I would've reported if there'd been any harm done.'

'How . . . going to explain . . . arti-sims? You . . . keeping an inventory, aren't you? Over.'

'Yes, sir. And last year, sir? How were the bullets in Phillip Loew's body accounted for? Over.'

'Loew . . . the missing .303 with him . . . assumed they were in the gun.'

'Thank you, sir.'

'. . . finished for now, Hollingford? Ov . . .'

'Not yet. Where was I, Bill?' Simon didn't add 'before I was so rudely interrupted' but the implication hung in the air. 'Oh yes—now I remember. Tony Colautti. He strikes me as someone about to blow. He has some secret he's desperate to keep hidden. And that secret, whatever it is, is connected with Phillip. I'm sure of it!'

'Secret? Colautti?' Bill repeated. 'Drugs, likely.'

'Find out. I know the answer's there somewhere, either back at Bellwood or possibly in Toronto. Even if Tony's secret is that he murdered Phillip we have to have a motive.' Simon's ears were aching now from pressing the earphones to his head.

'What about the wife? . . . kill to protect him? . . . stay silent . . . protect him?'

Anne's beautiful face crystallized before Simon's mind's eye. 'I don't know,' he replied slowly. 'Something's bothering her but I assumed it was Tony's behaviour. Maybe there's more to it . . .' He had been resisting this line of investigation but now had to acknowledge Anne had as much opportunity as the others to kill Phillip. And it was Anne who'd suggested he take the raft out on the ocean. And she'd been nearby when the stampede had erupted. 'I don't know,' Simon repeated unhappily.

'I'll . . . dig up . . . her,' Bill declared.

'Colonel, when will we be able to get the body?' Simon heard Bill ask.

'. . . not sure . . . fogged in at Resolute, Iqaluit and . . . er Lake. Is it clear where you are, Hollingford? Over.'

'For the moment, but clouds are rolling in. Over.'

'I'll try to arrange something as soon as possible. Keep me posted on your weather. Over.' This sentence boomed through a momentary cessation in the static.

'Will do.' Simon cleared his throat. 'Bill, any news on the, umm, inquiry?'

'Not yet . . . indication which way it'll go,' Bill answered. Again the static intruded.

'Call tomorrow, Bill, same time, same station. Over and out.' Simon removed the headphones and massaged his sore ears before shutting down the radio and restoring its dust cover—not that dust was a problem in the incredibly clean air. He checked his watch—he'd been on the radio for half an hour. He slumped on his packing crate and put his head in his hands. Here he was, in the middle of nowhere, investigating a murder solo, and he wasn't even sure he was still a policeman. He smiled grimly. It must have choked his superintendent to agree to this arrangement. 'Bastard,' Simon hissed. 'Why is he gunning for me?'

He shoved his personal worries to the back of his mind and rose stiffly to his feet. He sauntered out into the brightness and then stopped dead in shock. Tony was standing about twenty-five feet from the radio tent, his mouth opening and closing like a fish gasping in the air. Spying Simon, he scuttled out of sight into the gloomy interior of his tent, leaving Simon gaping in his turn. What had Tony heard? Why was he here? What would he do? Simon's heart pounded. From that distance Tony might have heard nothing . . . in any case, he could only have heard Simon's end of the conversation. What had he said? Simon frowned. The weather was the last topic, but before that? Tony and Anne. 'Damn,' he whispered. But it was possible Tony had just arrived. Maybe he was as surprised to see Simon as Simon was to see him. Or, since Simon had complained of radio problems, he'd assume that was the reason for the unscheduled call. Don't panic, Simon admonished himself. The best course of action is to say nothing unless Tony himself brings up the topic.

After rinsing his coffee cup, Simon gathered up his drawing materials. He dawdled a little, giving Tony an opportunity to approach him, but the man stayed hidden in his tent. With a last look back, Simon headed out to join Viola. He was preparing a series of sketches to illustrate a paper she was writing about juvenile musk ox behaviour, but he intended to ask the lady a few tactful questions about Eric as well.

With his binoculars, he quickly located his quarry on a ridge a good hour's walk away. While he couldn't spot Viola herself, he was familiar enough with musk oxen to be able to identify 'her' herd even from this distance. Its three massive males, one with its tusk broken off above the curve, were distinctive and accompanying them were four smaller males, fifteen females of various ages and ten juveniles. They had a characteristic formation they adopted when they foraged across the tundra. Two of the largest males roamed out in front and the one with the mutilated tusk stayed aloof in the rear. Fortunately for Viola this group rarely strayed far from the lush valley floor.

There was a definite nip in the freshening wind, so Simon huddled down into the bulky army issue parka. The temperature was well below the freezing point.

Viola popped into view a hundred yards away and waved at him. The herd was angling closer as it grazed on the low willows and reindeer moss, so finally he stopped and waited for her to join him.

'Getting cold, isn't it,' she said, shivering in her pink ski jacket. 'Snow, do you think?' She checked the sky anxiously.

'Could be, but not for a few hours I'd say. Would you like to borrow my parka?'

Viola laughed with genuine pleasure. 'So chivalry isn't dead after all. No, thank you, Simon, I'm a tough old girl and it's not that cold.' Pointing towards the nearby herd, she continued, 'They don't even notice it's colder; in fact they probably prefer it.'

The two stood in companionable silence for a few minutes watching the grazing animals and then, as the herd moved

on, they followed. Viola explained the points she wished
Simon to illustrate and waved her arms enthusiastically as
she pantomimed the activity. All the while they shadowed
the animals as the herd floated with deceptive speed across
the rough terrain. Simon closely observed the interactions
of the juvenile males and noted the behaviour Viola indicated. He made a few quick sketches to catch the dynamics
of the encounters—the thrust of the tusks, the attenuated
charges—but drawing while matching Viola's brisk pace
was difficult. Soon he put away his pencil and merely
observed. The finished sketches would come later.

'Have you given any more thought to your "accident"?'
he asked, breaking the silence.

'A little, I suppose,' Viola replied diffidently.

'Any conclusions?'

She shook her head slowly. 'The whole incident was
bizarre.'

Simon rubbed his chin. He'd forgotten to shave that
morning and the stubble felt like sandpaper. 'How well do
you know these people, Vi?'

She studied his face, narrowing her eyes until the crows'
feet radiated like gullies from their corners. Then she
shrugged and said, 'Some of them very well. Others, like
Joan, hardly at all, or at least no better than you do.'

'I understand you've known Eric for years,' Simon
prompted.

'Goodness, yes, we go back a long way, Eric and I. We've
known each other since graduate school. He was quite the
peacock even then, always grabbing the limelight, but just
as charming as he is now, when he chooses to be.' Viola
shivered and pulled her toque down over her ears while
glancing anxiously at the sky. 'Another half-hour and I'm
going to call it quits for today.' She swerved left, mirroring
the movements of the herd.

'Were you great friends?'

Viola cast a quizzical glance at Simon before replying.
'Eric and I, you mean? We got along.' Her tone conveyed
more than she intended.

'Did you meet his wife before they married?'

'No, but Eric introduced us shortly after at a conference in Chicago.' For once, she seemed reluctant to meet his gaze.

'Have you seen much of him since then? Are you still close?'

'I didn't say we were close,' Viola protested quickly. Too quickly.

The musk oxens' trek turned one hundred and eighty degrees and the humans ran to get out of the way. 'Unpredictable buggers,' she mumbled fondly.

'Were you surprised Eric got married?' Simon asked when they were safely to the side.

Viola noted the time and direction change in her field book before she responded. 'At first I wondered, but when I met Lynda I understood.'

'Oh?'

Viola glanced at him out of the corner of her eye. She knew she was being pumped and Simon knew she knew. He would have to weigh her answers accordingly. 'Lynda doted on him,' she replied, choosing her words with care. 'She was besotted. Maybe she still is, for that matter. Eric got a live-in groupie as well as a willing slave.' Viola's voice was shaded with bitterness.

'Lucky Eric,' Simon remarked mildly.

'Yes. Wouldn't we all like such service? Eric wanted to be the centre of the universe and he is the centre, at least of Lynda's world. She'll take anything from him and still come back for more; and believe me, she's taken a lot.'

Viola pushed a wayward strand of grey hair back under her hood before adding more calmly, 'Don't get me wrong, I like Eric, I always have. He's intelligent, witty, sophisticated and often charming. Who knows?' She shrugged, 'Maybe I'm just a little jealous of his success, both personal and scientific, but everything always comes up roses for Eric Karnot.'

'He's had some tragedy in his life,' Simon pointed out. 'After all, just last year his stepson disappeared.'

'True, although they weren't very close at the time. I think Phillip finally objected to the way Eric treated his mother. Whatever faults Phillip might have had, and he had many, he did love his mother.'

'How did Eric mistreat Lynda? I can't picture him as a wife-beater, somehow.'

'Of course he isn't a wife-beater.' She stopped and pointed at a lagging calf. 'See that one? Watch him home in on his mother.' Sure enough, within seconds the little one was back at her side. Viola chuckled. 'Just like humans. They don't like being alone, but one of the adults would have rounded him up soon if he hadn't returned of his own accord.'

'About Eric and Lynda?' Simon prompted as they started walking again.

'Nosey, aren't you?' Viola commented without heat. 'But so am I, for that matter, and Eric *is* fascinating. I'm sure he never hit Lynda but he hasn't been the most faithful and supportive of husbands. And he did walk out on her a few years back.'

'But they're together again . . .'

'Eric probably needed the constant ego massage she provided more than he thought he did. He hasn't mended his ways, but they are back together again—and happy as far as I can tell. And rich too. Eric wins again! Typical,' she muttered.

'Rich?'

'Just before they got back together, Lynda's aunt won a big lottery. When the old lady died, Lynda inherited the money.'

At this moment their attention was caught by another sudden swing in direction by the herd and they had to scramble to stay out of the way.

'Reminds me of that stampede,' Simon panted, sliding backwards on the gravelly slope. The herd passed so close he could smell the earthly richness of their thick brown coats and feel the impact of their hooves on the hard ground. Again he realized how close to death Viola had come. 'Do you think it could have been Eric who started the stampede?' he asked when they slowed down again.

'Of course not. Why would he?' Viola bent over to catch her breath.

'You'd know better than I. Old times' sake, perhaps?'

Viola shot him an angry look. 'I'm sure he wouldn't,' she repeated, but the conviction was gone from her voice.

CHAPTER 8

Simon frowned as he studied the sky. A swell of roiling, angry clouds surged in from the west. A diffuse, pallid glow enshrouded the landscape and everyone gathering at camp felt edgy, awaiting the inevitable storm. They weren't worried about a gentle snowfall—at this time of year, below freezing temperatures were bound to be short-lived. But if the wind picked up, the chill factor would plummet and the blowing snow would make navigation uncertain. As the small group waited for their still absent companions to return, memories of the previous year's tragedy were at the forefront of everyone's thoughts.

Anne, Wally, Eric and Joan still hadn't arrived and Simon wasn't the only one casting anxious glances at the horizon. In the dimness the field of view seemed strangely attenuated and for the first time since his arrival on Bathurst Island Simon felt closed in. He needed something to do, some physical activity.

To steady his nerves, Simon jogged along the antenna checking that all the gay wires and poles were secure against the approaching storm. At the end of his line he peered into the distance once again. Eric was barrelling up the final hill at a speed suggesting a family of hungry polar bears hard on his heels. The scientist spotted Simon and gave him a tired wave as he slackened his pace for the final stretch.

'Cutting it fine, aren't you, Eric?' Simon inquired as he landed a hearty slap on Eric's shoulder.

'Fine? Are you kidding? It won't show for another hour at least!' he panted, fighting for breath. 'Everyone else here?'

'Anne, Wally and Joan are still out.'

A crease marred Eric's patrician brow but he said nothing as the two of them hurried to the sanctuary represented by their few hundred pounds of gear.

Eric's return was greeted with relief by the others and just as everyone inevitably gravitated towards him, another figure swam into sight on the perimeter of the gloom. Wally was safely back, unharmed and obviously unchanged as he impatiently brushed off Tony's diffident welcome.

Tersely Eric gave instructions to double-check the tent pegs and to top up the fuel in the small stoves. Caring for their scientific equipment rated top priority and the radio tent was again piled high with crates and boxes. Simon had to clamber over an obstacle course to get to his radio. As his hands ran over its familiar knobs and buttons it occurred to him that it might be difficult to have a private chat with Sergeant Harkness if the entire expedition was snowbound and confined to camp. It might prove necessary to reveal his gruesome discovery after all.

A voice, half scream, half shout, brought him snapping out of his reverie.

'Simon! Simon!'

Anne's distraught voice propelled Simon's heart into his mouth. Charging from the tent, he spied the woman stumbling down the hill towards him. Everyone surged forward. Tony got to her first but she shook him off and struggled on towards Simon, clinging to him with astonishing strength. 'I found him! I found him!' she gasped, breathless and white.

'Who?' Simon took her elbows and shook her gently as his heart sank. 'Who?'

'Phillip. He's dead,' she shrieked through her ragged breathing.

Simon tried to read the expressions of those crushed

around them but Anne was tugging distractedly on his coat sleeve.

'Simon,' she insisted again and he turned back to her.

'Yes?'

'There was blood, Simon . . . I think . . . I think he was . . .' Anne couldn't finish.

'You think he was shot,' Simon finished for her.

Anne nodded. 'I'm not crazy?'

'No, you're not crazy.' He squeezed her shoulders. 'Phillip *was* shot, probably by a .303.' He pointed dramatically to a rifle leaning up against a tent. 'Like that one.'

After a moment of stunned silence, everyone began talking at once. While the cacophony raged in his ears, Simon studied the faces around him. He blocked out the strident voices and saw only their mouths opening and closing in meaningless pantomime. Wally's expression stood out. After one fishlike gape he clamped his mouth shut. A look of satisfaction flickered across his face as he retreated to the periphery of the crowd.

Simon turned his attention to the others. Eric was performing his 'concerned leader' routine—too perfectly for Simon's taste, and the others were looking from one to another, shaking their heads and denying belief.

Except Tony Colautti. Tony was standing motionless now, complexion ashen and eyes staring. Then his voice rose over the others. 'No. No! It can't be!' he shrieked and made to strike Simon.

But Tony's tortured face ran into Jeff's fist and the man crumpled to the frozen ground as the others looked on, aghast.

Jeff winced and rubbed his hand. 'I didn't mean to hit him that hard . . .'

Anne gave a cry, and abandoned Simon to throw herself down at Tony's side. A dribble of blood trickled from a gash on his right cheek and Anne dabbed ineffectually at it with her glove.

'Get away from me.' Tony struck her hand away and

pushed himself to his feet. Anne cowered on the ground, whimpering.

Again Tony rushed Simon and this time he managed to grab a handful of his coat. 'You're wrong!' he cried in a strangled voice. 'Phillip died in the storm, that's all! It was the storm!' He twisted the coat in his fists and tried to shake Simon.

Simon's fingers locked on Tony's wrists. With a jerk he freed himself but didn't release his hold. 'I found the body two days ago,' he said, staring into the man's wild eyes. 'There are two bullet holes in his chest.'

The certainty with which he spoke had its effect on Tony and on the others as well. The protests of outright disbelief died out to be replaced by doubt and confusion. Tony moaned and sagged. When Simon let him go he turned and ran blindly to his tent, shoving aside those in his way.

'Tony . . .' Anne started to follow but kind hands reached out to restrain her. She stopped, dazed.

Viola put her arm awkwardly around her friend's waist. 'Come to my tent until Tony's feeling better,' she murmured. Anne let herself be led away. The silence held until the two women disappeared into the tent but then the questions flooded forth.

Simon held up his hands to stop the deluge. 'Hold on. If you'll give me a chance, I'll explain.'

The hubbub died down and they clustered together a few feet in front of him. The group had not yet classified Detective-Inspector Hollingford as the enemy but he knew that would come soon enough. For the moment he was merely an outsider, a bearer of bad news.

'Two days ago—after I did the bird survey for you, Eric —I went for a walk on the far side of the valley. I don't really know why I did—I guess I simply wanted to see what was there. Anyway, I found one of those ice bridges across a stream and it was so beautiful I just had to touch it.' He shook his head. 'Was I sorry! As I ran my fingers along it, a chunk of ice broke off, and a human hand reached out for me.' Simon shuddered. 'At least it seemed to . . .'

'Well, go on, man,' Eric snapped at him. 'So you found a body. What makes you say it's Phillip? And why shot?'

Simon rested his foot on an upturned crate and leaned forward. 'It was quite a while before I noticed the discolouration on those stiff fingers, but when I did I knew what it was. Blood leaves quite a distinctive stain when it ages.'

This simple comment broke the remaining bonds linking Simon to the other expedition members. His profession blazed forth in everyone's mind and he became separate, he became someone to be wary of, someone slightly disreputable. Simon felt the chill. He didn't mind. As he was ostracized, he felt the familiar mantle of the investigator falling around him and he knew he would be more comfortable doing his job from outside the circle.

'I chipped away most of the ice over him—enough to see two bullet holes in his chest—and I know bullet holes when I see them.' Simon studied his audience. 'Phillip was shot all right. In fact, he was murdered.'

The words hung in the air like plague bacteria, contaminating everyone they touched and unconsciously the knot of listeners moved farther away from Simon.

'Maybe it was an accident . . .' Jeff suggested.

'How could it be? Who would accidentally shoot a man and then leave him to die?' Simon asked.

'Maybe whoever did it thought he was a bear or something.'

'Shooting polar bears is a serious matter, not to mention against the law, unless you're in mortal danger. And if the distance was too great for proper identification you wouldn't be in much danger, would you? Besides, a confrontation with a bear isn't the type of incident people keep to themselves.'

The scientists shuffled uncomfortably but Jeff had another suggestion. 'Maybe it was suicide?'

'Unless your arms were as long as a gorilla's you wouldn't be able to reach the trigger with the barrel against your chest. And there are no powder burns. It was definitely murder.' Simon began pacing slowly in front of them. 'I covered the body with ice again to keep it preserved, but it must have melted by the time Anne spotted it.'

'But you didn't say anything.' It was an accusation not a statement and it came from Eric.

'No,' Simon agreed calmly, 'I didn't—at least not to anyone here. I did tell Colonel Fernald, however, and asked him to notify the proper authorities.'

'And just who are the "proper authorities"?' Eric demanded. 'You must've noticed there isn't a cop shop down at the next corner.'

'It turned out to be an interesting problem, actually,' Simon replied with a calm which further infuriated Eric. 'Is it an armed forces matter? After all, this is a defence department sponsored expedition. What about the RCMP? This is usually their jurisdiction. What about the Ontario police? The victim is from their region of the country. However, after all parties discussed the issue it was decided that for the time being it is *my* jurisdiction, since I'm here.' Simon smiled grimly. 'So, Eric, *I* am the proper authority and I chose to say nothing.'

'Nonsense!' Eric exploded.

'Ask Colonel Fernald,' Simon invited.

'This is outrageous! First you find our colleague, dead, and you say nothing. Then you discover, or say you do, that it's murder.' The blood vessels stood out on Eric's forehead as his voice rose higher and higher. 'And now you claim you're in charge of an investigation that no one knows is going on! Do you think we're a bunch of idiots? I demand,' he sputtered, waving his finger in Simon's face, 'I *demand* to see Phillip's body for myself and I will most certainly talk to Colonel Fernald and have you thrown off the case!'

Eric stormed off to the radio tent and started flinging boxes out of his way. The scientists cringed as they pictured their precious equipment shattering into countless pieces, but they stood irresolute, looking from Simon to the tent and back to Simon.

'I assume you're telling us the truth about all this?' The

hoarse question came from Viola who'd slipped back out
of her tent to join the others.

Simon nodded. 'I'm afraid so.'

'Why didn't you tell us?' Jeff asked.

'Because Resolute is still fogged in and there's no way to
get us and Phillip's body out of here.'

'Why do we have to leave?'

'The body must be examined by forensic specialists
as soon as possible,' Simon replied, then hesitated for a
moment before continuing. 'And I wasn't prepared to keep
a twenty-four-hour guard over the corpse.'

'You wouldn't have had to guard it,' Viola objected.

'I couldn't be sure of that. Don't you see? The murderer
is here again this year.' Simon said this knowing that their
minds had resisted following the chain of events to this
inescapable conclusion.

'No . . .' But even as Viola spoke, Simon could see the
realization dawning on them all. It was not a pleasant
thought and it left them speechless.

'I think I'd better help Eric before he busts the radio.'
Simon disengaged himself from the silent cluster, but
paused and turned again to address them. 'Keep a watch
for Joan, she's not back yet and the weather's getting worse.
Let me know when she comes.'

Eric, it appeared, had a good command of dockyard voc-
abulary and was using it to the full as he wildly twiddled
knobs on the radio.

'Want help?' Simon asked.

'No!' Eric spat, but, realizing that he was getting nowhere
on his own, he moved aside with ill grace. 'Get Colonel
Fernald.'

Simon readjusted the frequency and threw the switches
in the proper order before donning the headset.

'This is Victor Echo 8735. Come in, Viking. Over.'

Response was instantaneous and clear, much to Simon's
annoyance. Why hadn't it been like this when Bill was
available, he wondered? And he would have preferred it if
Eric had had trouble talking to the Colonel—who knew

what the officer might choose to say? None the less, Simon asked for the Colonel and, as soon as Simon acknowledged him, Eric snatched the earphones off Simon's head and clamped them to his own.

'What's this I hear about Hollingford being in charge?' Eric shouted into the microphone.

Simon winced for the Colonel's ears and watched Eric's blood pressure rise even higher as he listened to the reply.

'This is my expedition, Colonel, I'll have you know, and I don't take orders from anyone, even you!'

Simon couldn't hear what Colonel Fernald was saying but from the belligerent expression on Eric's face he had a pretty good idea.

'I'm not one of your lackeys, Fernald, you can't force me to do anything,' Eric fumed but with less conviction this time. 'Aren't civilian charges like "obstruction of justice" outside your purview?'

Again Simon could only watch Eric's face to track the other end of the conversation but the expression was now composed equally of fury and defeat so he supposed the Colonel was making some telling points.

'I hope you realize we have only Hollingford's word that there was any crime committed . . . You may have confidence in him but I don't! . . . Just when are you going to get that corpse out of this place and let us get back to work?' Eric saw Simon's face and added more quietly, 'I know he's my son, but he's been missing for so long it's hard to realize . . . Thank you for your sympathy but we're not shutting down the expedition. Phillip would have wanted us to go on . . . Then we'll finish it without your damn help if we have to.' Eric's already thin lips disappeared altogether. 'We'll see about that, Colonel—don't bet on it. I'll let Hollingford do his nasty job but I remain in charge of the expedition and that's that. Over and out!'

Eric tore the headset off and threw a smouldering look at Simon. 'You'd better talk to your buddy—I've had more than enough,' he said through tight lips and stalked for the door, ruining his exit by tripping over a crate. He kicked it viciously before hurling himself out of the tent.

'Hollingford here, Colonel. Over.'

'I thought you were going to keep this under wraps until we could get to you. Over.'

'I was, but Dr Anne Colautti stumbled across the body this afternoon and blabbed before I could stop her. Over.'

'Does this change the situation? Over.'

'It does, but maybe for the better. At least there's no need to pussyfoot around any more. I can come straight out with my questions. Over.'

'Do you think Karnot will cooperate? Over.'

'No, but he won't actively hinder me . . . for now. Over.'

'How's your weather? Over.'

'Deteriorating. Low cloud, rising winds, fog, and we're anticipating snow. Over.'

'The fog's lifting at Baker Lake so this end may soon be clear enough for take-off. Over.'

'Unless you arrived in the next hour I don't think you'd be able to land here. Over.'

'Not possible, Hollingford. You'll have to hold on until your weather clears again—which may be a while if our meteorologist's any good. Keep me posted. Over.'

As Simon shut down the radio he felt alone. If the anticipated storm did break, he'd be trapped, like a pigeon among cats, in this tiny camp with seven unhappy people. They'd be suspicious of one another, but united in their antipathy towards him. Still, Simon comforted himself, the weather made an effective watchdog. At least he wouldn't have to babysit the corpse.

A shout in the distance brought him back to the present. From the door of the tent he saw Jeff waving madly at a figure in the distance. Joan jogged up the slope towards them, acknowledging Jeff's frantic signals with a tired shout. Everyone except Tony gathered to greet her.

'Thank God you're OK.' Eric took the heavy sample bag from her as he spoke.

'We were so worried about you,' Jeff exclaimed.

'Welcome home.' Viola hurried to help her off with her pack.

Joan's face, glistening from exertion, twisted in surprise at their enthusiasm. 'You'd think I was returning from the dead!' she quipped in bewilderment and then became even more puzzled as her light-hearted crack instantly snuffed out the high spirits. 'What's wrong?' she questioned.

It was Jeff who finally replied. 'Phillip's body has been found.'

'Oh.' Joan pulled off her gloves and slapped them rhythmically against her thigh. 'We knew he couldn't still be alive . . .'

'True, but . . .'

'So the mystery's solved.' Joan shrugged, collected her bag again and started to move on towards her tent.

'Not really.' Viola cleared her throat nervously.

'Yeah?' Joan asked over her shoulder as she walked.

'He didn't die of exposure.'

'So? Did he fall and crack his skull or something?' Joan stopped and turned around.

'Not exactly. He was shot.'

Dropping her sack, she stared at Viola. 'Say that again?'

'Phillip was shot. Murdered.'

Joan stood motionless and then with slow deliberation pulled the toque from her head and shook out her hair. 'Well, well, well . . . Isn't that intriguing. I guess someone else hated the guy even more than I did.' Joan flashed an unpleasant smile, picked up her samples again and turned on her heel.

The others stared open-mouthed at her retreating back.

Simon was hunched on his cot, his mittened hands tucked into his armpits and his toque pulled low over his ears. Wally was a dark, sullen shadow on the bunk opposite, a vague outline in the gloom. He was being difficult.

'Wally, you must answer my questions.'

'Why?'

'So I can find out who murdered Phillip.'

'I don't care who did it just as long as the bastard's dead.'

'Did you kill him?' Simon could barely make out the slight shake of the head and the disconcerting flash of yellow teeth. 'You hated him, didn't you?'

Silence.

'You blamed him for the death of your son, Scott,' Simon said, applying shock tactics.

'Keep my son out of this!' Venom hissed across the tent.

'How can I? He and Phillip were lovers.'

Wally lunged across the small gap, knocking Simon back against the canvas wall. He locked his hands around the policeman's neck.

The pressure of thumbs against his adam's apple brought tears of pain to Simon's eyes. He scrabbled at the death grip but his mittens got in the way. As he tore them off, stars burst before his eyes and Wally's distorted face blurred. Hands free at last, Simon grabbed Wally's index fingers and bent them backwards. The thumbs dug deeper into his flesh. As the sound of the sea roared in his ears Simon prayed his consciousness would outlast Wally's fingers.

His tongue was forcing its way past his lips when Simon felt rather than heard Wally's left finger crack and the pressure on his throat suddenly ceased. He fell forward on his cot, gasping and retching, still blind and deaf. When his paroxysms ceased he lay still.

At last he opened his eyes and found he could see again. Wally's shadowy form lay motionless on his bed, but Simon could feel his baleful gaze. Tentatively he fingered his bruised throat. When he couldn't find a hole punched clear through to his spinal cord, his spirits rose despite the thin stream of blood trickling down his neck.

Sit up! his brain commanded his body. It obeyed—slowly—but it obeyed, and Simon again sat hunched on his cot as if nothing had happened. But his mitts were on the floor and his neck was on fire. He warily eyed Wally. 'What the hell did you do that for? Are you crazy?' Simon coughed up blood as his chest spasmed. Wally didn't move. 'Are you trying to prove you're capable of murder?' Simon wiped his shaking hand over his forehead and it came away clammy with sweat. He wanted just to curl into a ball and succumb to his pain but he'd be damned if he'd let Wally succeed in putting him off. He sat up straighter. 'What were you doing the day Phillip was killed?' Simon's voice was a harsh croak. He grimaced and rubbed his neck.

Wally sat up like a corpse rising from a coffin. His dead eyes stared, only a tic at the corner of the left one betraying his recent fit of rage.

Simon leaned forward to grab Wally's jacket and shake the man but Wally shrank away.

After huddling silent for a few minutes more, Wally shrugged in a tired fashion and began a listless recital. 'I left camp early and went east towards the coast looking for some fresh dung. I kept mostly to the higher ground but I did go down into the wetter areas sometimes. It was a poor day for collecting.' Wally paused and his adam's apple bobbed up and down unattractively. 'I didn't notice the storm clouds coming until around two or two-thirty when I started back. By three the snow was really coming down so I headed for the IBP station . . . 'bout a mile away. I got there just before four. It was a miracle I didn't miss it in the snow.' His tone made Simon think he wouldn't have cared either way.

'Did you see anyone else during the day?'

'No . . . Yes. Someone, maybe Joan, to the south.' Wally's lips tightened and the tic grew more pronounced.

'On the other side of the Pass or in the Pass itself?'

'In the middle of the Pass.'

'What makes you say it was Joan?'

Wally shrugged. 'Maybe it wasn't.'

'Was this person carrying a gun?'

'Don't know.'

'Were they moving slowly or quickly?' Silence. Simon persisted. 'What time was this?'

'Noon.' Wally had turned his face to the wall and Simon could barely hear him.

'Could it have been Phillip?'

'Maybe.'

Simon could only whisper now and sweat glistened on his forehead from the effort of talking. The neck of his sweater was damp from the steady ooze of blood. 'Did you or Jeff get to the IBP station first?'

'He did.'

'And you both remained there for almost two days?'

Again the silence stretched until Simon felt he'd snap, but at last Wally grunted, 'Yes.'

Simon knew there were more questions to ask but he couldn't remember them. All he wanted was to lie back on his cot and go to sleep, but was it a good idea? You weren't supposed to sleep after a head injury . . . what about after near-strangulation? Besides, Wally still sat like a malignant toad only a couple of feet away. His company wasn't conducive to relaxation. Groaning, Simon struggled to his feet. His vision blurred for a moment but cleared as he cautiously made his way to the door of the tent and flung it wide. He left Wally to enjoy the frigid blast which poured in behind him.

The icy wind clawed at Simon's face and hands but it revived him. His curly hair was blown straight by the howling wind as he staggered against it to Viola's tent.

'Shut the damn flap!' greeted him. Joan scowled but her expression changed when she noticed his livid neck and its smear of blood.

'What happened?' Viola sprang up from her seat on a packing crate.

'Wally doesn't like people mentioning his son,' Simon croaked.

'It looks like he almost killed you!'

'It feels like it too. He may be over later for first aid—I had to break one of his fingers.'

'A street brawl,' Joan sneered as she unearthed the first aid kit.

'I prefer to call it a tent tussle.'

Joan wiped Simon's neck with an alcohol-soaked swab, taking no pains to be gentle. He gritted his teeth and didn't flinch while Viola, clucking anxiously, hovered at his shoulder.

When Joan had finished, Viola examined the wounds. 'Fingernails. That's what cut you. Wally must've been serious.'

'You shouldn't pry where you're not wanted,' was Joan's comment. She slapped two Band-Aids on to the cuts.

'If I were to ask you some questions would you react like he just did?'

'Maybe you should wait till you're feeling stronger before you take me on.' Joan's teeth flashed in a parody of a smile.

'Viola's here to referee.'

Joan shrugged. 'Have it your way. I don't have much of a record of cooperation with the cops.'

'Perhaps you'll have mercy on an invalid.'

'Don't count on it.'

'He has to ask us some questions in the circumstances.' Viola tried to smooth the atmosphere.

Joan shot her an angry look but said nothing.

'Did you like Dr Loew, Miss Winik?'

'*Ms* Winik. No, I didn't, Detective-Inspector Hollingford.'

Simon's head begun to swim. He peered around looking for somewhere to sit and Viola thrust her packing crate at him. Eyes and ears wide, she perched like an owl on her cot.

Simon sat down and took several deep breaths. 'Why didn't you like him?'

Joan sprawled on her cot, one knee bent in a parody of seduction. 'I told you already. He was an exploiter.'

'Of you?'

'Of Nature. People. His position. I loathe selfish people.'

'Didn't you have a more personal reason for disliking Phillip?'

Joan's hard blue eyes stared insolently at Simon. She ran

her fingers through her dark hair and tossed it defiantly. 'No. I disliked him on principle.'

'I think there's more to it than that.'

Joan hunched her thin shoulders. 'Think what you like —it's nothing to me.'

Simon shifted his position. The crate creaked under him but held. 'Where you from?'

Joan's brows snapped together. Simon knew he'd thrown her off balance by backing off. She'd been prepared for a fight.

'Saskatchewan . . .' she replied hesitantly, looking for a trap and finding none.

'Whereabouts? I've been to Saskatchewan a couple of times.'

'Some place so remote you'd never have heard of it, asshole.'

'Joan!' Viola admonished, but Simon waved her to silence.

'Don't worry, I've been called worse names by better people.' He caught the shadow of annoyance flitting over Joan's face. 'Could it be somewhere near The Winik Wilderness Camp?' he asked casually, 'The Winik Wilderness Camp where Phillip Loew was shot at?'

Joan drew in her breath sharply. 'Bastard!'

'Who? Me or Phillip?'

Joan swung her feet to the floor. 'It's all lies. I never laid eyes on Phillip until last summer. The day before we came north.'

'Where?'

'Winnipeg. At the Holiday Inn. That's where we all mustered for the expedition.' A raised eyebrow in Viola's direction elicited a tiny nod of agreement.

'You'd never seen him before? Never spoke to him on the 'phone?'

'No. I told you. Are you a slow learner?'

'Viola, did it look to you as if they were strangers?'

'I don't know.' Viola wriggled uncomfortably. 'They never talked much but then Joan isn't very . . . sociable.'

A smirk settled on Joan's face. She shifted around to sit cross-legged on the cot.

'You implied before that he'd done you some personal damage,' Simon pressed.

'I lied.'

'Did it have something to do with the mine near your family's camp?' He crossed his legs. 'The mine's expansion, sanctioned by Phillip's favourable environmental impact study, couldn't have done much for the wildlife population. No wonder you took a pot shot at him—you knew what his report would do to the family business.'

'Just speculation, Mr Detective. No one could prove anything then, and you can't now.'

'I don't have to—for now,' Simon said calmly. Her expression told him he'd guessed right. 'For the moment I care more about the shots which killed Phillip than the ones which missed.' His throat was throbbing and he wanted to get this interview over and go to bed. Taking on Joan while he was so below par had been a stupid idea. 'How about being a good girl and telling me where you were and what you were doing the day he disappeared?'

Joan cocked her head to one side and chewed her lip. When she noticed Viola's anxious gaze she shrugged her shoulders. 'Oh, very well—the information won't help you anyway. I was west of here. Taking soil temperature measurements.'

'In the Pass or on the south side?'

'Good try, Mr Nosey. This side.'

'Who saw you?' Simon asked, willing himself to pay attention and not let Joan see the difficulty he was having.

'How should I know?'

'Whom did you see?'

'*Whom* did I see?' she mocked. 'I saw no one.'

'Someone saw you in the middle of the Pass that day.'

Joan swung her feet to the floor and sat up abruptly. 'They're lying!'

'Maybe you're lying.'

Joan reclined again with studied disinterest. 'Prove it.'

'When did you get back to camp?'

'I dunno. The storm had already started.'

'Who was here when you arrived?'

'Vi. Anne. Maybe Tony—I'm not sure.'

'Which direction did she come in from, Viola?'

'The west, I think,' Viola mumbled. 'Not from the Pass.'

Joan's smirk broadened.

'Easy enough to arrange in those conditions,' Simon countered.

'You can't prove otherwise.'

Simon rose stiffly. 'It's been fun, Joan, but I've got to go. See you around.' He started for the door.

'Doesn't Viola get the third degree? Or do you reserve that treatment for us ex-cons?'

'All in good time,' he replied, heading reluctantly into the storm. As the tent flap slapped shut behind him he heard Viola's 'Ex-con?' on the wind.

Simon blew across the compound in a mad flurry of driving snow. He wanted his bed but Wally had tied their tent door closed from the inside. 'Open up!' Nothing. The wind ululated in the tent ropes—a lonely, wild sound. 'Open the door, damn it!' Simon joggled the tent. 'I'll pull out the goddamn pegs and crawl under if I have to.'

At last the tension on the door eased and Simon tumbled in with the snow. He re-strapped the door and turned in time to see Wally wrapping himself in his bag. The man lay down and pointedly turned his head to the canvas wall. Simon removed only jacket and boots before following suit but he remained facing outward, unwilling to turn his back on Wally. While reassuring himself that pain and apprehension would keep him awake, Simon fell asleep.

He woke to find a shadow bending over him.

'Wally!' Simon threw his arms up in front of his mangled neck and groaned involuntarily as pain shot through his damaged throat. He waited for the assault, but it didn't come.

'It's Eric. Pull yourself together.'

When the knives piercing his neck had shrunk to mere

skewer size and the stars he was seeing to specks, Simon gingerly sat up, keeping his upper torso and head rigid. The dried blood on his sweater was hard and scratchy and its characteristic metallic smell made his stomach quiver. Inside the tent the light was poor as outside the wind still howled and shook the canvas like an immense cat playing with a mouse.

'What do you want, Eric?' Simon's throat was so dry he could barely talk.

'I heard about your "accident". Will you be OK?'

'I think so. Thanks for your concern.'

'It's seven-thirty—almost time for the radio check. Under these conditions it's essential that we keep in touch with Resolute. I trust you will be capable of carrying out your duty to this expedition, Mr Hollingford.'

'I trust so, Dr Karnot.' Simon held his head in his hands while he fought off the fog of sleep. The cold was intense and he shivered.

'Sit down.' He waved Eric to the deserted cot across from him. 'Where's Wally?'

'Working in the storage tent.'

'And the others?'

'All minding their own business.'

'Unlike me. Right you are. But since I have your un-divided attention at the moment I'll stick my neck out again. What was your relationship with Phillip like?'

Eric tried to stretch out his long legs but in the cramped space it was difficult. He directed a piercing glance at the policeman, his lips set in a thin dark line over the startling white of his goatee. 'Not close, but cordial.'

'That's not what I hear.'

'It is none the less true. I am the only father Phillip knew and he my only son. We valued each other.'

'Phillip was furious when you left his mother.'

'Tongues are busy, aren't they?' Eric stroked his beard with his gloved fingers. 'But Lynda and I are happily re-married now.'

'Over Phillip's objections.'

Eric shrugged. 'Phillip wanted his mother to be happy. Lynda wanted me, so Phillip accepted the situation.'

'Maybe he didn't. Maybe you killed him.' Simon sensed the change in Eric's breathing and his hand went protectively to his neck.

Eric started to rise. 'If you've finished insulting me, I think I'll leave now,' he said icily, but he seemed to have no designs on Simon's neck.

'Wait.' Simon held up his hand. 'Tell me what you were doing the day Phillip died.'

Eric stared down his thin nose at Simon for a long minute before reseating himself. 'For Phillip's sake I'll humour you. My activities were much the same as always. I toured my observation sites, counted birds and took notes.'

'Which sites did you visit?'

'The ones in the Pass itself. They are the most productive.'

'That morning, did you leave before or after Phillip did?'

'I have no idea.'

'You had a rifle with you?'

'Of course. It's important for the team leader to give a good example,' Eric replied.

'When did you get to the site closest to the other side of the Pass?'

'About noon . . . maybe a quarter after.'

'Did you see anyone else while you were there?' Simon asked.

'No. I was bird-watching, not people-watching. I did catch a beautiful display of aggression between a snowy owl and a long-tailed jaeger if you feel that's relevant.' Eric's nasty smile dropped the temperature another few degrees.

Simon ignored the provocation—he'd make sure the man ate crow eventually. 'What time did you leave there?'

'Two o'clock. I had a schedule to keep and a side trip to murder my son would have put my timing off.'

'And then you proceeded to your last site which is on the way back?' Simon asked, again ignoring Eric's sarcasm.

'Yes. I got to my last station at two-twenty-five and

started observing at two-thirty. By three-fifteen, when my observation period was over, the snow had already started.'

'Did you see anyone while you were at that last site?'

'No.'

'How long did it usually take you to get from there to base camp?'

'An hour.'

'But you didn't get back until eight o'clock,' Simon challenged, leaning forward.

'As I have told you, Hollingford, if you could but remember, I first attempted to weather the storm at the blind. By five o'clock I knew it was impossible so I decided to try for camp. It was a difficult decision but there was no other option.'

'And it took you three hours to make a journey which usually took one?' Simon didn't try to keep the scepticism out of his voice.

'Conditions were far from ideal.' Eric dismissed the question with a wave of his tapered fingers.

'How did you navigate? Everyone else thinks it would be impossible under those conditions.'

'I'm very familiar with the terrain, and used the ponds as guides. I followed around their edges and only went cross-country when I knew the next pond was very close. Using that circuitous route it took three hours and would likely take two even under perfect weather conditions. Plus, I was very lucky.' Eric inclined his head graciously. 'I admit that freely. It was quite possible that I would not survive.'

'But you did.'

'Evidently.'

'Did you hear any gunshots?'

'No.'

'When you got back to camp what did you do about the missing men?'

'A search party was out of the question so I ordered the camp illuminated as much as possible and shot off rounds every hour.'

'Very sensible.' Simon was silent for a moment, fingering his sore neck. 'I won't keep you any longer.'

Eric extricated himself from the cramped bunk, pulled his hood up and examined his watch. 'Don't forget the radio check, Hollingford. That's your primary duty and it's now three minutes to eight.'

'Arrogant prick,' Simon mumbled under his breath.

After the radio check and a meal, both highly unsatisfactory, Simon needed some sympathetic company. Tony was working in the storage tent, so, with her watchdog out of the way, it was a good time to visit Anne. He even had hopes for some nurturing treatment at her hands. He hurried across the compound and scratched at her tent.

'Come in.'

He ducked inside. 'Sorry about the snow,' he gasped, brushing the thick covering from his head and shoulders. 'It's wicked out there.'

Anne was sitting cross-legged on her cot with an untidy sheaf of notes spread in front of her. The Coleman lantern's harsh white glare highlighted her gloved hands but her face was in shadow. 'I heard about your fight with Wally. Are you all right?'

'I'll live. Next time I'll be a little more circumspect with my questions.'

Anne unwound her legs and swung them to the ground before lifting her huge eyes to Simon's face. 'Is that why you're here? To ask me questions?'

'It makes a good excuse.' A smile flickered over Simon's features. 'And I do need to know a few details about your movements the day Phillip died—just to corroborate other stories, OK? I won't upset you.'

'I won't lunge for your neck, if that's what you're worried about.'

'Damn, I was counting on it. What would it take to make you attack?'

Anne rose fluidly from the low cot to lean against the tent's centre pole. The distance between them was now less than two feet and the intervening space was charged with energy. Anne tipped her face up towards Simon's. 'I don't know. Tell me my eyebrows are too thick.'

'Your eyebrows are too thick.'

It wasn't precisely an attack but the space between them shrank to less than nothing. Simon put his arms around her. She stiffened but didn't pull away.

'How do the Inuit manage?' Simon murmured some minutes later. They'd tossed toques and gloves aside but their bulky parkas proved to be severely constraining.

'Centuries of evolution,' Anne whispered. She sighed and melded her body as close to his as she could. Ignoring the throbbing in his throat and the niggling doubt in his mind, Simon responded.

A scrabbling at the tent door yanked the pair back to reality with a jolt. Anne flew to her cot, keeping her face carefully in the shadow. Simon, quick to recover, bent to retrieve his mitts and toque and stuffed them in his pocket just as Tony burst into the tent. 'What the hell are you doing here?'

'Asking questions. You're just in time to join the fun.'

Tony peered suspiciously at them both but Simon's bland stare and Anne's bent head defeated him. 'I'm not telling you nothing, Hollingford.' Tony jabbed a finger at Simon's chest, 'And neither is my wife.'

Simon stared at the newcomer. 'You want your finger broken too?' Tony drew back a pace and jammed his hand into his pocket. Simon turned back to Anne. 'You were just going to tell me what you did the day Phillip was killed.'

'Um . . . yes.' Anne cleared her throat, still staring at her lap where her fingers interlaced nervously.

'I, um . . . I think I was the last one to leave camp that morning. I had a sore throat, you see, and I wasn't feeling too well. I just sat around, drank a couple of cups of coffee and sorted my notes . . . until about eleven.'

'And at eleven o'clock?'

'Well, I, umm . . . I decided I couldn't waste the entire

day so I went to change the charts at a couple of my closer stations.'

'Which way did you go?' Simon asked gently.

'Down to the Pass for one site and back up on this side for the other.'

'Did you see any of your colleagues?'

'I wasn't really looking . . .'

'But did you see anyone just by chance?' Simon insisted, back on the chase.

'I saw Eric at his blind on the big pond—at least, he was close to it so I assumed that's where he was going. And I saw Tony on the far side of the Pass. He was extracting a core just above the swampy level.'

'You don't have to tell him anything, Anne. Shut up!' Tony took a threatening step towards her but Simon blocked his path and Tony sullenly backed off, fingering his already swollen nose. Simon's fist would do more damage than Jeff's had.

Anne ignored her husband and looked directly at Simon for the first time since she'd started her recital. She gestured nervously with her slim white hands. 'Everything was very normal.'

'When did you get back to camp?'

'Just after Viola.'

'No one else was there? Just you and Vi?'

'Yes. But by that time the snow was coming down thick and fast and we were starting to worry about the others.'

'Did you carry a rifle that day?'

'No. I wasn't planning to be gone long.'

'When you did take one, was it one of the .22s or a .303?'

'A .22.'

Simon had never seen her with a .303. 'When you saw Eric and Tony earlier in the day, were they carrying rifles?'

'Tony was working when I saw him, so even if he had done it would've been on the ground,' she prevaricated.

'Didn't you see him leave camp that morning?'

Anne shook her head yet again, her eyes wide and frightened like a trapped animal's. The warm glow which had enlivened them just minutes before had vanished. 'No.' She nervously brushed back her hair and stretched out her hand to grab her toque. With it squashed down on her head her face looked drawn and pale.

Simon hated himself for tormenting her, but the questions had to be asked—best get it over with. She couldn't have had anything to do with Phillip's death, could she? And he'd be able to soothe away her worries again later . . . 'How well did you know Phillip?'

'Not well. We . . . um, we just nodded at each other in the hall at the college or made small talk if we were in the elevator together. We didn't socialize.'

'And you, Tony? How well did you know him?'

Tony picked his nose nervously. 'I don't have to answer.'

'You can refuse, of course, but I'll wonder why. Something to hide, maybe?'

'I've nothing to hide! I hardly knew Phillip. We were colleagues, that's all—sat on a few committees together— that sort of thing.'

The veins in Tony's neck stood out like cords. Simon could even see the pulse hammering below his sweaty skin.

'You voted in favour of his tenure,' Simon said.

'So?'

'So six months previously you'd been opposed.'

Tony fidgeted with his jacket zipper and licked his white lips. 'I changed my mind,' he mumbled at last with a venomous glance at his wife.

'Anne didn't tell me,' Simon lied.

'There's no law against changing my mind.'

'What caused the switch?'

'Too many people were on his case over nothing. I thought he could use a break.'

'And what did he do for you in return?'

'Nothing! He didn't do anything.' Tony's voice had an edge of hysteria as it climbed the octaves.

'Did you vote in favour of Phillip's tenure, Anne?' Simon asked but his gaze remained firmly fixed on Tony.

Anne shook her fair head slightly and continued staring at her hands. 'I'm an adjunct faculty member so I didn't get a vote.'

'Tony, have you ever been to Phillip's Toronto apartment?'

A sickly hue passed over Tony's face and his mouth opened and shut like a landed fish. 'No,' he croaked.

'But you knew he had an apartment in Toronto?'

'No, I didn't know.'

'And you didn't know he dealt in drugs.'

He shook his head frantically. Despite the frigid temperature, sweat beaded on Tony's pasty forehead. Fear had completely replaced fight.

'What were you doing the day Phillip died?'

'Nothing. Nothing at all—I swear it.' Tony licked his lips yet again.

'No sampling? No data collecting?'

'Just my usual stuff—nothing different.'

'Did you see Phillip that morning?'

'In passing.' Tony swallowed hard. 'Just wished him luck.'

'Luck?'

The reptilian tongue flickered again over his narrow lips. 'On his fossil hunt. The night before Phillip had mentioned going to the south side to look for some.'

'Who heard this?' Simon asked sharply.

'Everyone, I suppose. It was at dinner.' A flash of cunning flickered in Tony's eyes as he realized the significance.

'Did you hear Phillip say he was going south?' Simon turned to Anne, who resolutely kept her eyes down and her head bent.

'I guess so. I didn't pay much attention.'

Simon studied her for a long moment before returning his attention to her husband. 'Where were you working that day, Tony?'

The man took a couple of deep breaths before he answered. 'Here and there. I made a kind of circle taking samples in different types of terrain.'

'Anne, and others I might add, say they saw you on the far hills.'

'I was there, briefly, but just on the edge. I didn't kill Phillip!' Tony's voice cracked with emotion.

Simon's confidence soared. He had him on the ropes. All he had to do was finish him off. 'How long were you over there?'

'Maybe an hour, an hour and a half.' Tony gulped convulsively and clenched his fists to control their shaking.

'Did you see Phillip?'

Tony shook his head violently, unable to speak. He was holding on to his self-possession by a thread and when he became aware of Anne's furtive stare he almost lost his grip completely.

'Did you see anyone else?'

'Just Eric,' he jerked out.

'Where?'

'At the big pond.'

'Did you hear any shots?'

'No! For God's sake, no!' he choked.

'When did you get back to camp?' Simon asked, backing off. He could wait to land the finishing punch. He had to find out what was destroying this pathetic man but he was humane enough to want to do it without witnesses.

'Late. Near four o'clock.' Tony chewed his thumbnail. His knuckles began to show telltale white spots.

'Where are your gloves, man?' Simon asked abruptly. 'For God's sake, put them on or you'll get frostbite!'

Tony stared blankly at his hands for a moment and then pulled his gloves from his pocket. As he pulled on the first one, its mate fell to the ground. Simon retrieved it for him and tossed it over. He waited until Tony had his thick mitts over the gloves before he returned to his questioning. 'Did you have any trouble getting back to camp that day?' he asked.

'Yeah.' Tony nodded. 'I almost didn't make it.'

'Were you worried about the missing expedition members?'

'Of course. I volunteered to go looking.'

'Even though you knew it was hopeless?'

'So? We should have done something!' Tony's voice had more than a quaver of hysteria to it now. Simon eased off again. He stole a glance at Anne, who huddled, head bowed, on her cot. Destroying her husband before her eyes wouldn't do their budding relationship any good, no matter how she felt about the jerk. But the man's craven attitude turned his stomach. He had to get away from Tony before he did something he'd regret.

'Thanks for your help,' Simon said abruptly and left the tent.

'Look what the wind blew in!' Viola smiled fleetingly at her visitor. 'My turn for the hot seat?'

'And for a hot chocolate.' Simon held out a steaming mug. 'A bribe.'

'I thought the witness was supposed to bribe the policeman, not the other way round.'

'I favour the element of surprise. It keeps the witness off-balance.' Simon squatted on a packing case. 'What've you been doing today?'

'Getting bored out of my mind. I hate this weather and I hate wasting time.'

'It's vicious out there.' Simon sipped his own drink. 'I think it's even colder now, if that's possible. I thought this was summer!'

'Definitely substandard even for Bathurst Island. It's going to play havoc with my studies.'

They listened to the ominous howl of the wind as it slapped and tore at the tent. Their reverie was broken suddenly as a commotion erupted outside.

'Let me in there!'

'Just wait a sec . . .'

The canvas wall bulged inward under someone's weight and then Wally burst through the door. Eric followed closely.

'What's going on?' Viola demanded.

Wally's head was weaving from side to side and his fists were clenched. Simon tensed for the attack but Wally looked right through him.

'Where's Joan? Where's that bitch?' Wally shouted.

'I don't know.' Viola shrank back.

'Where is she?' Wally took a threatening step but Eric smoothly slid in between them.

'I told you to cool it.' Eric kept a wary eye on Wally as he spoke. 'We'll discuss this like civilized people.'

'What the hell's going on?' Simon's voice rose over the hubbub.

'Wally says some of his notes are missing,' Eric explained.

'Not missing. Stolen,' Wally insisted.

'You don't know that.'

'They were in my briefcase and now they're not. That meddling slut took them!'

'You can't go around accusing people of—' Simon stopped to dodge out of range of Wally's swing.

Eric hung grimly on to his other arm. 'Calm down! We'll get to the bottom of this. We'll find your notes. Stop acting crazy.'

A dim flicker of reason returned to Wally's bulging eyes. 'She took them . . . ' he mumbled as he stood, uncertain.

'Come on, I'll take you back to your tent.' Eric steered the man out into the blizzard while casting a desperate glance back at Viola and Simon.

'Wow,' Viola breathed. 'Good thing Joan wasn't here.'

'I suggest you find her, warn her, and then bring her back here to stay out of Wally's way,' Simon advised crisply. 'Let's hope Eric has him under control.'

'Aren't you going to keep an eye on him?'

'No. I don't seem to have a soothing effect on our good Dr Gingras. Eric can take over my cot and I'll bunk with Jeff.' Simon thrust her gloves and toque at Viola. 'Get going now. Find Joan. And pray this weather lifts or we may have another murder on our hands.'

*

Simon wrapped his sleeping-bag around his legs and re-laxed. He felt much safer with his new room mate. Jeff seemed almost friendly.

'Thanks, I need that.' Simon passed the flask back to Jeff. 'What a day.'

Jeff took another gulp before stoppering the bottle and shoving it back under his bunk. 'So your mystery's been solved, Simon.'

'About Phillip? What makes you say that?'

'Isn't it obvious? Wally's a deranged killer. You're lucky to be still alive—you and Joan.'

'Granted he's not normal, but that doesn't make him Phillip's murderer,' Simon replied, pulling his toque down to his eyebrows.

'We can't have two homicidal maniacs among us.'

'Wally attacks with his hands. Phillip was shot,' Simon pointed out.

'You might've been shot too if he'd had a rifle handy.'

'There was one in the tent.'

'Then you're damn lucky he didn't use it.'

Simon leaned back, hands behind his neck, and contem-plated the billowing ceiling not far above his nose. 'What were you doing the day Phillip died?'

Jeff shook his head in disbelief. 'You don't give up, do you? You're not convinced it was Wally.'

'Humour me.'

'You're obsessed, you know.'

'Maybe. Did you see anyone near Phillip's location the day he died?'

Jeff's lips thinned. 'If you insist. I saw Tony near the far side of the Pass at noon or a bit before. And Joan not far from camp. That's it.'

'You spent the next two days at the IBP station?'

'Yeah. With Wally. Thank God he didn't turn on me.' Jeff shuddered dramatically.

Simon gave an involuntary snort and resumed his exam-ination of the wave pattern in the canvas above his head. His thoughts turned to Wally's missing notes. Someone had

see P. 59

had better luck finding a sample of Wally's handwriting than he'd had. Where did the man keep them? He'd have to ask—when Wally'd calmed down. And if Joan had taken them, she'd better give them back. He listened to the howling wind and the skitter of dry snow on the tent. He shivered and pulled his hood farther over his face. Where had Joan disappeared to in this weather?

CHAPTER 9

Simon was dozing when he heard someone scratching at the tent door. Before he could untangle himself from his sleeping-bag the flap snapped open and Viola blew in with the snow.

'Sorry about that,' she said, brushing the white coating from her parka. 'But I have to talk to you, Simon.'

'About what?' Simon asked while Jeff's eyes glittered with curiosity from his bunk on the other side of the tent.

'I've looked everywhere for Joan and I can't find her.'

Simon rubbed his chin with his mittened hand. 'What do you mean by "everywhere"?'

'I've checked all the other tents—even Tony's. She's not in camp.'

'She must be,' Jeff objected. 'Even Joan's not stupid enough to go wandering around in this weather.' He pulled his sleeping-bag more tightly around his neck.

'When did you last see her, Vi?' Simon asked.

'Seven or eight hours ago, I'd guess.'

'She didn't say where she was going?'

Viola shook her head.

'And you didn't ask?'

'Nope. She wasn't in great humour—you know what she's like—so I wasn't sorry to see her go. I was kinda hoping she'd stay away for a while.' Viola frowned with worry. 'Not this long, though.'

Simon swung his feet to the ground. 'I don't like the sound of this. We'd better organize a search.'

'Damn Joan,' Jeff cursed. 'Eric's not going to be pleased . . .' He hoisted himself to his feet. 'At this time of year the storm's bound to be short. Why couldn't she just wait it out like the rest of us?'

'Quit complaining and get ready,' Simon ordered. 'She must be close by.' He pulled his hood over his toque and put on a second pair of mitts. 'Let's go get Eric and Tony.'

'That woman's been nothing but trouble,' Eric fumed as the search-party gathered in the equipment tent. 'This stunt is the last straw. Joan is *never* coming on another of my expeditions.'

'Viola hasn't seen her for seven or eight hours—have any of you seen her more recently than that?' Simon asked the gathered scientists.

'She was in the equipment tent for a while,' Tony volunteered. 'Said she might make a collecting trip close to camp.' He wiped his nose on his sleeve. 'I told her I'd go with her . . . she shouldn't go alone. Besides, I left one of my corers near the glacial erratic and I wanted to pick it up.' All eyes were focused on him, but Tony didn't say any more.

'Well?' Simon demanded. 'Did you go?'

'No. She said she'd talk Eric into coming with her . . . wanted to talk to him about gyrfalcons or something crazy.'

Every head swivelled towards Eric. He was shaking his head. 'I never saw her, but if I'd known she was insisting on going out in this weather I'd have accompanied her . . . she has no sense of direction.'

Simon scanned the group. 'Anyone else see her?' Silence replied. 'OK, then. Let's get this show on the road.' He divided up the searchers into three groups. 'Eric, you and Tony team up and go west. Jeff, you and Viola take the east. Anne and I will search the Pass.'

'Just hang on a minute.' Eric held up his hands. '*I* am the leader here.'

'Then lead,' Simon shot back. 'There's no time to lose.'

Eric cleared his throat, looking for ways to improve on Simon's arrangements. 'Viola will come with me. Tony and Jeff search towards the east.'

Tony started forward but a fierce look from Eric stopped him. 'Got a problem, Tony?'

'No . . .'

'I don't know why you aren't making Wally come too,' Jeff complained, looking at the sullen man who hung on the outside of the circle.

'To look for Joan? Are you nuts?' Eric snorted. 'He'd sooner strangle her than save her.' He turned to Simon. 'Personally, I think this is a waste of time. She's probably just staying out of Wally's way. She'll be back when she thinks he's cooled off.'

'Maybe, but the weather's getting worse. I'd feel better if everyone were back here.'

Eric shrugged. 'Well, let's get going.' He took Viola's arm and shepherded her towards the door. 'Remember— stay together and fire a rifle if you need help.'

Simon raised his voice to be heard over the shrieking wind. 'Be back in an hour. If you have any doubts about your own safety come back sooner.'

The wind stole their breath away as Anne and Simon bent their heads against the gale. As they plodded on, the snow filling their eyes and noses and blurring the landscape, Simon tried to remain optimistic. After all, Joan was an experienced arctic researcher and while the visibility wasn't very good, it could have been worse. He squeezed Anne's hand. 'Don't worry,' he shouted. 'We'll find her.'

Anne clutched his hand even more tightly and nodded. She put her face close to Simon's. 'Joan said her best samples came from near that long narrow pond on the way to Eric's first blind. Let's try there.'

They veered to the right and walked on, calling Joan's name and straining to see through the snow and the gloom. At last Simon stopped and checked his watch. 'We've been out forty minutes now. We'd better turn around.'

'Let's steer a little to the left as we head back—we'll

cover more ground that way.' Anne pointed towards a pond barely visible in the haze. 'Let's go around the far side of that pond, OK?'

Simon grunted and pulled the edge of his hood down across his forehead. Anne grabbed his arm and they started moving again. Simon could feel her tension increase as her hope of finding Joan decreased.

As they approached the pond Anne stopped, her grip tightening convulsively. 'What's that?'

Simon peered in the direction she indicated. 'What's what?'

'That black hump sticking out of the ice . . . there . . . beside the biggest stone. It's too black and smooth to be rocks.' She let go of Simon and ran ahead to the pond's edge.

Simon followed reluctantly. 'This is no time for a scientific study . . .'

'I can't make it out,' Anne murmured. She raised her voice. 'Do you think the ice is strong enough to walk on?'

Simon tapped the surface of the pond with his foot. 'Maybe . . . I'm not sure.'

'I'm lighter than you are. I'll go.' Anne started across the slippery surface which had been open water just the day before. The ice cracked but didn't give way under her.

Simon bit back a warning shout. He saw her pause uncertainly as she approached the mysterious object. 'Well? What is it?' he called.

He saw her bend over and touch the black hump. She pulled her hand away as if burnt and stumbled backward. 'Simon . . .' Her wail rose on the wind.

Ignoring the ominous crackling under his feet, Simon raced across the fragile ice. 'What is it?' A horrible fear grew in his mind as he stared at Anne's white face. Catching up to her, he gripped her shoulders and swung his body between her and the object. Then he looked.

At first he could make nothing of the shapeless mass. Then he noted the texture. It was cloth, not rock. And it was dark green, not black as he'd first thought. It extended in two directions beneath the translucent ice and one end terminated in what looked like hair. Joan's hair. She floated face down in the ice-covered pond.

'We've got to get her out!' Anne tugged on his arm. 'She might still be alive. Cold water slows down the body functions . . .'

Simon shook his head. 'Not that much. Look how the ice has formed around her.' He swallowed hard. 'She's been here for hours . . .'

'We've got to try.' Anne tried to move around Simon but as she did the ice cracked and heaved. They clutched each other, balancing precariously. Water washed over their boots and waves slopped around Joan.

'No,' Simon said sharply. 'We've got to get off this ice or we'll end up with her.' He half dragged, half carried Anne towards the nearest bank. She struggled for a moment, then went quiet. Once on shore, Simon took her in his arms and hugged her tightly. 'I'm sorry, darling. I'm sorry. But there's nothing we can do . . .' He felt her body shudder as she sobbed dry sobs. To find two bodies, first Phillip and now Joan . . . 'Let's get back to camp.'

'And just leave her here?' Anne raised her stricken face to Simon's.

'Only for a little while. We need a rope . . . and some sort of a stretcher. I'll come back with Eric and Jeff.'

'I'll wait here.'

'No way.' Simon shook his head. 'Too dangerous. We'll go back to camp together. If the storm doesn't get any worse I'll bring Eric and Jeff back immediately.'

'I'm coming too.' Anne set her face determinedly. 'You might have trouble finding the spot again. Besides . . . I found her. She's my responsibility.'

They bent their heads to the wind and trudged home-ward in silence. Simon left their navigation to Anne as his mind raced. Accident? Suicide? Murder? he was as anxious as Anne to retrieve Joan's body but for a different reason.

CHAPTER 10

By the time Simon and Anne got back to camp they'd been gone almost two hours. As they entered Eric's tent amid a flurry of snow, the welcoming smell of coffee warmed their battered souls.

'You're late,' Eric accused. 'Some leader you'd make, Simon. You can't obey your own orders.' His voice trailed off as he had a look at their distraught faces. 'We didn't find Joan,' he continued more quietly. 'Neither did Jeff and Tony.'

'We did,' Anne groaned. 'Face down in a pond.'

'Oh my God!' Viola's eyes widened. 'She isn't dead, is she?'

'Yes . . . at least, she must be. The ice has formed around her.' As she spoke, Anne held her frozen hands towards the small stove. They trembled. She bit her lip and turned her head away. Tony put out a hand towards her but drew it back as she flinched from him. He coloured and retreated into the shadows.

'You poor girl,' Viola exclaimed. 'I'll get you some hot coffee.'

'But what happened to Joan?' Jeff asked. 'Those ponds aren't deep . . . it would be hard to drown.'

'I don't know what happened,' Simon replied wearily. 'We'll need a rope to get her out. As soon as we move her the ice is going to break up. Anne and I would've ended up in the water if we'd tried.'

Viola thrust a steaming mug at him. 'Wait till you've warmed up a bit,' she urged. 'You won't help Joan by freezing to death yourself.'

Simon sat down on the edge of Wally's bunk and looked into the man's haunted blue eyes. They darted around the tent, not fixing on anything. 'What've you got to say,

Wally?' Simon asked. 'You won't have to worry about someone stealing your notes any more.'

Wally's face contorted but almost instantly went blank again. He swallowed spasmodically, saying nothing.

'You're not implying Joan's death wasn't an accident . . .' Jeff stammered.

'Of course he isn't,' Eric snapped. 'Simon already said he didn't know what happened.'

Jeff shot a nervous glance at Wally but the man seemed far away, staring into space. Jeff leaned towards Eric and whispered, 'Wally's already attacked Simon and threatened Joan . . . We've got to be careful.' Jeff moved even closer to Eric. 'He's unbalanced.'

'Nonsense.' Eric gripped Jeff's arm for emphasis. 'Joan slipped in the muck of the pond and hit her head. Something like that, anyway.' He cast a malevolent scowl in Simon's direction. 'Unless, of course, our resident sleuth tries to make more of it.'

Simon cradled his head in his hands. God, how tired he was. If only he could sleep . . . This trip had turned into a nightmare. He could see his boss exclaiming over another unsolved case. Even if it did survive the inquiry, his career was on a fast train to nowhere. 'Hollingford,' he could hear his superintendent saying, 'maybe you should get back into uniform—you're obviously not cut out for investigative work. I hear they're looking for a new sergeant in Wawa . . .' He took a deep breath and lifted his head. 'We've got to bring Joan's body back here,' he insisted wearily. 'We can't just leave her.'

Eric bristled. 'It's all right to leave my son frozen inside some giant ice cube but it's not all right to leave some pain-in-the ass student floating in a goddamn pond. Is that what you're saying?'

Simon clenched his anger to his chest. 'We have to know how she died. I know how Phillip died.'

'So you say.'

Simon ignored the provocation. He got up and poured

himself another coffee—black this time. 'We must go now in case the storm gets worse.'

'You can count me out.' Eric's goatee quivered with rage.

'Fine.' Simon turned his back to Eric. 'Jeff?'

Jeff hesitated. 'Well . . . I suppose so.'

'I'll help.' The unexpected offer came from Tony. 'I've got some rope in the supply tent.' He inched his way past Anne and undid the door to the tent. 'I'll get it.'

'And I'll get you the collapsible litter from the first aid kit.' Viola's lips quivered. 'It was Joan's pride and joy. Now she's the one who needs it.' Viola followed Tony into the night.

'Right.' Simon drained his coffee and gathered up his toque and mitts. He studied Anne who huddled on Eric's cot. 'I can find my way . . . you don't need to come.' She didn't even look up. 'Are you OK?' he asked quietly.

'*I'll* look after Anne,' Eric announced, sitting beside her and putting an arm around her shoulders.

Anne stiffened. 'I'm fine,' she stammered, jumping up. 'If you don't need me, Simon, I'll think I'll just go lie down in my tent.' She ducked out and, with a mocking smile at Eric, Simon followed.

'*Are* you all right?' he asked again, catching up with her.

'No . . . But don't worry about me. Get Joan back here. Tell me how she died.' Anne raised her eyes to his. 'And why.'

When Simon reached out to caress her face, she grasped his hand and pressed it to her moist cheek. Her eyes were luminous with tears. At that moment Simon wanted more than anything else to make her smile again. 'It'll be OK,' he whispered. 'I promise.' Just at that moment Tony reappeared carrying a rope. He stopped in his tracks while Anne disappeared into her tent.

Tony controlled himself with a visible effort. 'My wife seems to like you,' he said hoarsely.

'And I like her. You're a very fortunate man.'

Feeling the irony of Simon's words, Tony flushed. He poised on the balls of his feet, fists clenched. Simon braced himself, but even as he did he saw the light go out of Tony. 'Let's get Joan,' Tony growled. He brushed his mittened hand over his scarlet cheeks. 'Where's Jeff?'

'Right here.' Jeff had a long pole—the handle of a plank-ton net—over his shoulder and the bundle containing the litter under his arm. 'Which way?'

Although the snow had stopped, at least temporarily, the temperature had plummeted. Only anxiety kept the trio warm as Jeff hustled along at Simon's side and Tony followed closely. Simon chose each step with care, making sure of the route. When they'd been walking for twenty minutes, Jeff tapped Simon on the shoulder. 'Yeah?' Simon panted.

'Can we stop a second?'

Simon slowed. 'Why?'

Jeff licked his lips. 'I've never seen a dead body . . . I mean . . . except at a funeral . . . when they're all fixed up.'

'Me neither,' Tony mumbled.

'What does she look like?' Jeff cleared his throat. 'I've . . . umm . . . I've heard drowning victims are the worst . . .'

'Only if they've been in the water a long time,' Simon explained impatiently. 'Joan only died a few hours ago.'

'Will she be . . . stiff?' Tony asked. 'Rigor mortis and all that?'

'She's likely *frozen* stiff,' Simon retorted. 'And we will be too if we don't get moving.' He plunged ahead. 'Not much farther,' he called over his shoulder.

A few minutes later he halted at the edge of the pond. 'She's over there.' He pointed. 'See?'

The lump in the ice was no longer black—snow and ice now covered her jacket, making her part of the monochrome landscape. If Simon and Anne had been much later they never would have recognized the amorphous hump as the missing woman.

Jeff cautiously stepped on to the ice. Simon followed at what he hoped was a safe distance. 'The ice will be weaker near her,' he warned.

But Jeff was oblivious of Simon. Joan attracted him like

fire attacks moths. He inched closer. Still he couldn't see
the human form represented by the swelling in the ice. 'Are
you sure that's her?'

'I'm sure.' Simon surveyed the scene, trying to decide
the best way to proceed. 'Go get the rope from Tony. Make
sure he hangs on to one end of it.' Simon turned back to
Tony. 'You stay on shore,' he yelled. Tony didn't need
convincing. He looked sorry that he'd come.

When Jeff returned with one end of the rope, Simon
approached Joan. Truth to tell he wasn't any happier about
the situation than his companions but pride forced him on.
Pride and curiosity. He edged forward. The ice rumbled
beneath him. He dropped to the ice, lying flat. When both
his heart and the ice became silent again he wiggled forward. 'Gotta lose some weight,' he mumbled to himself.
'Soon be as heavy as Bill if I'm not careful.' He reached for
Joan's jacket, but his fingers found little purchase on the
slippery material. With his closed fist he pounded the ice
around her head. All he accomplished was sore knuckles.
He wriggled closer again and grasped her hood. Its ice
shroud shattered as he pulled it back. Seeing Joan's black
hair glistening in the ice didn't help his equilibrium. He
swallowed and breathed deeply. Now she looked much
more like the human she'd been—not an inanimate icicle.
He squeezed his eyes shut. Dammit, he knew this woman.
He hadn't liked her, but that didn't matter. No one
deserved to die like this.

'What are you doing, Simon? Jeff sidled closer.

Simon opened his eyes and mentally shook himself. You
can't afford to mess this up, he cautioned himself. He
twisted around and squinted at his companions. 'Hand me
that pole, Jeff.' The geologist poked the end of it towards
him, staying well away from the corpse.

Simon chipped the ice with the metal-sheathed end. By
the time he freed Joan's head and upper body from its
brittle shroud his arms were aching from working at such
an impossible angle. 'Now the rope, Jeff, but crawl up,' he
warned, 'I've weakened the ice.'

Jeff squirmed forward as Tony paid out rope. 'Now what?' Jeff gasped, his eyes riveted on Joan's body.

'Now . . .' Simon grunted, 'now I tie this under her arms and then we pull.' He grabbed the rope Jeff tossed to him. He sat up, yanked off his mitts and stuffed them in his pocket. Then he undid his parka and pulled it off. He tossed it to Jeff. 'Keep this dry. Move back beside Tony. There's no point in us all falling in.'

He inched forward again on his elbows and knees, feeling the surface pitch under him. As he approached the edge of the ice, chunks started breaking off, floating free and drifting up against Joan's body. He stopped to plan his approach. How could he get the rope around her without crawling off the ice into the frigid water? 'I can't do it,' he mumbled. 'I have to get wet.'

He tossed the end of the rope across her back. It sank out of sight on the far side. 'Now all I have to do is catch the end again.' He laughed. 'That's all.' He shuddered as he slid his arm into the frigid water and under the corpse. Using his toes he propelled his body forward on the ice, immersing his arm to the elbow, then to the shoulder. He stretched his fingers as far as he could, searching desperately for the rope. Nothing. He inched forward again. His entire shoulder was now submerged and he struggled to keep his head above water. He gripped Joan's jacket in his teeth and eased the body closer, right to the edge of the ice. 'Come on . . .' His fingers brushed against the rope but it bobbed out of reach. 'Damn,' he muttered as his face ground into the ice. He relaxed for a moment, gathering his courage.

He took a deep breath and plunged the upper half of his body into the water. He stretched and flailed for the rope. Again he felt it brush by his fingers, but this time a final lunge brought it into his grasp. Frantic to get the knot tied before his fingers froze completely, Simon yanked on the cord and drew it up. He scrambled backwards on the ice, tying a slip knot as he went. The ice cracked beneath his chest but he skittered backwards like a crab and managed to stay on the solid piece. 'Pull!' he yelled. 'Pull!' as he scrambled to his feet and ran for the shore.

Waiting just long enough to see Simon safely ashore, Tony and Jeff pulled, straining against the water and the rough edge of the ice. The body suddenly slid up on to the ice and the pair fell back as the resistance disappeared. Simon didn't even watch. He stripped off his sodden, already freezing sweater and shirt and plunged into his dry parka. He scrabbled at the pocket for his mitts but by now his hands were frozen to immobility. 'Help me,' he gasped. 'My mitts . . .'

Jeff regained his balance first and responded. He pulled out the mitts and shoved them on to Simon's hands. 'OK? Are you OK?'

Simon nodded, too cold to answer. He huddled into the down jacket. 'Hood,' he croaked. Jeff tugged it up and pulled it tight around Simon's face and neck.

'Can you wait for us to get her on the stretcher?' he asked, grey eyes clouded with worry. Simon nodded.

Tony had pulled the corpse to the edge of the pond where the stretcher lay assembled and waiting. With Jeff, he lifted the dead woman aboard and strapped her on. 'Let's go.'

Simon lurched forward, stumbling against a rock and falling. He struggled to his feet and ploughed ahead again.

'Wait!' Jeff dropped his end of the stretcher and walked back to Simon. 'Look.' He picked up a small object Simon's fall had dislodged and waved it in the air.

'What is it?' Tony asked impatiently, twisting to look. 'Oh . . .' The air left his lungs in a rush. He recognized that small ball-peen hammer.

Simon shivered so violently he couldn't see clearly but he recognized it too. 'Bring it,' he stammered, plunging forward in the direction of camp.

CHAPTER 11

Viola fed him hot chocolate and wrapped his hands and face in warm towels but still Simon shuddered uncontrollably. He'd dragged on countless layers of sweaters and socks to keep in his body heat, but, as he told Viola, he had no more body heat to keep in. 'You'll be fine,' she said bracingly, lighting a second stove. 'You don't even have much frostbite.' She shook her head and tut-tutted. 'Men are such babies.'

Simon's eyes returned yet again to the bunk opposite. Joan lay rigid and still—no amount of towels or hot drinks could warm *her* up. He heard the drip-drip of water running off her sodden clothes on to the reindeer moss beneath the cot. Simon staggered to his feet. 'Time I had a look.'

'Eric wants me to tell him when you're going to examine her . . .' Viola said uncertainly. 'He didn't want the body in here in the first place. Where's Jeff going to sleep?'

Simon brushed aside this complaint. 'My bunk, Joan's —it doesn't matter. What's important is that no one messes with the body till I've examined it.' He turned to Viola with a strained smile on his face. 'Want to help?'

'Umm . . . well . . . I don't think . . .' Viola stuttered, but then she stopped herself. She took a breath and straightened up. 'Of course.' She cleared her throat. 'What about Eric?'

'To hell with Eric,' Simon muttered through clenched teeth. 'He wouldn't help bring Joan back here, so he has no right to gawk at her.' He walked slowly over to the body and crouched beside it. He pulled back the sleeping-bag which covered her and brushed the dark hair from her face. 'Poor Joan . . . defensive, abrasive . . . prickly as a porcupine. Now this indignity.'

He stared at her. There were no marks on her face. He

worked down the zipper of her parka to examine her neck. Nothing. He opened her jacket and probed gently, searching for blood or other signs of injury.

'Looking for more bullet holes?' Viola asked hoarsely.

'Anything,' Simon replied. 'She didn't just jump into the pond and wait to die. That wasn't Joan's style.' He eased the jacket away from the dead woman. Just as he was about to toss it aside, he noticed the underarm seam was ripped. 'Did you notice this before?' he asked, pointing to the rip.

'No, but I'm not very observant where clothes are concerned. Is it important?'

'I don't know yet.' He put the jacket down and returned to the body. 'Help me turn her over. You take her feet.' Simon grasped Joan's shoulders and Viola reluctantly took her ankles. 'Now.' Joan rolled smoothly on to her stomach. Viola wiped her cold, wet hands on her jeans.

Simon's fingers roamed Joan's scalp. 'Ah.'

Viola's stomach lurched. 'What is it?'

'A cranial depression . . . skull fracture.' He bent over Joan's head and scrutinized the area where his fingers had found the injury. Even after he'd done his best to get her black hair out of the way, he couldn't see much. He straightened up at last, and stepped back. He looked with distaste at the dark clots of blood sticking to his fingers. He suppressed a shudder and wiped them on his towel. He took a lot of flak for his squeamishness from his associates on the force. He cleared his throat. 'I'd better have another opinion—see what you think, Vi.' Simon grasped her hand and pulled her over to the corpse. 'Here. Her hair's covering it up but you can't miss it.'

Viola's instinct fought against him but almost immediately her will triumphed. She let Simon guide her fingers.

'Feel it?' he asked.

Viola nodded, too traumatized to speak.

Simon shoved his emotions aside and tried to be objective. 'I'd say the indentation is fairly round, 'bout an inch in diameter and almost an inch deep. Agree?'

'Yes,' Viola whispered. She withdrew her hand and

examined her fingers. They were red. Her face was white.
She looked around, hands held stiffly in front of her. Wordlessly Simon handed her the cloth he'd used. She wiped her
hands with painstaking care, avoiding the red-brown stains
already drying on the towel.

'Let's turn her back over.' Simon grabbed the head and
waited for Viola to take the feet. Then he gently swept the
hair away from Joan's face.'

The tension was broken by a sound at the door. 'May I
come in? It's Anne.'

Simon pulled the sleeping-bag back over the corpse while
Viola kicked the soiled towel into a corner. 'All right,' he
called. 'Come on.' He and Viola watched as Anne slipped
through the tent flap and carefully closed it behind her.
When she turned to face them she averted her eyes from
the still form on the cot. 'Is there anything I can do to
help?' she whispered.

Simon shook his head. 'Thanks, but no. There's really
nothing to be done.'

The silence extended uncomfortably. Anne cleared her
throat and cast surreptitious glances at the corpse. 'May I
see her?'

Simon put his arm around her shoulder and felt her tension. 'Are you sure you want to?'

Anne nodded jerkily. 'I found her . . . but I didn't see
her face.' She let her head fall against him. 'I have to see
her face . . . to convince myself it's all true.'

'Come then, dear,' Viola said, taking her arm. Simon
released her and the older woman led her to the body.
'Ready?' Viola slid back the cover and Anne stared at her
former colleague. Simon watched her face but her expression remained blank, unreadable. He wondered how
she exercised such control. At last she sighed a long, shud-
dering sigh. 'OK,' she said. 'Joan really is dead.' She
squared her shoulders. 'What happened?'

Before Simon could answer, a flurry of noise erupted
outside. Eric burst through the door, face contorted and fist
raised. He bore down on Simon. 'You liar! You charlatan!'

He shook his fist at Simon, who retreated a step. 'I can use that radio too, you know . . . I'm a quick learner. Thought you'd hide your dirty past from us, did you?'

'Eric, what are you doing?' Viola grabbed his arm but Eric shook her off.

'Hollingford's got you under his spell too, I see. I thought you were smarter than that.' He turned his furious gaze back to Simon as he snarled, 'Fernald told me a few things about you . . . you're not quite the lily-white cop you try to portray.'

Anne's face reflected her confusion. 'What are you talking about?'

Eric swept her with his contempt. 'Your lover-boy's been suspended from the police force—for brutality. How do you like that? Beat up some innocent accountant in his own home.' He spat out a harsh laugh. 'We've been dancing to the tune of a crooked cop!'

He whirled back to Simon again. 'Get out of here! *I'm* taking charge.' His face was blotched with red and his goatee stood straight out in fury. He lunged out to push Simon away from the body but Simon was ready. He caught Eric's arm and in one smooth motion twisted it behind his back.

'I'm not going anywhere. My suspension's been lifted until I hand this case and *two* murder victims over to the proper authorities.'

Eric sputtered, 'Let go of me!' Simon relaxed his grip. Cursing, Eric jerked himself free, but had the sense to move out of reach. 'Look, Viola,' he shouted, 'now he's claiming Joan was murdered too. This man's suffering delusions.' He rubbed his hands over his face and fought to lower his voice. More under control now, he pleaded his case to the two women. 'Not only does he insist Phillip was murdered, but now he's trying to convince us this tragic accident is a murder too.' He threw out his hands. 'The man's dangerous.'

Viola looked uncertainly from Simon to Eric while Anne stood wide-eyed and speechless.

'Well, Viola?' Simon asked into the sudden silence. 'Was Joan murdered or did she hit herself on the back of the head?'

'I don't know . . . Maybe she slipped and hit her head on a rock.'

'A perfectly round rock? No sharp points? No bits of reindeer moss to stick in the wound?' Simon asked.

'So you say,' Eric interrupted. 'Now I suppose we're supposed to take your word Joan was bashed on the head.'

Viola held up her hand to stop him. 'I examined the wound too. It's just as Simon described it—very smooth and regular.' She frowned in thought. 'And it's near the crown of her head, not a part you'd hit if you fell.'

Eric's complexion glowed even redder. He didn't like to be crossed by the members of his team. He opened his mouth to argue but Anne forestalled him.

Her face had taken on a grey tinge. 'Jeff said you found a hammer at the edge of the pond . . .' Her voice trailed off and she sat heavily on Simon's bed. She covered her face with her hands. 'Oh no. Oh no.'

Eric's beard jutted belligerently. 'I heard nothing of this . . .'

'If you'd shown some interest in Joan, you might have found out,' Viola retorted. 'Jeff found a small hammer beside the pond where they found her.'

'Whose?'

Viola nibbled her lip. 'It looked like Wally's,' she whispered.

Five minutes later, everyone was clustered around Wally in the tent he now shared with Eric. Simon held the hammer. 'This is yours, isn't it?' he asked for the second time.

Wally sat hunched on his cot, staring at the ground. He had his arms wrapped around himself and rocked gently back and forth.

'I found it near where we found Joan,' Jeff accused. 'And she was hit on the head.'

Simon shot a sharp glance at Jeff but held his tongue. His own questions hadn't elicited any answers from Wally

—maybe one of the others would goad him into a response.

'Well? Well, man? How'd it get there?' Eric demanded. 'Speak up.'

Tony's lip curled. 'I bet he killed her over his damn notes.' He shook his head. 'Dung. A woman's dead because of some pile of shit. What kinda man are you?'

'She stole my notes.' Wally spoke so quietly they almost didn't hear him.

'So you killed her?' Jeff's voice cracked as he strained to grasp the idea.

'No.' Wally shook his head. 'She stole my notes.' He reached into his parka. Simon held his breath and poised on the balls of his feet. The air whistled from his lungs as Wally withdrew a fistful of paper and held it up. 'She had them . . . she's a thief.' Wally swallowed convulsively. 'I made her give them back.' He seemingly gazed into space but he saw Eric's hand flash out to take the notes. 'No! They're mine.' He tried to stuff them back under his jacket but Eric already had a grip on the sheaf of paper. They struggled, an even match until Tony grabbed Wally's arm to help Eric.

'Got them,' Eric gasped triumphantly, with a superior smile in Simon's direction.

'So what?' Simon asked.

'They're evidence.'

'Of what? Wally already said Joan had them and he made her give back. They don't prove he killed her for them.'

Eric was momentarily deflated, but almost immediately his nasty smile returned. 'For a cop—or ex-cop I should say—you don't know much about evidence. You're getting your fingerprints all over that hammer.' He paused, as if to acknowledge the expected applause.

Simon again punctured his balloon. 'You really think someone wielded this metal hammer with their bare hands at ten below zero?' He held out his own hands and gestured to the others. 'We're all wearing mitts.' He plucked a sheet of Wally's notes from Eric's limp grip. 'I will take this, however.'

Ignoring Eric's sputtering, he examined the sheet, fully expecting to see the same handwriting he'd found on the note in Phillip's backpack. He would compare the papers directly later, but he could picture the note clearly in his mind. He frowned, willing a match. The writing on the warning note had been spare and unadorned, the letters well formed but without superfluous strokes. It slanted to the left. In Wally's field notes the writing sloped to the right. Simon knew this aspect was the first one changed by someone trying to disguise their handwriting, but the whole character of the script differed. The words in Wally's notes were broken up into short sections and no more than three letters were ever joined together. Wally's writing was cramped—tall and thin rather than plump and attenuated like that in the hate letter. He was no expert, but Simon was willing to bet Wally Gingras had not written the note. He stroked his chin.

'So?' Eric asked belligerently. 'Don't stand there growing mould. What are you planning to do? There are arrangements to be made, and if you're not going to make them, I will.'

Simon looked up at this. 'What do you mean?'

'What do I mean?' Eric barked. 'This man has killed twice. We've got to take steps to ensure he doesn't strike again.' His piercing eyes swept the group. 'We're all at risk. Wally must be restrained.'

'But . . .' Viola squeaked.

'No buts. I'm in charge of this expedition.' Here he glared at Simon, daring him to challenge this statement. 'Enough is enough. Wally will be confined to his tent until the army can pick him up.'

Simon lounged against the centre pole of the tent. 'You're trying and convicting him, then? No due process? No innocent till proven guilty?' He smiled bleakly. 'I always knew you were an arrogant prick.'

Jeff shuffled his feet nervously. 'You're being unfair to

Eric. I have to agree with him—Wally's unbalanced.' His eyes darted around, flitting to every face except Wally's. 'Poor man . . . we've been friends for years . . . but he's not himself.'

Simon ignored Jeff and turned his attention back to the accused. 'Well, Wally? Anything to say in your defence?'

Wally's tongue flickered along his lips. 'I have work to do,' he mumbled hoarsely. 'I can't stay here.'

He started to get up but Tony roughly shoved him back. 'You're not going anywhere.' Tony stood over him like a big game hunter over his fallen prey. Simon noticed Anne shrink back. Was it Wally or Tony who frightened her, he wondered?

'Wally, tell us what happened,' Viola pleaded. She knelt on one knee beside him and put her hand on his shoulder. 'It's OK to tell us—we're your friends. We want to help.'

Wally's mouth worked but no sound emerged.

Seeing Wally was incapable of telling a coherent story, Simon decided to try simple questions. 'Did you see Joan today?' he asked.

'Of course he did,' Eric spat. 'He already told us that.'

Simon glared at him. 'Keep out of this.' He faced Wally again. 'Never mind Eric, just answer my question. Did you see Joan today?'

Wally nodded.

'Where?'

Wally stared at his boots.

'In camp here?' Simon suggested. Wally shook his head. 'In the Pass, then?'

'I told her to give me back my notes.'

'And did she?'

'She laughed at me.' He ran his hand through his lank hair and it stood out like clown fluff around his ears. 'She waved my own notes in my face.' Emotion at last flashed in the man's eyes. Was it rage? Righteous indignation? Simon wasn't sure but at least Wally was talking. 'And then?' he prompted. He could feel the collective breath of the audience being held.

'I tried to grab them but . . . I missed.' He frowned. 'She ran a few feet and stopped. She laughed at me.'

'So you chased her?' Simon didn't like leading the witness but Wally was a difficult subject.

Wally nodded. 'I caught her jacket . . . It ripped but she didn't get away from me.' Wally smiled, his yellow teeth gleaming like caution lights in the dimness. Simon remembered the rip under the arm of the dead woman's jacket. 'I took my notes away from her,' Wally continued.

'Did Joan get angry then?'

Wally sucked on his crooked teeth and lowered his head. 'She laughed . . . said she had copies . . . said she'd use my data whether I liked it or not.'

'Sounds like her,' Viola murmured.

'So you hit her with your hammer,' Tony said.

'No.' Wally searched out Tony and blinked at him. His eyes goggled from behind his Coke-bottle lenses. 'She ran away. I yelled at her to stop, but she didn't.'

'A likely story,' Eric snorted.

'Which way did she go?' Simon asked. 'Towards camp?'

Eric turned his back in disgust. 'Why does the man persist in this charade?' he asked the room at large. 'Can't Hollingford admit I'm right?'

Wally was nodding. 'The weather was getting worse. I waited a few minutes . . . didn't want to run into the bitch. Then I started back too.' He struggled to his feet. 'Snow's stopped now. Gotta finish my work.'

Eric blocked the door. 'You're staying here, where we can keep an eye on you.'

A low growl formed in Wally's throat. A full-fledged howl ripped from his mouth as he charged. He butted Eric in the stomach and pushed him aside like a rag doll. Before anyone else could react, Wally grabbed the rifle standing by the tent door and vanished into the night.

'Nice one, Eric,' Simon said acidly. 'Now we're going to lose another member of this expedition.' He watched Jeff help Eric to his feet and support him to the cot recently vacated by Wally. Eric dropped to the bed and doubled over, gasping for breath. Anne rushed up. 'Are you all right? Can I get you something?'

'Leave me alone.' Eric thrust her away.

Viola took her arm and pulled her back. 'Let him get his breath,' she advised. 'He'll be fine.'

'What about Wally?' Anne asked. 'He'll freeze out there. He doesn't have his scarf, or his toque.' She pointed to the dirty woollen garments at the end of the bed.

Eric coughed. 'Let him. It's better than he deserves.'

'Simon?' Anne turned her worried frown to him.

'Yeah, I'll look for him. The rest of you stay inside.' Simon grabbed Wally's bundle of clothes and shoved them in his pockets.

'And we'll stay together,' Tony added, 'until that madman's been found and restrained. He might murder us in our beds.'

'Do whatever you like,' Simon replied as he donned his outer garments and headed once again into the cold. He decided the first thing he'd do when he got back south was keep going. The equator sounded about right.

The sun had dipped to the horizon, where it was hidden behind a thick bank of clouds, but it wasn't exactly dark. Overhead the stars glimmered in the midnight blue of the sky, imparting a silvery, otherworldly sheen to the undulating blanket of snow. He had no difficulty finding a set of footprints which left the circle of the camp. Is it worth following the trail or not, he wondered? Simon was sure Wally would return to camp within the hour. He might hide in the equipment tent, but he wouldn't stay away for long, not with the temperature so far below zero. Simon hesitated at the edge of the circle of tents. The footprints held a straight line to the north-east—towards the IBP station. 'I wonder . . .'

Simon jogged into the silver night, following the line of impressions in the snow. He startled an arctic fox, a streak of cream against the blue-white of the snow. It disappeared as swiftly as it had appeared, leaving only it's delicate prints on the blank white page.

Simon narrowed his eyes and compared the lengths of

his stride and Wally's. He'd soon catch up, he concluded, so he had to decide what he was going to do. He slowed to a brisk walk as he considered the situation. On the face of it, the evidence weighed strongly against the man. Wally made no secret of his dislike for Joan, in fact he admitted confronting her about the stolen notes. And his hammer, undoubtedly the murder weapon, had been found at the scene of the crime. But in Simon's experience Wally didn't go in for weapons—he attacked with his bare hands. He'd tried to strangle Simon, and he'd punched and butted Eric. Joan was bashed on the head and that required close, physical contact, but Phillip had been shot—an impersonal act. Could Wally have done both deeds?

Simon threw back his head and breathed deeply. The frigid air caught at his throat and he coughed out clouds of vapour which hung around his face and frosted the fur trim on his hood. He needed to clear his mind before he tackled a possible murderer. If only the handwriting had matched . . . that would have made it so much simpler. '*You'll pay in full for S.'s death . . .*' that's what the note said. Was 'S' really Wally's son? If so, who'd written the letter? If not, who else had suffered at Phillip's hands?

He started jogging again. Cloaked by the snow, the ground looked smoother than it actually was. Simon missed his footing and fell headlong on to the frozen tundra. 'Dammit!' He spat out a mouthful of snow and struggled to a sitting position. He fingered his nose . . . still in one piece despite the pain, though it might be swollen by morning. He wriggled his ankles. No damage, but he'd better be more careful. He stood up, brushed the snow from his pants and jacket and started out again along the trail. He peered ahead but still couldn't see Wally. He was half way to the IBP station and approaching the huge coral boulder which loomed like a massive milestone in the wilderness of white. If I can't spot Wally from there, he decided, I'll turn back. After all, I know where he's going and he'll be safe even without his toque and scarf. That quonset hut has everything he needs for a couple of days.

The intricate pattern of fossils embedded in the coral erratic lent it a texture of silver velvet lacking in the ordinary basalt rock. The feeble light, shining from behind Simon, stretched his long shadow towards the rock and melded it with the deep shadow crouched on the far side of the obelisk. The combined pool of black sucked all detail from the terrain beyond and the faint trail of footprints led straight into the inky blackness. As Simon approached the rock, he slowed, trying to watch ahead as well as keep an eye on the terrain. The shadow swallowed him and for an instant he was blind. A stinging blow to his temple sent him flying. A heavy body landed on top of him, forcing the air from his lungs. An arm squeezed his windpipe. Simon levered the arm from his neck. 'What the hell do you think you're doing?' he gasped out between ragged breaths. A knee caught him in the groin and Simon doubled over, unable to defend himself from the blows raining down on his head. The thick parka hood deadened most of the impact. 'Wally . . . for God's sake . . .'

As suddenly as the attack began, it ceased. Simon heard the muffled thud of retreating footsteps. 'Wally . . .' he called, as loudly as he could manage. 'I want to talk to you.'

'Leave me alone!' The anguished cry echoed in the silent night. 'Just leave me alone.'

Simon saw a running figure cross from the shadow into the pallid light. 'I've got your toque,' Simon yelled, scrambling to his feet. 'And your scarf.' The blurred figure didn't even slow down. Simon waved the toque over his head, but he knew Wally couldn't see him. 'I'll leave them here beside the rock,' he called. 'I'm going back to camp, so you can get your things whenever you like.'

Simon rolled the scarf up inside Wally's toque and placed them on a patch of clear ground in the lee of the boulder. He leaned against the rock while he caught his breath. He laughed without humour. 'At least I'm warm now . . .'

As he retraced his steps, Simon's thoughts inevitably revolved around the strange man who'd attacked him without warning and then run away before he'd done any real damage. He was definitely unstable, violent even, but was he a killer? The others evidently thought so. Wally's flight made 'tent' arrest impossible but there were no guarantees he'd stay at the IBP station. A wild card was on the loose.

CHAPTER 12

Simon was bone tired by time he got to camp and in no mood to argue with Eric or anyone else. 'If you're that scared of Wally, find him yourself,' he told the expedition leader. 'I've been tramping around outside in the snow and the cold all day while you've been toasting yourself in here. I'm going to bed.'

He marched off towards his tent, but Jeff caught up to him and grabbed his sleeve. 'Where am I supposed to sleep?' he asked. 'There's a corpse in my bed, remember.'

Simon shrugged. 'I've got all the information I can from the body, so you can move her. Put her in the food tent.'

'I can't do that. What would Viola say?'

'Then put her in the radio tent. I don't care.' He yawned. 'Right now I don't care about anything except sleep. I'm even too tired to eat.'

Jeff followed Simon into their tent and eyed the corpse warily. 'Did you have to put her in *my* sleeping-bag?'

Simon's reply sounded muffled as he bent to pull off his boots. 'She's not in the bag, she's under it, and it's not your bag anyway. Yours is over there, untouched by dead flesh.' He pointed to a heap on the ground. He slithered into his bed. 'Good night.'

Jeff turned around, his mouth open. 'Aren't you going to help me?'

'She only weighs about a hundred and ten pounds and you're always going on about what great shape you're in.'

'Simon,' Jeff whined, 'who's going to open up the tent for me?'

Simon pulled his sleeping-bag over his head and ground his teeth in frustration. Then he snapped open the covers and dragged himself back out of bed. 'Let's make this quick.'

With Joan stowed in the radio tent and Jeff snoring peacefully across from him, Simon finally relaxed. His mind swirled with questions but even this couldn't keep him awake. Murderer on the loose or not, he slept like a baby.

In the morning the storm attacked their outpost with renewed vigour, and, in the white-out conditions, Simon's repeated attempts to contact Resolute were rewarded with nothing but static. The miserable group huddled in their tents, for the most part zipped into their down bags. While Wally remained everyone's favourite suspect, silent, mutual suspicion killed any wish for conversation. They lay there in the gloom and listened as the icy tongue of the wind penetrated the tents in a thousand places and uttered whistles and howls of delight as it knifed through their puny defences.

Simon scurried across the open circle to Viola's tent. Anne was with her and they were bent over their notes but they didn't look as if their minds were on them. Simon sat on Joan's empty cot out of the pool of light thrown by the propane lamp.

Anne's eyes, when she met his, mirrored both hope and fear. He felt Eric's accusations hanging in the air between them.

'What can we do for you?' Viola asked, putting her notes aside and sitting back. The harsh glare of the lamp accentuated the deep lines in her face but her eyes sparked with life and energy.

'For starters, I'd like to know why you came back to the exact same spot two years running.'

The two women looked at each other briefly and then Anne answered in a soft, hesitant voice. Her hands moved restlessly in her lap. 'The armed forces really made the decision. They were willing to provide transportation and accommodation to this site and this site only.'

'Why so specific?'

'Bureaucratic intransigence,' Viola explained drily. 'Granted it had to be within helicopter distance of Resolute, but that could've taken us anywhere on Bathurst Island, Cornwallis Island or Devon Island. But Cornwallis has been well studied already, another group was scheduled for Devon Island, and they had military exercises planned for the south of Bathurst Island. So here we are.'

'And what was the reaction to the decision?'

'Some of us were pleased and some weren't,' Viola replied. 'What would you expect? It depends on what you're studying.'

Simon raised an eyebrow.

'Well, take me, for example. I was thrilled,' Viola explained. 'Long-term studies are best for understanding animal behaviour. Ideally, I'd be here ten years running.'

'Same for me,' Anne added. 'Any ecosystem research needs at least two years' information—otherwise you can't infer anything meaningful from the data set. In fact, before we were sure we would get back here with the military, Viola and I kicked around the idea of mounting our own expedition.'

'And would you have?' Simon asked curiously.

Anne rubbed her fingers and thumb together suggestively. 'Money. It's always a question of money. I doubt if we could've picked up the tab by ourselves. Ecological stuff isn't well funded, especially with women in charge.' Anne pulled off her toque and ran her fingers through her hair. 'And I'm not a real academic, remember. I'm just an unpaid adjunct.'

'Is there anyone who didn't want to come back here?' Simon asked.

'Jeff, for one. He says he's had enough of Polar Bear Pass, geologically speaking,' Viola explained.

'And Eric,' Anne added. 'He collects exotic locations like other people collect stamps, so he hates to waste time repeating himself.' A familiar shadow crossed her face.

She's thinking of Tony, Simon concluded, I know that look. He frowned.

'Different sites would be more useful to Tony's work too,' Anne said sadly, confirming Simon's suspicion. 'But let's face it—' she spread her palms in front of her—'we go where anyone will take us. Except for Eric and Wally, none of us has the funds for independent arctic research.'

'Eric did come back here, though,' Simon pointed out.

'True,' Viola agreed, 'but he likes lording it over his inferiors. If he went off by himself there'd be no one to order around. Besides, it *is* a good spot for bird-watching.'

'And Colonel Fernald appointed him group leader again this year?' Simon asked.

'He appointed himself, but I have to admit he's a very good leader,' Viola said, a little grudgingly.

'So you two were in favour of this site, Eric and Jeff opposed it, Tony wasn't too pleased, and Wally didn't care. Is that a fair summary?'

The two women nodded in unison. 'Why do you want to know?' Anne asked.

Simon drummed his fingers along his thigh as he considered his answer. 'One person knew that if Phillip's body turned up all hell'd break loose. Now if you were that person, would you want to come back?'

'I suppose not,' Viola replied. She smiled at Anne. 'I guess that lets us off the hook.'

Simon nodded. 'That's one way of looking at it. But, on the other hand, you might want to come back, locate his body yourself and hide it permanently. After all, the person who shot him would have the best idea where to look.'

'Oh.' Viola's smile faded and Anne looked close to tears.

'Don't take it personally,' Simon said. 'I'm merely pointing out the difficulties.'

'I thought we'd decided Wally had killed Phillip . . . and Joan,' Anne wailed. 'Now you're accusing us!'

'I'm certainly not discounting Wally, but there's no real proof. A few solid facts would be most welcome at this point.'

'The hammer . . .' Viola said.

Simon shook his head. 'Anyone could've put it there. Wally makes a great scapegoat.'

'But no one else had a reason to kill Joan,' Anne murmured.

'No reason that we, or at least I, know of,' Simon corrected. 'But there's a lot I don't know.' Simon turned to Viola, his brow creased. 'For example, you know something you're not telling me.'

Viola's piercing eyes widened in a picture of innocence. 'Of course not! What makes you say that?'

'The way you act when I'm asking questions. I can't put my finger on it but there's something you don't want me to ask. What is it?'

Viola slowly shook her head. 'Nope. I know nothing related to Phillip's death. Or Joan's. Absolutely nothing.'

'But you do know something, don't you?'

Viola didn't deny it. 'It is not my secret to tell,' she finally answered, 'and I won't hurt a friend needlessly.'

'I'd hardly call helping solve a murder "needless",' Simon retorted.

'If my information would help I'd tell you, but it won't.'

'How can you be so sure?' Simon stood up and loomed over her. Viola shifted on her cot but held her ground. 'I know people, and I know this person is incapable of murder.'

'Anyone is capable of murder if pushed hard enough. You can take my word for that.'

'I disagree,' Viola replied calmly, standing up herself and forcing Simon to back off.

'You could be charged with obstruction of justice,' he threatened.

'You can't prove I know anything,' she retorted, 'and what could you do about it if you could? Arrest me? We're all jailed by this damnable weather anyway.'

'That's telling him!' Anne smiled.

'*Et tu, Brute?*' Simon asked mournfully.

Viola plonked her toque on her head and drew on her

mitts. 'I'm going to get myself some lunch. Then I'm going to talk with Jeff about the mineral content of the bedrock.' She threw a coy look at Simon. 'I promise I won't leave town, Officer.'

After Viola departed in a flurry of snow, Simon and Anne remained in uncomfortable silence. Anne stared at her lap and Simon stared at his boots. At last he cleared his throat. 'I know you're thinking about what Eric said . . . about my being suspended for assaulting a man.'

'It doesn't sound like you . . .' Anne whispered. 'Is it true?'

Simon compressed his lips. 'Sort of,' he mumbled.

'Tell me about it.' Anne stood up, walked across the tent and sat down beside him. She put her small hand on his arm and looked into his eyes. 'Tell me.'

'It's a long story . . .' Even now, a month after the charge was laid, bile rose in Simon's throat. He twisted his bootlace in his fingers. 'A man . . . a subhuman actually . . . Delio . . . says I assaulted him . . . that I used excessive force when I arrested him.'

Anne's question hung in the air even though she never voiced it.

'I grabbed him by his collar . . . hit him once or twice,' Simon said hoarsely.

Anne studied him. She couldn't see much of his face— he had turned away and was staring blindly at the wall of the tent. 'You had a reason?' she murmured softly. She released his arm and ran her hand lightly down his back.

Simon shifted on the cot. What should he tell her? How could he convey his outrage . . . his frustration? He cleared his throat. 'The last case I worked on—am still working on, though I've been officially taken off the case—was about this little girl. Jennifer.' Simon wiped his hand across his eyes. The laughing, pixie-like face in her photograph haunted him night and day. 'She was twelve when she died. Drug overdose.' Simon licked his dry lips and fumbled for the canteen in his pocket. He drank deeply. Anne watched but didn't interrupt.

'I was supposed to find out who supplied the drugs.'
Simon paused. 'I did.' His gorge rose as Delio's urbane face
swam before him.

'That's terrific,' Anne congratulated him.

Simon laughed bitterly. 'You think so? What do you
know?' He sprang to his feet and paced angrily. '*I* know
he was the source. The crown attorney knows it . . . but
they say there's not enough evidence to get a conviction.'
Simon turned on Anne and shook his fist at her. 'Delio
had a knife—I saw it. He was going to use it on me but
I got him first.' Simon flung himself back on to the cot.
'They couldn't find the knife afterwards, but I know he
had it. He's thumbing his nose at all of us and going
scot free while I get hung out to dry.' Simon clenched
and unclenched his hands. 'Delio's still in business. More
Jennifers are going to die.' His mouth stretched in a
soundless howl of anguish.

Anne put her arm around his shoulder. She had no idea
of the procedure followed in such cases. 'They believed him
instead of you?' she asked in a small voice.

Simon shrugged angrily. 'Must have. I've been suspended while they "investigate".'

'I suppose they have to,' Anne murmured.

'Yeah, right. Pillory me while a child-killer goes free.'
Simon shook off Anne's comforting hand. 'Why do I bother?
Phillip Loew had the right idea. Look out for number one
and to hell with everyone else.'

Simon stomped out into the storm. For once the stinging cold felt good. The unshed tears froze to his lashes
as his breath caught in his throat. He laughed a soundless,
bitter laugh. Way to go, man. Not only have you jeop-
ardized your job, but you're alienating the only person
here who doesn't think you're a monster. He paused to
tighten his hood and the biting wind and icy snow blew
painfully in his face until he turned his back to the gale.
The radio tent lay only a few feet away but it was barely
visible. The driving snow was a moving wall of white;
each spicule a tiny cutting edge ready to attack exposed

flesh and flay it in seconds. Simon sprinted the short distance to his goal, though the force of the wind forced his straight-line course into a drunken curve. He fumbled clumsily at the ties holding the door shut and finally lunged inside into the relative calm. It was less windy inside, but not less cold. Simon peered at the thermometer hanging from the centre pole, squinting at the mercury. Minus fifteen Fahrenheit—not that cold for a brisk walk or a good ski run when you knew a warm hearth and a hearty meal awaited you, but as an indoor temperature with only tepid slop to eat, it left a lot to be desired.

He coaxed the radio to life. Static shrieked and howled in his ears and no amount of knob-twiddling improved the situation. 'Got to talk to Fernald,' he grunted. 'Got to let him know there's been another murder.' He checked the batteries. The cold was draining their power but the level was still acceptable. It had to be the aerial.

Simon beat his way through the blizzard back to his tent and as soon as he opened the door a wall of warmth hit him. The temperature inside was a balmy ten degrees Fahrenheit thanks to two lanterns, a Coleman stove and two human bodies, Eric and Jeff. As soon as Simon entered the murmur of conversation stopped as if a radio had been switched off.

'Don't let me disturb you,' he commented sarcastically, 'I've just come for more mittens and another toque. I think the antenna's down.'

The men watched Simon in silence as he hurriedly grabbed his gear and disappeared again, letting a good blast of arctic air enter as he left.

The aerial hugged the ground for fifty feet or so after it slid out from under the tent wall. This arrangement wasn't ideal for radio function, but for safety reasons Simon had decided to run the wire away from camp before raising it into the air on slim metal poles. To follow it, he almost had to crawl on hands and knees as he traced the wire from insulator to insulator, hidden beneath the drifting snow. In places where the tundra had been blown bare his task was easier, but in hollows the snow had already accumulated to the depth of a foot.

Simon straightened with a sigh of relief when he got to the first pole and the wire took to the air. He looked back the way he'd come. The camp was already lost in the whirling snow. He craned his neck in vain to see the top of the post. The aerial itself was stretched a good twenty feet overhead and was completely invisible, but he'd strung the support wires connecting the posts at shoulder height. He used these as a guide as he made his way slowly along. From the first pole to the last the distance was two hundred and seventy feet—the same as the radio wavelength he was using. Now he wished he'd been less enthusiastic and settled for a half-wave antenna. He consoled himself with the thought that it was precisely in these adverse conditions that his long antenna was beneficial. But it was these same conditions which hid the indistinct outline of another well-muffled person following the same trail just a few minutes behind him.

Finally, face and fingers numb, Simon reached the end where a coil of extra wire hung from the final support. The last three posts had been lying down, covered in snow, and he'd practically had to crawl the last sixty feet. When he eased himself upright the fury of the wind blasted his exposed face and he withdrew as far as possible into the shelter of his fur-rimmed hood. Turning his back to the wind, Simon jury-rigged repairs, working his way back along the aerial. The combination of numb hands, wind, swirling snow, and gloom conspired against him and the thirty-minute job had become a marathon of endurance.

Suddenly, without warning, the sharp end of the guide wire ran through his gloved hand. Simon stared at his empty palm. It wasn't possible! Less than an hour ago it had run, unbroken, from the radio tent to the final support. Since the wire was loosely hung from post to post the strain of the wind couldn't have snapped it. And where was the other end?

Simon halted in his tracks and stared ahead, eyes

narrowed against the driving ice crystals. The snow created an opaque, swirling curtain in the beam of his torch. There was no sign of pole or wire. Behind him he could see one post at the extreme edge of the flashlight's range, but one post was not enough to give him the bearing to the camp.

Simon fought his rising panic. He willed the knot in his stomach to dissolve and concentrated on breathing slowly and deeply. He mentally braced himself. One step at a time.

He located the last pole again and stumbled towards it, afraid that it too would vanish. But it was solid and real and he hugged it to his chest. Now what, he wondered? There had to be a method for finding his way home. His mind seemed as frozen as his body. Think, he commanded himself. He huddled deeper into his parka and tucked his hands inside his sleeves. He stamped his feet but he couldn't feel the ground any more, just the shock of the impact as it transmitted itself up his spinal cord.

He jerked to attention. More wire—that was it. He needed more wire. He remembered the coil hanging from the end pole.

Fighting his fear, he switched off his flashlight to conserve its power. Taking the guide wire in his hand, he jogged blindly back the way he'd come. When he arrived at the end, he clicked on his light and fumbled in his pocket for the wire-cutters. It took two long minutes for his nerveless hands to grasp the cutters and sever the wire. Just as the strand parted, the torch rolled off his knee and went out. His heart lurched. His panic rose as he scrabbled in the snow in wider and wider circles. He twisted around in fright and his foot kicked something hard. It was the flashlight and when he picked it up with shaking hands both it and his hope burst into life. His heart returned to its usual anatomical location.

On feet he could no longer feel, Simon hastened back along the antenna, the extra loops of wire hung over his shoulder. One, two, three, four posts. Simon stopped. This should be it. Again it took agonizing minutes to do the simplest of jobs; this time to tie one end of the coil to the support. He took the time to make the attachment extra secure because his life depended on the knot holding. This completed, he slowly paid out the wire, backing off from the post as he did so. Soon his anchor was out of sight in the driving snow and he had to trust the thin strand of steel which tethered him to it.

Simon estimated he had forty-five feet of wire—not nearly enough to get him to camp but enough to swing him past the next post in the series. Then the aerial could again be his guide. He started a slow, clockwise circle at the extremity of his rope. Simon's eyes were red and strained as he fought to maintain his focus along the beam of his flashlight, but everything was blurred and unclear, like snow on a poorly tuned television set. He could imagine he saw all sorts of things in the dancing pattern. He felt he'd been circling for hours when a post suddenly sprang into being in the flickering light. His heart leapt as he raced for it and then clung to it like a burr. But something about it caught his eye. It was painted red. Simon had used only one red pole and it was the third last one. He'd made a full circle and found nothing!

This time his battle with panic and despair was harder to win. He wanted to run blindly forward, letting instinct take him home, but a thread of sanity held him back. Forty-five feet should have been enough to bridge the gap between the posts—they were only forty feet apart. He refused to acknowledge this discrepancy. He must have miscalculated the length of his line. He needed more. Again he travelled out to the end post and cut an additional length of wire to attach to his old tether. Now he could walk a circle with a radius of over eighty feet.

Simon began tracing the enlarged arc. His flashlight was definitely dimmer now and he could no longer convince himself it was an optical illusion. Although its assistance was mainly psychological, speed became even more important as the beam of his torch shrank. He stumbled forward like a drunkard. He had lost all feeling in his extremities; below the knees and elbows he had ceased to exist. Will-power and reflex were all that kept him going.

In the end he almost missed it. His numbed brain responded sluggishly to what his eyes reported but the message registered at last and Simon stopped and stared at the beautiful sight. There, only ten feet away was a pole.

As he stared at it his smile faded. From the pole, wires stretched out in two directions. One led away from him, aligned with his guide wire and leading to the radio. The other headed out at right-angles to the first—a configuration Simon had never made. Both wires were taut. Both were attached to something. One had been moved.

The cold in his heart equalled the cold in his limbs as realization flooded through Simon. The antenna had been deliberately cut. Someone wanted him dead. His knees threatened to buckle under him.

Forcing this thought aside, Simon bridged the gap between his wire and the antenna just as his flashlight flickered. Mesmerized, he watched the bulb turn yellow, fade to the strength of a glowing cigarette and then die away to darkness. Simon clutched the wire with his numb hands and stumbled back along the path he'd taken so light-heartedly three hours before. He literally tripped over the edge of the radio tent where the wire vanished inside. Safe! For now.

CHAPTER 13

Simon staggered into Viola's tent. She was talking with Anne but one look at his white face stopped her in mid-sentence.

Viola gently removed his ice-encrusted mitts while Anne turned up the heat on the small stove and prepared a pot of lukewarm water. While Simon soaked his hands in this, the woman pulled off his boots and gently rubbed his frozen feet. Viola clucked constantly like a mother hen.

Eric poked his head in the tent door. 'There you are,' he exclaimed in annoyance. 'What are you doing in here? You should be working on the radio—we've simply got to contact Resolute.'

'That might be difficult without an antenna,' Simon retorted.

'What do you mean? I thought you'd gone to fix it.'

Briefly Simon explained what had happened. 'It wasn't an accident,' he concluded. 'Someone wants to kill me.'

'How can you say that?' Viola protested in disbelief.

'Delusions,' Eric declared. 'No one wants to kill you.'

'Poles don't walk by themselves. On my way out the line was straight. On my way back the wire was cut and at least two poles had been moved.' Simon hoisted himself to his feet. 'Everyone is to spend the night with a buddy and keep an eye on each other,' he ordered, hobbling for the door. 'I'll stay with Jeff in our tent. Eric, you stick with Tony. The women can look after each other. Good night.'

'Wait.' Eric grabbed his arm. 'What about Wally? If the posts were moved it was likely him.'

Simon turned tiredly. 'That's one of the reasons I don't want anyone spending the night alone. We can't find him in this weather . . . we can't even fix the antenna until the storm clears. Sleeping is the most useful way to spend the time.' He shook off Eric's grip and left. Behind him he heard Eric shouting, 'Who the hell does he think he is . . . ?'

By the next morning Simon had recovered some of his strength and felt warm again at last. When he opened his eyes, he felt Jeff's gaze on him.

'Finally woke up, I see,' Jeff muttered. 'I've got better things to do than babysit you.' He got to his feet. 'Wally could've come in here last night with a machine-gun blazing and you wouldn't have heard a thing.'

Simon lifted his wrist. A thin fishing line cut through the air six inches in front of the door. 'I don't think so.' He swung his feet to the floor. 'Now that my brain's thawed, I have a couple of questions for you.'

Jeff frowned and shuffled his feet.

'Did you move those damn posts?' Simon demanded abruptly.

'Of course not.'

'Then why are you so edgy? What's wrong?'

'The situation's getting serious,' Jeff mumbled. 'If someone really did try to kill you . . .'

'They did.'

'I shouldn't say anything . . .'

'If you know something, Jeff . . .'

'I don't know, precisely, and it happened last year. Joan
mentioned she saw Phillip and Eric having a quarrel.'

'About what?'

'I don't know but they each threatened to tell Mrs Karnot something about the other.'

'What?'

Jeff shrugged. 'I don't know. I don't think Joan knew
either.'

'When did this argument supposedly take place?'

'Just a couple of days before Phillip was lost last year.'

'Did she tell any one else? Did she confront Eric?'

Jeff shrugged again. 'That's all I know.' He headed for
the door. 'I don't know why I told you . . . Eric and Phillip
often argued. It wasn't anything new.'

Simon stayed in the tent a few moments longer. Why
had Jeff told him? The story seemed so vague . . . almost
manufactured. From all Simon had heard, arguments between the two were common—there was little love lost
between Phillip and his stepfather. Or Phillip and Joan, or
Phillip and Wally. And what about Phillip and Tony? What
was the connection there?

Simon rubbed his chin thoughtfully. Maybe Jeff was
pointing a finger at Eric to direct Simon's attention away
from himself. But if that was the case, what secret was Jeff
hiding? Why would he have wanted to murder Phillip? And
Joan. Simon sighed. It was hard enough getting a handle
on one murder, but two . . . Where was the association?

The atmosphere crackled with tension in the Colautti tent.
Anne had tried one more time to get Tony to talk to her.

'But if you'd just tell me what's wrong . . .' she pleaded.

Anguish honed the edge of his whiplike tongue. 'Can't you see I don't want to talk to you?' He shook his fist in her face. 'I don't want to see your goddamn rabbit face! I don't want to hear your snivelling voice! I don't want you near me. Bitch! Get away from me!' he howled, shrieking louder even than the storm. He stared at his quivering fist. With a final wail, he lashed out. Anne's head snapped back and she went sprawling.

She lay stunned on the ice-hard ground. Finally she struggled to her feet, her face snow white except for a red weal spreading over her temple and cheekbone. 'I won't bother you any more, Tony,' she said softly. She opened the door flap and stepped out into the blizzard. Outside in the wind and snow she stood, hatless and gloveless, letting the icy blasts blow through her mind, revelling in the pain and cold. It felt good, physical pain; so much healthier and cleaner than the long months of emotional torture. At last, frozen and snow-covered, she walked like an automaton to Viola's tent.

Tony watched her leave. Then he threw himself down on his cot and wallowed in self-loathing.

Simon huddled anxiously over the radio transmitter, searching for a signal from Resolute. With help from Viola and Jeff he'd repaired the truncated aerial. They'd re-erected the five remaining support poles as well as the weather conditions permitted, but Simon was not sure it was enough. He'd watched their faces closely as they surveyed the damage. Their concern seemed genuine to him but he wasn't totally convinced.

The fourth time Simon sent out his call signal he heard a faint response through the static.

'Viking here. You're very faint. Over.'

Relief flooded Simon and he fine-tuned the signal, eliminating some of the crackle but boosting the volume only slightly. 'Is this better? Over.' Simon yelled into the microphone.

'Yes. How's the weather? Over.'

'Visibility ten feet, high winds, snow. But you've got to get us out. There's been another death.'

'Hold on for Colonel Fernald.'

Simon held on, praying the connection would hold. Unsettling clicks and whistles played in his headset.

'Hollingford? Are you still there?'

'You've got to get us out of here, Colonel,' Simon yelled through the static. 'There's been another murder. Winik's dead.'

'We can't do it in this weather. You'll have to hold on. Over.'

'When will you be able to come?' Simon asked desperately.

'. . . as the weather clears. Keep me post . . .' The Colonel's voice faded as the background cacophony swelled to engulf it. Simon twiddled and swore but the connection was lost. He slumped back on his packing crate.

As he sat there, his eyes strayed to the emergency medical chart hanging on the side of the radio cabinet. It was something he'd stared at many times before, but this time something clicked. Simon snatched down the sheet and ran his eyes over the blood types of the expedition members. Yes, he was right. Wally had blood type O positive. But about the only part of the coroner's report he'd heard when Bill read it was Scott Gingras's blood type, AB−, a very rare type indeed, and one which couldn't be fathered by O positive. Wally Gingras was not Scott's father.

Simon sprang to his feet and paced in the cramped quarters of the tent. He re-ran the conversation with Bill in his head. Yes, Bill had said AB-, he was certain. Simon absently scratched his two-day beard. Had Scott been adopted? Simon remembered Viola commenting on how sick Wally's wife had been during her pregnancy, so that was out. Did Wally know Scott wasn't his son? And who *was* the father? On a hunch Simon examined the medical list again. Everyone on the list, including himself, was Rhesus positive except Jeff Jost. And Jeff was type B, quite rare and definitely a potential father for an AB− son. Jeff and the Gingrases had been close friends ... maybe Mrs Gingras was an even closer friend than anyone thought. Simon slammed the lid on the radio and hurried out.

Jeff looked up anxiously when Simon entered the tent. 'Did you get through to Resolute?'

'Yeah, but they can't pick us up till the weather improves.'

'They have to,' Jeff sputtered. 'This is an emergency.'

'Dying in a plane crash wouldn't be an improvement,' Simon replied. He held out a piece of paper to Jeff. 'Could you write something down for me?'

Jeff raised an eyebrow. 'My fingers are hurting,' Simon lied. 'Frostbite must be worse than Viola thought.'

Jeff took the paper and spread it on a book. He held a pen poised above it. 'Well?'

Simon cleared his throat. '*Phillip. Sweating yet? Next time your mailbox may contain . . .*' Jeff had started to write but now sat staring at the page. 'Recognize it, don't you,' Simon said quietly. He took the paper from Jeff's limp fingers and studied the writing. It was a kind of flowing printing, the way he wrote his field notes. 'The note you sent Phillip was written, not printed, but the same hand wrote it.'

Jeff's lips quivered but he said nothing. He goggled at Simon and swallowed convulsively.

'Does Wally know you're Scott's father?' Simon asked abruptly, going for shock tactics.

Jeff jerked like a marionette hauled to attention, shock draining his face of blood and leaving it blanched. His reaction erased Simon's remaining doubts.

'I don't know what you're talking about,' Jeff stammered.

Simon merely raised an eyebrow.

Jeff reiterated his feeble denial. 'What on earth do you mean?'

'Exactly what I said. You are Scott Gingras's natural father. Does Wally know this?'

Jeff's tense shoulders sagged in defeat. 'No,' he whispered, 'he doesn't. And don't tell him!' he warned Simon in sudden alarm.

'Scott was born about three years after the Gingrases were married, as I recall.'

Jeff nodded. 'Muriel and I had known each other for a long time before she married Wally and . . . well . . .'

'Why did she marry him?' Simon asked.

'I suppose because I wasn't ready for "commitment", that horrible word, and Wally was. She hadn't planned to continue the affair, but . . . it just . . . happened . . .'

'I see. And Wally never knew?'

Jeff shook his head dismally.

'You're sure?'

'I'm sure. Wally was madly in love with Muriel and doted on Scott, but he's very strait-laced.'

'No wonder you were upset when Scott died. So you wrote a threatening letter to Phillip.' Simon waved the original in the air. 'It was very stupid to handwrite it. Hate mail should be done with cutouts, or at least a typewriter. I would've thought an intelligent man like you would be above such basic errors.'

Jeff drooped. His skin took on a sickly hue, emphasizing his wrinkles and giving his skin the texture of worn leather. Even his hair seemed more limp. He shrank into himself.

'The letter says Phillip would pay . . .' Simon let his words trail off suggestively.

Jost looked up, terrified. Sweat formed on his upper lip and he rubbed his clammy hands on his parka.

'Phillip is dead, Jeff. Murdered. He *has* paid.'

'But I didn't kill him! It was just a threat. To scare him. I could never kill anyone,' Jeff protested.

'You had the means, Jeff, you were carrying a rifle that day. You had a motive—hatred and revenge. You even had the opportunity. You were seen near the other side of the Pass in the early afternoon. And you were late getting to shelter.'

'Everyone was late,' Jeff pointed out, 'and besides, I could never have got all the way across the Pass to the IBP station in the snow. You know that. Hell, you couldn't even get back from the end of the antenna!' Jeff relaxed a little, realizing he'd scored a telling point.

Simon cursed inwardly. No matter who he accused, they could all fall back on that inescapable defence.

Jeff recovered his wits and went on the attack. 'Don't forget about Joan. If the same person who murdered Phillip killed her—and surely you can't suppose we have two murderers on the loose—what would you cite as my motive for that? I had no reason to kill her.' He stood up and approached Simon, eyes blazing. 'And what about the stampede, eh? I like Viola. Then there's the antenna business.' Jeff waggled his finger in Simon's face. 'What reason do I have for killing you?'

'The same one anyone else has,' Simon retorted. 'To stop my investigation.'

'I did not kill Phillip.' Jeff shoved his hands in his pocket and leaned against the centre tent post. 'Personally, I have no interest in uncovering his murderer. Whoever it was, he or she deserves a medal.' Jeff leaned forward, a less pugnacious expression on his face. 'What I do care about, Simon, is Wally. He doesn't know about Scott and Muriel. Please don't tell him; it could serve no useful purpose.'

'No promises, but if it's irrelevant I won't go out of my way to tell him.' Simon pulled his toque over his ears. 'A lot of dirty linen gets aired during a murder case, and some of it inevitably blows off the line.'

Simon headed for the supply tent to dig out something to eat. As he rummaged through endless boxes of breakfasts he thought about Jeff. It looked like he'd found another prime suspect. But Jeff definitely wasn't around when the arti-sim stampeded the musk oxen. Was this crucial? Were the two murders, the stampede and the attempts on his life all perpetrated by the same person? Simon selected his unappetizing lunch and scurried back to the relative warmth of his tent.

Despite having muffled up well before braving the storm, Simon's breath was torn away from his mouth as he stepped out into the blizzard. Drifts had accumulated on the wind-ward side of the tents now that the blow had settled in the north-west. If this is summer, Simon thought, I sure don't want to be here in the winter. He admired the people and animals who lived in the north year round but he had no intention of joining them.

He scuttled for Tony's tent, where the man now resided in solitary squalor. Simon blundered right in without permission.

Tony was awake, huddled miserably in his sleeping-bag, but he started up when the blast of frigid air hit his face. 'What the hell do you want?' he demanded, surly with dislike and apprehension.

'I just want to ask you a few questions,' Simon replied amiably, searching without success for somewhere to sit.

'I don't want to answer any,' Tony declared, hunching his shoulder and turning his back to Simon.

'Then I'll simply speculate aloud.' Simon propped his bulky form against the tent post.

'I can't stop you,' Tony mumbled, 'but I'm not listening.'

'I want to theorize about your relationship to the late Phillip Leow. You know, that stone cold dead corpse lying in the ice on the far side of the Pass.' Simon noted with satisfaction the convulsive shudder beneath the down covering. He began his story. 'For a considerable time after your arrival at Bellwood, you were unimpressed by Phillip, considering him less than an asset to the biology depart-ment. But the time came for the aforementioned Phillip to be considered for tenure and an opposition group was formed, spearheaded by Dr Wally Gingras, no friend of the deceased.

'So Phillip needed some supporters and he decided to cultivate Dr Anthony Colautti, a hard-working, fun-loving, but ultimately light-weight scientist. But what could he dangle in front of Colautti's nose?' Simon paused. 'Any suggestions, Tony?' He watched Tony pull his sleeping-bag over his head and spoke a little louder. 'No? Then I'll have to speculate.' Simon eased his weight on to his other leg.

'Phillip could offer his support in the department, but at the time his influence wasn't great—even his powerful step-father was distressingly neutral. Phillip could offer to lobby for industrial contracts for him, maybe, but Colautti was a confirmed academic and not ambitious enough to compro-mise his position. He could offer drugs, since Phillip was both a user and a pusher.' Simon noted the sudden stiffen-ing beneath the sleeping-bag. 'Or,' Simon articulated slowly, 'he could offer sexual favours since Phillip was gay and Colautti was . . . reluctantly bisexual, shall we say?'

'No!'

'You visited Phillip at his Toronto apartment and he used that place for two things—drugs and sex.'

'I've never been to that damn apartment! I don't even know where it is.' Tony, still tangled in his sleeping-bag, sat up and hugged himself defensively.

'Come on, Tony, your visits weren't as secret as you thought,' Simon needled. 'Even Anne knows you called on him.'

'I've never even been to the Parkway Apartments.'

'So you do know where Phillip's apartment was.'

'No! I . . .' Tony ducked his head between his knees. 'Go away.'

Tired of standing, Simon cleared a space on Anne's bunk and sat down. 'Now we come to Bathurst Island last sum-mer,' he continued. 'Phillip is getting bored with Tony, his lover, who has served his purpose and so he withdraws his favours. Tony gets frantic and begs his lover to take him back. Phillip refuses, taunts him, maybe threatens to tell his wife, and Colautti shoots him in a rage.'

Tony flung off the sleeping-bag and clapped his hands over his ears to keep out these monstrous accusations. 'You're wrong. I didn't kill him! I couldn't. I needed him,' he sobbed uncontrollably.

Simon ignored this outburst and continued his dis-passionate recital. 'After the second shot, Phillip falls to the ground but he's not dead. Not yet. A few more agonizing hours of stumbling around in the snow must be endured before death draws him in. But Colautii either doesn't know or doesn't care his victim isn't dead and scurries back to camp, arriving in the nick of time. He joins his companions in speculating about the whereabouts of the missing men . . .'

By this time Tony was moaning and rocking back and forth on his cot, cradling himself and whimpering. Simon detested himself for what he was doing but he couldn't afford to be gentle. He flayed his victim with the lash of his words. 'When the storm cleared Colautii desperately searched for the body to hide the evidence of his crime. He let everyone believe he was frantic to rescue Phillip. But, although he didn't find Phillip's body, neither did anyone else. He thinks he's safe.' Simon permitted himself a bleak smile and stretched out his legs.

'How dismayed Colautii was to discover another expedition was headed for Polar Bear Pass again the next year. He couldn't afford to protest the location too violently or to refuse to go. He could only pray the body would stay hidden.'

'But then he discovered that Viola Leggett knew his secret. Oh, not that Colautii was a murderer, but that he had been cheating on his wife, and with a man. She might tell Anne, so he started a stampede hoping to silence her. But that didn't work, did it? Then Anne herself discovered Phillip's body and, horror of horrors, there was a policeman on the scene ready to investigate. Another person to stop.'

While Tony whimpered like a trapped animal, Simon fought his disgust for the man. 'First he tried to drown the policeman, but his plan failed. Then he waited until the cop had gone out into the storm and then cut the wire which would guide him back. Too bad it didn't work, Tony,' Simon commiserated sarcastically.

'You're wrong. All wrong,' Tony croaked, his throat constricted with tears of fear and shame.

'Am I? Simon asked. 'It makes a very convincing scenario, I think. You did have an affair with Phillip, didn't you?' he demanded.

When Tony didn't answer Simon pressured. 'We'll find proof when we start digging, you know. If you wrote any letters Phillip would be the type to keep them—blackmail would be his style.'

'But I didn't sign them,' Tony protested and then, realizing what he'd said, covered his face with his hands and wept.

'And Phillip did dump you,' Simon attacked relentlessly.

Tony nodded miserably. 'But I didn't kill him. I swear it!' he protested desperately. 'I didn't . . .' he repeated in despair.

'You started the stampede,' Simon accused.

'She knew. Viola knew about Phillip and me. She said I should explain to Anne—can you believe it? I was afraid she would tell . . .' Tony's voice was thick with tears. 'But I was glad Viola wasn't hurt,' he choked. 'I must've been crazy.'

'Viola wouldn't have revealed your secret, Tony, but she is right. You must tell Anne. You have to.'

'I can't,' Tony wailed, running a damp hand over his blotched face. 'She hates me enough already. And I love her,' he whispered almost inaudibly, his mind drifting away from Simon.

'Did you cut the antenna wire?' Simon asked, although he knew what the man would say.

'No,' Tony mumbled. His shame was public knowledge now. Simon slipped out of the tent and into the storm but Tony didn't even notice he'd gone. A peace, of sorts, came over him and he knew his time of hiding and lying was at an end. He would tell everything and face the consequences as a whole human being. He would lose Anne but it was only right to have to pay the price of his sins.

Simon hurried to his tent, fighting the gale force wind all the way. Was the snow letting up a bit? Maybe. He wasn't sure, but thought he could see a couple of feet farther than when he'd left. He fastened the tent door against the storm and lit the stove, glad to have the tent to himself. While he waited for the water to boil he crouched beside the stove, seeking warmth for his throbbing hands and feet. He felt a bit more confident now than he had when he woke up. Information was finally starting to shake lose.

He'd started his recital to Tony to irritate him—to goad him into letting something slip. But as he watched Tony's writhing silhouette under the covers, Simon knew he'd discovered the key to his behaviour. Blaming him for the stampede had also been a shot in the dark, but Viola was very perceptive and it was exactly the type of secret she'd never tell. But would Tony know that? As Simon spun his tale, the attempt on Viola's life and Tony's sordid affair locked together in his mind. It fitted. Serendipity, Simon thought, as he stirred his tea. His work often involved playing hunches and he was good at the game.

Simon cradled his cup in his hands. The warmth slipped over his fingers like lambswool gloves and he gave himself up to the enjoyment of the sensation. When he returned to cold reality, however, his spirits sank again. None of his other suspects were likely to crack as Tony had. Wally, Eric and Jeff; they all had motives. So did Anne if she knew about Tony's affair. Maybe her confusion was an act. Simon frowned at this possibility but couldn't dismiss it. Jealousy was a strong motive. Anne or any one of them could have made a detour and done the deed, but it would have been impossible to shoot Phillip, unheard, before the storm, and after the blizzard began, no one could get back to camp. Simon sighed. There had to be an answer.

He began pacing in the cramped tent. On top of everything else he was worried about Wally. He was pretty sure the man would be safe at the IBP station if he had the sense to stay there, but sense didn't seem to be Wally's strong suit. If he left while the storm was raging he could be lost. Even dead. Simon refused to give in to the common fear that Wally lurked just out of sight, waiting to snuff out another life.

He was just draining his coffee mug when a muffled figure appeared in his doorway.

'Simon?' Anne called quietly. 'May I come in?'

'Of course.' Simon ushered her in. They stood awkwardly in the middle of the tent.

'Cold, isn't it?' Simon commented, then bit his lip in annoyance. He'd never been good at small talk.

Anne nodded her head slightly without lifting her gaze from her boots.

'Coffee?'

The delicate head was shaken.

Simon slipped his hand under her chin and tilted it up. The red welt stood out against her pallor. 'Did Tony do that?'

Anne dropped her eyes. Her nod was barely perceptible.

'The bastard!' Simon's voice was tight and controlled. He'd been much too easy on the man.

Tears rolled silently down Anne's cheeks but she didn't sob. She didn't brush them away. She didn't move.

Simon gathered her into his arms. 'Don't worry. He won't bother you any more.'

Gradually Anne's stiff body relaxed. 'Maybe I'll have that coffee now.' A glimmer of a smile flickered across her face when at last they drew apart.

CHAPTER 14

In the morning the sky glowed crystal blue and the wind whispered sweet nothings around the circle of tents. Simon checked the thermometer beside the radio and smiled— above freezing and still rising. Already a tell tale drip-drip sounded from all quarters. Simon donned his sunglasses to protect his eyes from the painful dazzle of sun on snow and began peeling off layers of clothing.

Along with the storm, the radio interference disappeared. Eric marched into the tent to give Colonel Fernald a piece of his mind, but when he emerged one look at his face betrayed his failure.

'Well?' Viola asked. 'Do we all have to leave?'

'Yes, dammit. Fernald won't budge . . . I told him we'd round up Wally and hand him over, but the Colonel says we're all under suspicion.' Eric slammed his fist into his palm. 'That's Hollingford's doing, I'll bet. To anyone with half a brain it's perfectly obvious Wally's the killer.' His goatee bristled with rage and he glared at Viola. 'Start packing and go tell the others to do the same.' He stomped off but before he got five paces he turned around. 'And tell Hollingford to stay out of my way or there'll be another corpse.' He disappeared into his tent. If there had been a door to slam he would have knocked it off its hinges.

Simon had talked to Resolute before Eric and wisely made himself scarce. He slogged through the wet snow and slush towards the IBP station, anxious to find Wally before the helicopter arrived. The squat outline of the quonset huts remained maddeningly distant as he tramped up and down the hills and every time he crossed a stream the ice threatened to break under him. Soon his feet were as sodden as the first day he'd arrived. The rifle bouncing uncomfortably on his shoulder reminded him at every step that Wally, too, had a gun.

He slowed as he climbed the last hill to the station, trying to make his approach as soundless as possible. The snow helped him, masking the crunch of his boots on the gravelly terrain. He studied each dip and shadow, as he searched for a glimpse of his quarry. Ah . . . there he was, standing beside the open door of the second hut. Simon eased his gun from his shoulder and balanced it in his hand, trying to be both prepared and non-threatening at the same time.

'Hello there,' Simon called when he was still thirty yards away. He didn't want to startle the man, and he needed room to manœuvre if Wally attacked. Wally's head jerked up, but his face was in shadow and Simon couldn't read his expression. Simon edged up while Wally kicked at some ancient dung poking through the melting snow. 'We were worried about you,' Simon said.

Wally grunted his disbelief.

'We were worried,' Simon repeated, coming to a halt a

few feet away from the man, 'and I wanted to ask for your help.'

'With what?' Yellow eyes darted here and there, but never settled.

'I wanted to ask if you have a theory about Phillip's death.'

'No,' Wally mumbled after a pause so long Simon wondered if he'd heard the question.

'A terrible tragedy . . .' Simon commented provocatively.

A quiver shuddered through Wally's gaunt frame. 'Retributive justice,' Wally spat out. 'The murderer was himself murdered.'

'Phillip didn't kill anyone,' Simon objected.

Wally turned away, again kicking at the patch of dung. Displacement behaviour, Simon decided, baiting him again. 'Unless you mean the unfortunate death of your son, Scott?' Simon stepped back, but not quickly enough.

'I warned you . . .' Life flashed in the dead eyes as he twisted Simon's sleeve in his yellow claw.

'Your son committed suicide by jumping off Phillip's balcony.' Simon wriggled out of Wally's grasp and put more space between them.

'It wasn't suicide.' Wally ground his teeth. 'That bastard used my boy and then threw him away. He murdered Scott!'

'Is that why you shot him?' Simon asked.

The blaze had died down but fire still smouldered in Wally's eyes. 'I'm glad someone did. Someone had the guts to give Phillip exactly what he deserved.'

'You hated him, Wally. Doesn't that make you the most likely candidate?'

Wally licked his narrow lips with a furred tongue and pushed back his lank hair. His eyes cooled into bloodshot, glassy marbles. 'I didn't have the nerve,' he whispered in a voice full of self-loathing. 'I wanted to do it . . . God, how I wanted to see him squirm . . . watch him die . . . but I didn't have the guts.' Head down, oblivious of Simon's presence, Wally shifted into the dimness of the quonset hut.

Simon followed, keeping his distance until his eyes adjusted to the low light. 'What about Joan?' he asked. His voice echoed accusingly in the metal building.

Wally's head lolled from side to side. 'She can have my notes . . . I don't care any more.'

Simon rubbed his chin. 'Joan's dead, Wally. Don't you remember? She was hit over the head with your hammer and thrown in a pond.'

'Oh yeah . . . Eric thinks I did it.' Wally sat heavily on a packing crate.

'Did you?'

Wally gave him a death's head grin. 'If I couldn't kill Phillip for murdering my son, I could hardly kill an incompetent student for taking my notes.'

Simon agreed with the logic of his statement but didn't completely trust Wally to act in accordance with it. He stayed out of arm's reach, surreptitiously searching the gloom for the gun. He spotted it propped up in the corner, out of reach. 'Time for you to come back to camp,' Simon told him. 'We're all going home.' He sidled over to Wally's gun, picked it up and cracked it open. It wasn't loaded. 'Let's go, old man.' Simon gently grasped Wally by the arm and urged him to get up. 'We don't want to miss the plane.'

Simon did a cursory job of tidying the hut while Wally sat on his haunches and watched. Simon felt his empty eyes drilling into his back and hurried even more. 'That's it,' he said, straightening up the last of the cartons. 'We'll take your empty food cans with us and leave everything else here.' He crammed the cans into his pocket, wrinkling his nose in distaste. He wished he'd brought his backpack.

To Simon's surprise, Wally didn't protest about returning to camp. Simon walked a little behind him and to the side, just out of arm's reach. They were silent during the long walk back, but the birds more than made up for it as they screeched and trilled, celebrating the return of spring.

Everyone managed to be present when the two men

arrived back in the circle of tents. 'You found him,' Anne commented, breaking the silence. 'Where were you, Wally?'

'At the IBP station,' Simon answered as Wally scurried past her without speaking.

'Where do you think you're going?' Jeff demanded, as Wally opened the flap of the equipment tent.

Simon put a restraining hand on Jeff's arm. 'He's going to pack his things. Leave him alone.'

Jeff shook Simon off. 'You'd better keep an eye on him, then. I don't want a knife in my back.'

'You watch him. I've got other things to do.' Simon turned to Viola. 'How's the packing going?'

Now Tony jumped in with both feet. 'What do you mean —you've got other things to do?' He stepped in front of Simon and poked his stubby finger in his face. 'You brought him here . . . you're the cop,' he shouted. 'Protect us.'

Simon's lip curled. 'It's broad daylight. There are five of you and one of him. His gun isn't loaded and Eric already has his hammer. Be a man.' He started to walk away.

Tony balled his fists and punched out. Simon dodged with ease. 'I've been charged with brutality, remember?' Simon sneered. 'Want me to demonstrate why?' Simon took a step towards Tony, who cringed away. Out of the corner of his eye he saw Anne cover her face and turn aside. Smart move, Hollingford, he told himself furiously, but he hid his chagrin. 'You people pack up the rest of the equipment. If I'm back in time, I'll help with the tents.'

Jeff tentatively put out his hand. 'What about . . . Joan?'

Simon shrugged. 'Someone'll have to crate up her stuff. She's sure as hell not going to do it.'

'That's not what I meant,' Jeff stammered. 'What will we do with . . . her body?'

'Move it outside on to a tarpaulin. The troops will bring a couple of bodybags.' He knew he sounded callous, but he was anxious to get going. Again he started to leave and again he was stopped.

'Where are you going?' Eric asked, speaking for the first time since Simon and Wally had returned. He'd decided to give Simon the silent treatment but curiosity got the better of him.

'To see if I can still find Phillip's body. The storm will have covered it up again.'

'I'm coming with you.'

'I don't know if that's a good idea,' Simon began, but Eric cut him off.

'My wife will want to know, Hollingford, and I insist. You can't stop me.'

Simon knew there was nothing he could do about it. 'Get Wally's trowel and come on, then.'

They walked in silence, skirting the frozen ponds and listening to the raucous cries of the thousands of birds as they wheeled and soared, released at last from their snowy imprisonment. Here and there the still carcase of a young nestling reminded them this freak summer storm had taken its toll.

Simon was timing their progress to the ice bridge forming Phillip's tomb. Even at a very brisk pace it was almost two hours before they reached the spot. While Simon began digging away the snow which had drifted over the body, Eric stood back and watched, a fixed expression on his face.

Simon almost didn't recognize the source of the moisture running down his face. He stood up and wiped his forehead. How long had it been since he'd been warm enough to sweat? He stripped off his parka and threw it on the tundra. Without its awkward bulk he progressed much faster. Suddenly he stopped in mid-stroke, heart racing. The dead hand again reached out for him. Eric took an involuntary step backward and sucked in his breath. Simon tore his gaze away from Phillip to study the dead man's stepfather, but Eric had regained his control and his face revealed nothing.

Simon dug gently until the head and torso were exposed. He stepped back, motioning the other man to approach. Eric stared long and hard before removing his glove and gently touching the frozen face and the beckoning hand. 'It really is Phillip.' His voice was subdued. 'And there's blood

. . . and what looks like a bullet wound.' He rubbed his temples and sighed. 'Poor Phillip, . . . poor Lynda.' He turned away and began slowly to return the way he'd come.

Simon repacked the body to protect it from the warming rays of the sun and erected the red flag he'd brought with him to mark the location for the rescue party. Then he jogged off to catch up with Eric.

'You were overheard, last summer, exchanging threats with your stepson,' Simon remarked, breaking the silence between them.

'By whom?'

'Joan, for one,' Simon replied.

Eric laughed shortly. 'And you believed her? She was just trying to save her own skin by shifting suspicion to me.'

'And then she hit herself over the head and drowned herself to make sure I was convinced?' Simon shook his head. 'I don't think we can pin Phillip's death on her.' He swerved to avoid a plover's nest. 'And yes, I did believe her. Phillip threatened to tell his mother about your "philandering", and you couldn't allow that. She might cut you off from her money!'

Eric laughed again. 'We understood each other, Phillip and I. We're two of a kind—out for number one. Yes, he threatened to tell Lynda about my dalliances, but he wouldn't have said anything. He knew I'd tell her he was gay, so you see, we had a stand-off. We'd both keep our mouths shut.'

'I'm sure your wife knew about Phillip's sexual proclivities . . . mothers always know. You had no hold over him.'

Eric continued as if Simon hadn't spoken. 'I certainly won't tell her now; Lynda has enough sorrow without the addition of that tawdry detail.'

Simon unbuttoned his sweater and pushed up the sleeves. The sun had real warmth in it now. 'You had opportunity to cut the antenna wire when I was out in the storm,' he pointed out.

'So did everyone else,' Eric countered, unruffled. He too

was stripping away his layers of clothing. Sweat glistened on his forehead.

Simon rubbed the itchy stubble on his chin. 'So what's your theory about the murder?'

Eric was surprised at the question. 'Why are you asking me? I'm a prime suspect, aren't I?'

'Oh yes, very prime. But if you aren't the murderer your views could be valuable. You know all the players and you were here at the time. And you're bright and observant.' Simon laid it on thick, knowing Eric wouldn't be able to resist showing off.

Eric bowed his head briefly, acknowledging the compliment as his due. 'My guess is that Joan killed Phillip.'

'And her motive?' Simon asked.

'Revenge, partly, and as a preventative measure as well, I expect. You are aware Joan and Phillip were old enemies?' he asked, turning to fix Simon with his penetrating stare.

'Yes, despite the fact you failed to mention it before.' Simon replied. 'The Northern Mining and Exploration affair.'

'Very good, Hollingford, you haven't been completely wasting your time.' He smiled thinly. 'Joan hadn't forgiven Phillip for the loss of the family business, so that provides a revenge motive. Then you take into account Joan was a fanatic when it came to environmental issues.' He raised an eyebrow at Simon. 'I presume you noticed?'

Simon nodded. 'It would be hard to miss.'

'Therefore,' Eric continued, 'since it was Phillip's assessment which permitted the mine to expand and ruined the area for wildlife, she viewed Phillip as a threat to Mother Nature herself—which gave her "just cause" for terminating the threat.'

'Was Joan in the vicinity of the shooting, though?' Simon asked, turning to look back at the low hills from his present position in the middle of the Pass.

'I didn't see her,' Eric admitted grudgingly, 'but I could easily have missed her. I've often thought how easy it is to move about unnoticed when all the potential watchers are scientists immersed in their projects.'

In the past couple of days Simon had become painfully aware of this fact which flew in the face of all his preconceived notions. 'Yes, everyone seems annoyingly dedicated.'

'And we know Joan was unprincipled since she stole Wally's notes,' Eric pointed out. 'Very unethical behaviour.'

'But not in the same league as murder,' Simon protested.

'Not to you, perhaps. It is a very important matter to scientists.'

Simon shot a sharp glance at Eric. He seemed serious. 'Then who killed Joan?'

'Wally, of course.'

'Over the notes.'

'Yes.' Eric turned to the policeman with a kindly smile on his face. 'So, you see, I have solved your mystery for you.' He clapped his hands together briskly. 'When you've explained the situation to the authorities, you can advise them to let us come back to finish our work . . . without Wally, of course.'

Eric was pushing the pace now. 'I've got to get back and pack up the rest of my equipment before the plane arrives,' he said to Simon. 'If you can't keep up . . .'

'Don't worry about me,' Simon replied, matching him stride for stride.

They returned to a scene where everyone was wandering around at loose ends. All the equipment and supplies were packed, but the tents still stood, waiting for Simon to receive the message that their flight was en route. One package lay apart from the rest. Joan's body was zipped into a sleeping-bag and covered with a tarpaulin. Everyone gave her a wide berth.

Well removed from the rest of the group, Anne wandered restlessly. Her connection with Bellwood College all but severed, and certain she'd never return to the north, she drank in the landscape. Even the presence of two dead bodies couldn't ruin her pleasure. They were all transitory,

unimportant figures in this landscape. Their petty jeal-
ousies and tragedies were irrelevant events. Anne breathed
deeply the pure shimmering air, willing it to cleanse her
spirit and her mind, to gently blow away the pain in her
soul. She focused her mind as well as her gaze on the austere
beauty around her.

'Anne?'

It was Tony.

'Yes?' Her voice was sharp, her defences ready for an
attack.

'I'd like to talk to you . . . that is, if you don't mind . . .'
Tony pleaded both with his eyes and his voice. He extended
and then quickly withdrew a beseeching hand.

The silence stretched.

'OK,' Anne replied neutrally.

They stood facing each other, not speaking, while Tony
searched for the words he needed. 'I'm sorry,' he finally
said in a voice dripping tears. 'I hurt you. And I love you.'

A small part of Anne wanted to reach out to comfort him,
to tell him it didn't matter, but the other part, suspicious
and puzzled, held her back. It was the second impulse that
won out. 'Yes, you hurt me,' she agreed in a steel-steady
voice. 'It's difficult to believe you love me.'

'I suppose it is,' Tony admitted, gripping his hands
together tightly until they were white with tension. 'Anne,
I can understand your feelings, but I do love you and I
always have. It's myself I hate and I've taken it out on you
. . . because I knew I didn't deserve you.'

Anne refused to melt. 'Meaningless words, Tony. I need
more explanation than that.'

'I know,' Tony agreed quietly, 'so I'll try to give you
one.'

Haltingly, Tony told his story and he told it all: the
infatuation, the infidelity, the guilt, the fear of discovery,
the deceit, the lies. As he spoke, both the speaker and the
listener stared into the distance, not meeting each other's
eyes. Anne wanted to clench her mind closed against the
words, against the pain, but she couldn't. She pressed her

fingers to her mouth to check the moan which rose to her lips. Each new revelation twisted the knife deeper into her heart. She felt faint.

When Tony finished his confession it hung, dark and smoky, in the clear air between them. Tony's face was drawn and pinched; all his colour had been washed away. His dark eyes were sunken and shrivelled. 'Can you forgive me, Anne?' he pleaded, at last turning to regard his wife.

Tears silently streamed down her face. She didn't look at him. 'Maybe,' she whispered to the wind.

'Can you still love me?' he begged.

Could she still love him? Everything in her upbringing rejected him . . . his betrayal. But she'd loved him so much before . . . 'I don't know.'

'Do you hate me?' Tony asked in despair.

Anne's brow creased. She glanced at her husband's strained face. 'I don't think so.'

'Can we try again?' Hope struggled into his eyes.

Anne stared at the Pass. Could she try again? Like a dentist with his pick, she carefully examined the nooks and crannies of her battered emotions and flinched each time a sensitive spot came under scrutiny. She shot a sideways look at Tony. She could erase his misery with a few simple words, but would they be honest words? A year ago . . . even a month ago . . . she would have lied for him . . . buried her doubts. But now? Simon's green eyes and crooked smile formed in her mind's eye. 'I honestly don't know, Tony.'

He gulped. 'That's more than I have a right to expect. I can wait . . .' He hovered at Anne's side but she stood silent, gazing out across the Pass. Tony turned away just as they were hailed from the campsite.

'Yo! Time to pack up! The plane's on its way!' Simon called.

Anne started, then smiled. 'Coming!'

Simon watched until he was sure they were coming. He'd seen Tony follow Anne up to the ridge and had considered stopping him, but Tony hadn't looked belligerent. From a

distance he couldn't tell what was happening, but he knew
Tony hadn't touched her. He smiled to see Anne jogging
towards him. Her husband stayed a few paces behind her.

In a short thirty minutes the five tents were dismantled,
rolled and squeezed with their hardware into their sacks.
Simon's temporary home had dissolved into a mountain of
crates and canvas. Joan's shrouded body lay to the side.

The members of the expedition stood in a ragged line,
searching the southern sky and straining their ears. Simon
paced behind them, a knot in his stomach. His instincts told
him if he left Polar Bear Pass with the murders unsolved he
would never learn the answer—and he needed a win here.
Even if the brutality charge were dismissed, his superiors
would still be on his back. They wanted some convictions
from him. The future loomed unpleasantly before his
mind's eye. He'd have to do something about his father too.
He couldn't keep the old man with him much longer—he
needed full-time attention. Simon hoped his brother would
back him up when it came to putting their father in a home.

'Sad to be leaving?' Anne asked him.

'What?' Simon looked up. 'Yeah, in a way.' He scratched
his head. 'This wasn't the type of vacation I was expecting.'

'More of a busman's holiday,' Anne agreed. 'Too bad.'

'Especially since I haven't found the murderer,' Simon
mumbled. He saw the shadows gathering on Anne's face.
'One good thing happened, however ... I met you.' His
crooked grin brought an answering smile to Anne's face.
'Bellwood University isn't that far from where I live.'

Before Anne could answer, Viola let out a shout. 'There
it is—a plane, not a helicopter.' They all strained their eyes
in the direction she pointed. The silver speck in the blue
distance grew in size as the drone came to them on the
wind. The pilot made a low pass, studying the terrain, then
roared away to make his approach for a landing on the
spine of the hill. The waiting party moved back down the
slope.

'I hope we'll be able to return soon,' Viola remarked
anxiously. 'I don't want to lose track of my herd.'

'If we manage to get back here within a week or two perhaps I'll be able to salvage some data,' Tony whined.

'I hope your blinds are sturdy,' Simon remarked to Eric.

'Oh, they are,' Eric replied, 'and I will insist we come back within two weeks at most.' He glanced at Wally, who stood near the mound of equipment. 'I hope they have a doctor in Resolute with some psychiatric training. I wouldn't want him attacking anyone else before they get him into hospital. Poor man . . .' Eric dismissed Wally from his mind. 'With a little luck they'll take a few statements at Resolute and let the others come back. I, of course, will have to go home with Phillip's body.'

To lighten the gloom which descended with Eric's last words Anne rushed into speech. 'Did your tagged snow bunting make it through the storm, Eric?'

'Yes, he did, I'm pleased to say.' Eric took his receiver from his pocket and swept the air in front of him. 'Yes, there he is now, south, south-east,' he reported with satisfaction, fixing the position.

'Do you always carry that receiver with you?' Simon asked.

'Most times. I check his location pretty frequently.'

'As you did with your gyrfalcon last year?'

'Yes, but he never strayed far from camp . . .' Eric's voice trailed away as he became aware of the expression on Simon's face.

'So that's how you did it,' Simon said softly, comprehension flooding him.

'Did what?' Eric's face drained of colour.

'Got back to camp in the storm after you shot Phillip,' Simon yelled over the roar of the plane.

'I don't know what you're talking about.'

'Oh yes you do. Your gyrfalcon was at camp that day; you knew that's where it would be. All you had to do was get out your receiver and head for that magic homing signal! Poor visibility wouldn't hamper you at all.' He slapped his thigh as the light dawned. 'And later you hid his pack so no one would find it and know where to look for his body.'

'No!' Eric screamed against the shriek of the braking engines.

No one noticed the perfect landing the old saddle jockey had executed. All eyes were on Eric and they were filled with dawning horror.

Even before the pilot had cut the engines a burly figure was running down the slope towards the assembled company. 'Simon!' Bill Harkness hailed his partner. 'Did you solve the case?' he asked in the sudden silence as the engines died.

Simon gripped Eric by the shoulder as a grim smile settled on his features. 'Yes, just in time.'

Eric shook him off. 'How dare you!' His patrician sneer had disappeared only for a moment. 'This is nonsense,' he blustered. 'No one's going to believe you.'

'Oh no? Take a look around,' Simon retorted. Every face was turned towards Eric and every face reflected revulsion. 'We all know you and Phillip hated each other. We know and *Phillip* knew you were cheating on your wife—your *rich* wife.' Simon's lip curled. 'You didn't want to lose your meal ticket.'

'You're crazy.' Eric swept the others with his gaze. 'He's crazy, I tell you.' He stepped backward but Bill Harkness blocked his path. Eric flushed and moved away. 'Next he'll be blaming Joan's death on me.'

Simon rubbed his chin. 'That's not a bad idea. You could've stolen Wally's hammer . . . anyone could have.'

'But only Wally had a reason for killing her.' Eric stabbed the air with his finger. 'Even you can't hang a motive for that one on me.'

Simon glanced at the other members of the expedition and read the hesitation in their expressions. 'Which one of you was the last to see Joan? Tony?'

Tony nodded.

'And what did you say Joan wanted to talk to Eric about?'

'Gyrfalcons.' He hesitated. 'And transmitters.'

Simon allowed himself a wintry grin. 'Joan sure as hell wasn't planning to put a transmitter on her bacteria.' He jerked his head at the shrouded corpse. 'Joan was smart. She figured out how Eric killed Phillip and decided to try her hand at blackmail.'

'All you have is the second-hand report of a neurotic queer,' Eric sneered. 'You'll never make it stick.'

Fighting a spurt of rage, Simon's grip tightened convulsively on Eric's shoulder. Eric staggered, off balance. Bill's large hand reached out. 'Easy, Simon. I'll take it from here.'

'Get him out of my sight,' Simon ordered.

Anne played with her spoon and stared at the grey formica table. The coffee shop was a neutral place to meet Simon. She wasn't ready for romantic dinners yet. 'I'm glad to hear the charges against you have been dropped.'

'Yeah.' Simon heaved a sigh of relief. 'Once in a while truth wins out.' He sat back in his chair. 'That's why they're letting me finish investigating Eric's unsavoury activities.'

'I feel sorry for Mrs Karnot. What a blow to find out your husband has murdered your only son.'

Simon nodded, staring at Anne's bent head. He watched the play of light on her shining hair and longed to reach out and touch it. Instead, he fingered the cleft in his chin. 'Eric killed Joan too, but he's not going to be tried for that —there's not enough evidence.' He cleared his throat. 'But we've nailed him for the death of Mrs Karnot's aunt.'

Anne looked up, a question in her eyes.

'She's the one Mrs Karnot inherited the money from —the one who died just a few months after winning the lottery.'

'I thought she was old . . .'

'She was, but an autopsy indicates she died of suffocation.'

'And you think Eric did that too?' Anne, put her hands to her temples and shook her head. 'I can't believe it. I've known Eric for years . . .'

'Eric claimed he was in England at the time she died,

but we can prove he's lying. According to immigration records, he made a lightning trip back to Canada at the crucial time.' Simon allowed himself a satisfied smile. 'And I have an eye-witness who places him within half a block of her house on the night she died. All in all, we've got him.'

Tears started in Anne's eyes. 'This has been a terrible summer. Phillip and Joan murdered . . . Eric arrested . . . Tony gay . . .' She fumbled in her pocket for a tissue.

Simon swallowed hard. 'What about you and Tony? Are you getting back together?'

Anne shook her head. 'I can't forget the last two years. I can forgive, but I can't forget.' She smiled wanly. 'We're friends again, though. He's letting me work in his lab until I get a real job.'

'How are the prospects?'

'It'll take a while, but I'll get one.'

Simon smiled his crooked grin. 'So you'll be around here a bit longer?'

Anne's smile broke like clear dawn. 'Looks like it.'

'Good.' Simon stretched out his hand and Anne nestled hers in it.